# Above a gathering storm

By

Reuven (Gutkin) Govrin

Production by eBookPro Publishing
www.ebook-pro.com

**Above a gathering storm**
Reuven (Gutkin) Govrin

Copyright © 2024 Reuven (Gutkin) Govrin

All rights reserved; no parts of this book may be reproduced or transmitted in any form or by any means, electronic or mechanical, including photocopying, recording, taping, or by any information retrieval system, without the permission, in writing, of the author.

Translation from Hebrew: Michael Waisfeld
Editing: Joya Peri
Contact: robby@giner-govrin.com

ISBN 9798308510741

*This book and all the main characters described herein are the product of the author's imagination. Any connection between the plot of the book and events that occurred in reality, as well as between the main characters described herein and names and figures or names of people living or deceased, or their likeness, is strictly coincidental.*

# Table of Contents

1975 ..................................................................................... 7

PART ONE ........................................................................ 13

PART TWO ..................................................................... 175

PART THREE .................................................................. 223

EPILOGUE ...................................................................... 305

ACKNOWLEDGMENTS ................................................. 311

DIARY'S – TRANSLATOR'S NOTES ............................... 315

1975

A barely perceptible tremor went through the heavy bulldozer. The front blade had hit something hard.

An inexperienced bulldozer operator might not have given it any thought, but this Dozer was skilled and experienced. He immediately stopped the large machine's movement, turned off the engine, and opened the cabin door.

The worksite was located southwest of Kfar Qassem, in central Israel. The giant bulldozer was pushing clumps of hard soil to level the ground as part of the construction for a new road. From cabin height, the Dozer saw the pile of broken orchard trees that he had uprooted, cleared, and piled up yesterday beside the area he was working in. Their torn roots jutted into the air, ragged and neglected. The image of the defeated orchard made him feel an unusual discomfort that wasn't typically characteristic of him at work.

He looked back at the wounded ground, trying to figure out what he had hit.

He stood on the track, jumped to the ground, and approached the edge of the large blade. At first, he noticed nothing within the cloud of dust billowing before him, so he returned to the bulldozer, grabbed a big shovel that was attached to the side, and began digging around the area.

A large metal lump, buried only about 20 centimeters deep in the ground, was revealed. He continued digging around it until he managed to expose its upper and front part. He knelt and examined the find carefully. It looked like the remains of pistons.

Interesting, what is this?

He continued digging. Slowly, a large, very rusty, bent and twisted engine emerged from the ground. It seemed to have been severely hit at the front. He gathered that the engine had been round in shape before, but found it difficult to be certain.

He decided to call the foreman before continuing.

"Yes, it looks like an engine," agreed the foreman, a big-bellied man of about fifty-five, wearing a light, wide-brimmed straw hat and round-frame sunglasses. "How could it have gotten here?"

The Dozer shrugged.

"I'll assign you more men and digging tools. We'll dig around and see what's buried here."

Little by little, the remains of an old plane were uncovered before the onlookers' eyes: First, they revealed remnants of a square metal frame which likely protected the plane's nose. Rotting pieces of wood were still attached to it. Then, the diggers exposed part of the cockpit, to which a rectangular remnant of some beam was attached. The cockpit's frame was missing, but one of its walls, mostly hidden under a layer of soil, could be identified.

The diggers continued working around the debris and revealed a wooden part of the plane's wing that was connected at its base to the surviving cockpit wall. In place of the rest of the wing was nothing but dark, organic decay. This plane had been buried under piles of earth many years ago.

The Dozer was already drenched in sweat and wiped his forehead with a handkerchief.

The foreman turned to him, "Take the keys to my truck and drive to the office. Inform management about the plane wreck we found and tell them I've decided to stop all earthworks here for now until we receive new orders."

The Dozer returned after an hour and a half with further instructions.

"Where the hell have you been?" asked the foreman. "What took you so long?" He didn't wait for a reply, and they both started walking towards the excavation site.

From a distance, the Dozer could see that most of the debris had been exposed. He could identify part of the plane's body and a bit of its tail. The central part was obscured by workers standing around it. It was clear that they were very excited, and as soon as one of the workers spotted them approaching, he motioned for them to come quickly.

They hastened their pace.

When they reached the wreckage, everyone moved aside to let them through. A brief glance at the plane's rear was enough for the Dozer to understand the cause of the uproar, and a shiver ran down his spine.

The plane's tail was adorned with a swastika.

# PART ONE

# Chapter 1

The stunning view of Tel Aviv unfolded outside the large windows of the conference room, with the Mediterranean Sea stretching from horizon to horizon between the towering office buildings and residential towers, bathed in the brilliant morning light. In the center of the room stood a long, dark, wooden table surrounded by identical chairs. In front of each chair was a clear, empty glass, a notepad, and a pen.

In the center of the table were several pitchers of clear water, a pack of tissues, and a white frame covered in glass, holding a newspaper clipping.

At the far end of the table was a chair for the person who would direct the meeting, Attorney David Rubin, his father's trusted confidant for many years.

Mark decided to sit in the chair next to the head of the table, fitting for someone who, at the end of the meeting, would become the largest shareholder of 'Citrus Investments' and probably one of the wealthiest people in the country. He regretted reaching this point only as he was approaching seventy, widowed and overweight, but better late than never.

It had been about four weeks since his father passed away at the luxurious retirement home where he had lived in recent years, and yesterday was the unveiling ceremony of his tombstone – a large and impressive volcanic rock monument towering over all the surrounding gravestones, just as his father had requested.

So typical of Dad. He always strove for that, at any cost. Always to be first, always to be the winner. In tenders, in court, in arguments, in everything.

Mark was, of course, the one who ended up paying the price every day. He hoped that at least the reward would finally come today.

Ten days ago, he had received an official letter from Attorney Rubin inviting him to today's meeting, where Rubin would read his father's will. He didn't understand the point of all this drama. Why couldn't they simply hand him a copy of the will and be done with it?

Knowing his father, he assumed these were his instructions and that there was no escaping honoring his wishes, even after his death. Their father didn't tell him or Lilly what was in the will, not even a hint. The fact that Dad chose him to replace himself as CEO when he retired from managing the conglomerate, rather than Lilly or an external professional manager, gave him the confidence that his seniority would also be reflected in the will.

As he slowly walked alongside the table towards the seat he chose, he reached for the framed newspaper clipping and read it. He remembered this news piece well. It was published the day after his father's death. He read it again, word by word, sentence by sentence:

*The businessman and agricultural entrepreneur, Michael Golber, passed away yesterday.*

*The billionaire, who established a grand business empire and managed 'Citrus Investments' for many years, died of old age.*

*The Minister of Agriculture eulogized Golber, saying:*

*"Michael Golber was a pillar of the Israeli agricultural world. He was one of the greatest businessmen in this field here. Noble-hearted, he was wholly dedicated to developing the economy and agriculture in Israel. There was no better ambassador for Israeli entrepreneurship and Israeli spirit than him."*

*Golber is most identified with the greatest success story of the private agricultural sector in Israel, 'Citrus Investments Group,' which he founded and turned from a local company into one of the leading agricultural equipment trading companies in Israel. He was one of the first orchard owners who, even before the establishment of the state, formed their own packing house. In the 1950s, he expanded his business and began importing agricultural equipment himself. Golber's struggles with the agricultural establishment led over the years to revolutionary changes regarding the right of private farmers to market their produce themselves.*

*He leaves behind a son and a daughter.*

Mark returned the frame to the table. People truly admired his father. Well, they didn't know him like he did.

In the background, he heard Lilly's voice echoing in the waiting room. Lilly, or Liliana by her formal name, was three years younger than him and had always been a fountain of optimism and positive thinking for him. The daily confrontations with their father, which began when he started working at the company, had exhausted him over the years.

Only thanks to her support and encouragement did he manage to survive the many years of working with his father and under his management, until his old man had retired a decade ago.

I owe her so much, he reminded himself.

Lilly's cheerful laughter was heard again, this time closer. In a moment, she would enter, and he would invite her to sit next to him.

This is it, the moment of truth. They were gathering together for one purpose. Today, they will finally know.

The conference room door opened and a woman of about sixty-seven entered. Her head was adorned with a mane of silver hair, her face was round, and her big smile lit up her stormy green eyes. She wore a fashionable dress in light colors, a turquoise stone necklace around her neck, and a large ring on her finger.

He got up to hug her.

"Hey Mark," she extended her arms for a hug, "you got here before me, as usual, no matter how hard I try to be on time."

They hugged tightly, and he gestured for her to sit in the chair to his left.

"Hey Lilly, it's always good to see you. I wish I had all that energy of yours."

Lilly had been widowed long before him, and he often wondered how she managed to stay so positive and optimistic. *I wish I were a bit more like her and less like...*

"So today is the day, right?" Lilly interrupted his thoughts. "Finally, you'll get ownership of 'Citrus.' There's no one more deserving than you."

"Not any more than you if you wanted it," he replied seriously.

Lilly nudged him in the ribs, "I'm fine without all that responsibility. I'm sure Dad took care of me. Everything is fine."

Lilly always took life lightly and accepted things as they were, even though her life was full of challenges and struggles. She resembled their mother in that way. Unlike her, Mark was always serious and took everything to heart.

"Do you think we'll finally find out how Dad built his empire from scratch?" Lilly remarked as she sat next to him.

"Not entirely from scratch. He did come to Israel with some small capital."

"I think he once said he arrived on one of the underground immigrant ships in the 1930s."

"I don't remember that. I only know that his first business was buying land near the sources of the Yarkon River, not far from the old train station by Rosh Ha'Ayin. He restored an orchard that was in bad shape and built a packing house next to it."

"Yes, the Bergs Orchard. That I know. I still remember how angry he was at us when we played and made noise there as children. Do you remember?" She smiled nostalgically.

"Yes, of course I remember. He never took us there again after that. Did you know that it's the only place he refused to sell despite it being unprofitable?"

The door opened, and his sons, Daniel and David, and Lilly's children, Tom and Hannah, entered, chatting among themselves.

Hannah went over to her mother and kissed her cheek.

"Hey Dad, hey Aunt Lilly," said David. Daniel also waved hello, and they all sat at the far end of the table.

"What are you doing here? I didn't know you were invited too," Mark said.

"Yes," Daniel replied, "Grandpa probably wanted the whole family here."

Dad still had to control everything, even now. What exactly did he bequeath them at his expense? Didn't Dad trust him to share generously with them? What other surprises were awaiting him today?

# Chapter 2

The conference room door opened and Attorney Rubin entered carrying a rectangular wooden box with an antique look. "Good morning," he said as he approached the head of the table. He placed the box down, shook hands with Mark and Lilly, and took his seat.

The attendees stopped what they were doing and turned their attention toward him. Silence fell.

Attorney Rubin, slightly older than Mark, was impressive in appearance. He stood at 1.9 meters tall, with a full head of graying hair covering his head and temples. His blue eyes conveyed wisdom and experience.

"How is everyone today? I know Mark and Lilly, of course. Who are the rest of you? Who belongs to whom here?"

Everyone began introducing themselves one by one.

"Okay, can we start already? I don't have all day," Mark announced.

"Mark, some of the people invited to the meeting have yet to arrive, so we'll all need to be patient. We cannot begin until everyone is present." His tone was authoritative as always.

"What do you mean? Who else needs to be here? All the family members are already here."

"Your father left very clear instructions regarding the invitees and the conduct of this meeting," Rubin said, placing a hand on the wooden box. "We will honor his instructions."

Everyone cast curious glances at the old box. It was hand-carved and partially covered in dark brown leather with lighter shades, adorned with shapes that had worn down over the years. A brass strip encircled the sides of the box, and there was a latch at the front made of brass as well, with a small lock wrapped in red wax. The silent box exuded mystery.

"Have you ever seen this?" Mark asked Lilly. She shook her head.

A moment later, the door opened again, and Miriam, the office manager, entered, accompanied by a man of about fifty with an Eastern European appearance. The man wore an outdated gray suit and a dark, faded tie. He carried a worn leather briefcase and wore a necklace with a golden cross around his neck. Miriam gestured for him to sit down.

"I apologize for being late," said the stranger in English with a pronounced Russian accent as he sat down. "I came here straight from the airport. It took the taxi driver a long time to get me here," he added.

Mark looked toward Miriam, who shrugged. From Lilly's expression, he could tell that she also had no idea who the man who had joined them was.

"You can invite the interpreter to join us as well now," Rubin said.

A short moment later, another person entered and sat next to the stranger.

Miriam sat to Rubin's right, placed a tape recorder on the table, and turned it on to record the meeting.

Rubin turned to the interpreter. "For the record, please ask our guest for his name."

The interpreter spoke to the stranger, who replied in Russian that his name was Alexander Mirkin from St. Petersburg. He presented his passport to the attorney.

"Now that everyone who was invited has arrived, we can finally begin. The meeting will be conducted in Hebrew. There is an interpreter here who will translate everything into Russian for Mr. Mirkin so he can follow along," Rubin said. He looked toward Mr. Mirkin to ensure he understood, and then added, "I'm now going to open the wooden box entrusted to me by the late Michael Golber."

Mr. Mirkin leaned toward the interpreter and whispered something quietly.

"Just a moment, sir. Before you begin, Mr. Mirkin would like to know why he is here, who Michael Golber is, and who these people in the room are. The invitation he received only mentioned an event for the reading of a will," the interpreter said.

Mark glared at Mr. Mirkin. This guy has a lot of nerve, he thought. European or Russian, some manners wouldn't hurt him. He wondered how Rubin would respond.

Unlike Mark, the attorney maintained his composure, or at least in appearance, and replied in a matter-of-fact tone, "I assume Mr. Mirkin will get answers to all his questions during the course of the meeting. In the meantime, we'll proceed as planned."

Everyone watched Attorney Rubin in silence.

"This box was entrusted to me by the late Michael Golber a few years ago. Today, the conditions for its opening and the reading of the will have been met. As you can see, I'm now breaking the wax seal and opening it with the key given to me by the deceased. I should add that I didn't draft the will and have no knowledge of its contents. Additionally, I don't know what's inside this wooden box."

The tension Mark felt only intensified, and he couldn't help but blurt out, "How could you not have been involved in drafting my father's will? I don't get it."

"Believe me, I was just as surprised as you," Rubin replied. "I offered to draft a will for your father countless times and he always replied that I was right and that he intended to take care of it, but he never told me he had already done so, until he entrusted me with this box. I have no explanation for why he kept this from me, and to some extent, I was disappointed, maybe even a little hurt. I struggle to understand why he didn't trust me on this matter."

Mark saw out of the corner of his eye that the interpreter was translating the exchange for Mirkin. I need to keep that in mind moving forward, he thought. Next time, I'll make sure to ask Rubin such questions privately.

The attorney set the lock aside and lifted the top of the box. Everyone waited to see what it held.

He revealed its contents to the attendees. The inner walls were lined with a delicate dark blue felt, and inside were several items stacked on top of each other. The very first item was a sealed white envelope with the words "Cover Letter and Instructions" handwritten on it. The envelope bore the unmistakable logo of 'Citrus' – a marquise diamond.

"Well, there's no doubt that Grandpa prepared this box," David said. "He was always a bit mysterious, wasn't he?"

"What a load of nonsense; what was mysterious about Grandpa?" Hannah replied.

"Well, you were his favorite grandchild, you grew up on his lap. Maybe he shared secrets with you that we don't know about," David suggested.

"Both of you, stop interrupting," Mark chastised. "Let's continue."

# Chapter 3

Rubin opened the envelope and pulled out a multi-page printed document. The first page, in bold letters, bore the words *"Instructions for Opening My Will."*

He flipped through the pages, each bearing the initials "M.G.," and reached the final page, which displayed the deceased's signature; he showed it to those present.

"Yes, that's my father's signature," Mark confirmed.

The document bore no date.

The attorney cleared his throat and began reading:

"My dearest family,
If you are sitting in the office of my long-time lawyer and confidant, David Rubin, it means that I have joined my beloved wife Frida, your mother and grandmother.
 I have had a life full of activity and accomplishments, and I am fully satisfied with it. I fought my competitors, defeated them, and succeeded in leaving you a financial empire. Take care of it! I worked very hard throughout all my days to build it. I founded it myself, but not alone. After nearly eighty years, it's time to do justice by the person who helped me most in my success."

It was naive to think that the will would be short and clear; after all, nothing could be 'clear cut' with Dad, Mark thought. He wiped the beads of sweat that had accumulated on his forehead threatening to drip into his eyes. Lilly also began to shift uncomfortably in her seat.

He glanced at Rubin and met his gaze, directed at both him and Lilly. He recognized a sense of unease and confusion in the old man's eyes too.

Attorney Rubin continued reading:

> "It's important for me that you know that knowledge is everything. The wealth I leave you is meaningless if you don't understand where I came from and what drove me. During my life, I never found the time or the mental strength to properly tell you. Now the time has come.
>
> I assume you are wondering who the stranger sitting among you is, if indeed Attorney Rubin succeeded in locating and inviting him to this meeting as I instructed."

Mark could almost feel his father's presence in the room, pointing his index finger at Mr. Mirkin, who sat to Lilly's left, his head slightly tilted toward the interpreter, listening quietly to every word.

> "The answer to that will become clear later, so please be patient."

Rubin paused his reading, took a sip from the glass of water in front of him, and continued.

Mark pulled the nearby pitcher of water closer and poured a glass for Lilly and himself. They both took a sip, as if preparing for what was to come.

> "I now ask you to take out the brown envelope marked with the number '1' from the wooden box in front of you and present its contents to the attendees."

The brown envelope was pulled out. It was heavy and stiff. Attorney Rubin took out a thick booklet from within with the title

"Translation" written on its first page in large print. Below, in smaller letters, were the words "Translation of the Diary from Latvian to Hebrew."

Latvian? Mark wondered. What more tricks does Dad have in store for us? To the best of my knowledge, Dad hasn't been to Latvia since he left many years ago, and I don't recall him having any contact or connection with anyone from there. And what does this have to do with this Mister Mirkin? This time he kept his questions to himself.

A look of surprise appeared on Mr. Mirkin's face upon hearing the reference to the Latvian language, but he said nothing.

Rubin also pulled out a thick, very old-looking notebook with a black cover from the same envelope. The cover was partially torn and deeply creased. A large brown stain marred the front. The notebook's pages were yellow and crumbling at the edges, some torn. One could see dense handwriting in a foreign language, with some parts faded and hard to make out.

The attorney began reading from the cover letter, placing the old notebook on the table in front of him.

> "I instruct the translation to be read to those present before proceeding to read my will, even if the reading of the translation takes more than one meeting."

"What does that mean? The whole booklet?" Lilly asked Mark.

"Seems like it," he shrugged. "Is this standard? We're not going to sit here for days. Why don't you give it to us to read in our own time? For now, let's move on to the will. That's what we came here for, isn't it?"

"As your father instructed, and we *will* honor his last wishes, yes, we will all sit here, however long it takes, and I will read this booklet through to the end. Perhaps before we start, we should clear our schedules accordingly."

Mr. Mirkin raised his hand and spoke to the interpreter.

"Mr. Mirkin wants to mention that he's only here for three days.

He doesn't understand his connection to all of this and, in any case, cannot stay longer."

"Is he trying to run the show now?" Mark raised his voice slightly.

"Mark, please," Attorney Rubin intervened before anyone else could speak. "Tell him that we'll do our best to finish within that timeframe," he said to the interpreter, then turned to Miriam.

"Please clear my schedule completely for the next three days. Also, ensure that food and drinks are brought in here at 10 AM and 2 PM each day." He addressed the attendees, "If we finish earlier, all the better; otherwise, take into account that this is the schedule from now on. If anyone wants a hot drink or to use the bathroom, now's the time. I wish to begin, and with minimal interruptions."

Ten minutes later, everyone was back in their seats. The room was completely silent. Everyone was waiting for the translation to be read.

Attorney Rubin carefully and somewhat questioningly took hold of the thick booklet and began reading:

### "Riga, Latvia, Friday, May 25, 1934.

I've decided to keep a diary. Today was a very important day for me, not because I turned seventeen yesterday, but because from this day on, I know what I want to do with my life, and it's not exactly what was planned for me. I have no idea where this will lead.

My name is Mihails, but everyone calls me Miku. This is how you start a diary, by stating your name, right? Otherwise, how will anyone know who wrote it? Someone will surely read it someday.

I live in Riga, Latvia, obviously. My home address situation is a bit complicated..."

# Chapter 4

**Riga, Latvia, Friday, May 25, 1934**

. . . I was born on May 24, 1917. My mother, Inga, died when I was a year old. I don't remember her. My father, Martin, never remarried, and since he spends most of his day at the factory he owns with my grandfather, Ernest, I live in two places. On weekends, I stay with my father in our apartment at 10 Antonias[1] Street, and during the week, I sleep at my grandparents', Hilda and Ernest, at 3 Alberta Street. The two homes are a two-minute walk apart.

My day began with breakfast in the large dining room at my grandparents'.

Grandpa told us about what he'd read in the newspaper. It was about the new government formed by Karlis Ulmanis[2] after the coup he'd carried out about ten days ago and the dissolution of the parliament. I've heard people talking about it everywhere in the past few days.

Grandpa finished eating and said, "I won't be home for lunch today."

"Why?" Grandma wondered. Grandpa always comes home for lunch.

"I mean to attend the reception planned for the pilot Herberts Cukurs, in Spilve."

Grandpa was referring to the Spilve Aerodrome[3] on the other side of the Daugava.[4]

"You can use the time to finally instruct Martha to wax the dining table, so it shines."

I looked up and stared at Grandma. If there's anything she hates, it's Grandpa 'advising' her on what to do. She, of course, didn't disappoint. Her gaze fixed on him. It felt like a combination of 'How dare you intrude on my territory?' and 'Since when are you interested in planes and flights?'

I asked Grandpa to explain what it was about. He smiled, and I think he was grateful for the distraction. I'm sure he preferred looking at me rather than at her.

"Herberts Cukurs is a pilot in our air force. He built a single-engine plane all by himself, and last August he took off with it and flew west and south for several months, from city to city, from country to country, until he reached Gambia. Another pilot named Nicholas Pullins[5] tried to do so last year and crashed on his way to Berlin."

"Gambia?" I asked, "Where's Gambia?"

"In Africa," Grandpa replied. "It's an almost unbelievable feat, like the flight of that American, Lindbergh, who flew from America to Europe in 1927. Cukurs made the return trip from Gambia by plane as well, and he landed in Liepaja[6] a week ago. Today, he'll fly to Riga and land at our aerodrome, Spilve. There's a reception ceremony planned for him there."

As Grandpa spoke, I could vividly picture Cukurs flying in the skies above all those countries. I got excited and asked him to take me with him. I wanted to see this hero myself.

Grandpa seemed surprised that I wanted to join him and, before he could answer, Grandma intervened, "It's a great idea, Ernest. Take the boy with you. It's an extra birthday present for him. I'm sure you'll have a great time together," she said with a slight note of cynicism.

"Okay," he sighed, "as long as you don't cause me any trouble. Stay by my side the whole time and do exactly what you're told."

"Sure, sure. Thank you, Grandpa. Thanks, Grandma," I said immediately, probably too loudly, because their housekeeper Martha, who was standing nearby, raised her head and gave me a chastising look for breaking their strict etiquette rules.

Dad's parents passed away many years ago. My mom was an only child, and so is my dad, and I'm his only son, which means I'm the heir to the entire family fortune. As a result, I always have to behave perfectly. Grandma and Martha always tell me, "One day you'll be responsible for everything you see here, and it's about time you start behaving accordingly."

I was forced to do my homework, learn to play the piano, and keep up my German, in addition to Latvian and Russian. They just don't understand that I'm seventeen already; I'm not a little boy anymore. At least I'm done with the piano lessons for good.

I was a bit excited when Grandpa and I left. I had never seen an aerodrome with my own eyes before.

Attorney Rubin raised his eyes from the text. Everyone was looking at him, waiting for him to continue. "I see there are translator's footnotes here, I suggest we don't dwell on them now and review them at the end." He gently turned the page and continued.

# Chapter 5

Spilve is a large field covered in green grass. Grandpa pointed to the administration buildings and offices nearby, as well as to the hangars intended for storing aircraft.

Within the grassy field was a long, narrow, cut path. Grandpa said that this was likely the runway Cukurs would land on later.

There were a lot of people there, with many boys who I think were about my age. They were all bunched together, and one of them looked familiar to me.

As I got closer, I recognized Mikhail. He used to be a year above me at the 'Erich-German' private school, which is very close to my house, and we were on good terms back then. Mikhail transferred to another school over a year ago, and I hadn't seen him since. He was supposed to graduate last year.

"Am I the only one who finds it strange that his friend's name was Mikhail, just like his? What, weren't there any other names for boys in 1934?" Hannah remarked, taking advantage of Rubin's pause for breath. He lifted his eyes from the document.

"But everyone called him Miku, and maybe it was a common name. Why does it matter now?" replied Lilly.

"It just caught my attention," she smiled at Rubin. He, for his part, returned to the booklet in his hands and continued.

Mikhail couldn't see me from where I was standing. I told Grandpa that I recognized some friends, and he agreed to let me move away from him. I approached Mikhail from behind and surprised him with a tap on the shoulder.

He turned around, smiled at me, and extended his hand for a handshake.

I noticed the overalls he was wearing.

"What are you doing here?" I asked him.

"I'm working here as an apprentice mechanic. I started last Monday and I've been shadowing the chief mechanic here ever since, wherever he goes. I have good hands and I love working with engines so, for now, I'm really enjoying the work here."

It sounded strange to me. Almost everyone studying with me is planning to enroll in university after high school. "But why didn't you go to university?"

"I registered, I registered alright, for Riga Polytechnic. I wanted to study engineering..." his tone changed, "... but they didn't accept me because I'm Jewish..."

Mikhail paused for a moment and stared straight into my eyes. I didn't know how to respond, so I remained silent and waited for him to continue.

He told me that the Polytechnic had decided that the number of Jews admitted each year wouldn't exceed 10 percent "because, according to them, that's our share of the population in Latvia. It even has a name, 'Numerus Clausus.' Since I wasn't a particularly outstanding student, I couldn't make it into the group that got admitted."

I'd already heard that universities limit the admission of Jews, but this was the first time I'd met someone who was personally affected by it.

"So, I didn't have much choice. I looked for a job at Spilve as an apprentice mechanic. I hope I can get accepted to the Polytechnic next year, and in the meantime, I'll gain a profession and experience. So, since last Monday, I come here by bike every day except Saturday."

"Why don't you work at your father's bakery? Wouldn't that be better for you?"

"The last thing I want is to work with my father. I'm not interested in baking bread, and besides, my two older brothers already work there, and I'd just find myself constantly following their orders." Mikhail rolled his eyes. "I love engines and planes, so working here suits me."

He told me about the Latvian school he transferred to and the sports he was introduced to; they taught them winter skiing, boxing, discus throwing, and shot put. He sounded enthusiastic. I wasn't surprised. He was considered the athletic type and one of the strongest boys in our school. Mikhail also told me that he'd joined the Scouts and that last summer he even spent almost a month in camp.

"I could only dream of doing these things; my grandparents would never allow me."

Mikhail chuckled. "And how did you end up here today?"

"My grandpa received an invitation. I've never really seen a plane, so I decided to join him."

"You made a smart choice. Planes are amazing! You can't stop looking at them; they're like metal birds among real birds." Mikhail spread his arms, demonstrating flight in an imaginary sky.

"And they're also the peak of technology. That's why I chose to study aircraft mechanics. I promise you—you'll love them too. Now, I have to takeoff back to work. It was good seeing you here. Should we try meeting up again?"

"Gladly."

After talking to Mikhail, I noticed that police officers in peaked caps and long, thick coats were directing the crowd to walk toward an area enclosed by ropes and marking posts in front of one of the hangars. The gathering crowd grew denser and wasn't allowed to roam around the rest of the aerodrome.

I found Grandpa and stood beside him, waiting with everyone else, until the sound of an engine came from above. We raised our heads and saw a plane emerging from the gray sky, flying parallel to the runway on its other end. Just as Mikhail said, from the ground it looked like a large bird gliding in the sky. To think that Cukurs flew inside that thing alone to Africa and back, over jungles, high mountains, and raging rivers. It's incredible, chilling, and even frightening.

I tried to imagine what it looked like. The only time I saw the world from above was when I'd climbed with a friend up to the observation deck of St. Peter's,[7] but that's still far from the height a plane can reach. I wish I could see what Cukurs saw.

Excited calls rose from all directions. I took advantage of the moment when Grandpa and everyone around him were looking up to squeeze through and reach the front row of the crowd, so that no one would block my view of the plane landing.

The wing closest to us tilted down, and the plane turned until it straightened in the direction of the runway, then gradually descended until its wheels touched the ground.

At that moment, people from the crowd broke past the ropes and began running towards the plane, which was still taxiing on the landing strip. The police officers shouted that it was dangerous and that they had to return, but the crowd that got through simply ignored them and continued running until they stood at the edge of the runway, waiting for the plane to come back towards them.

I ducked under the barrier rope and joined the last people who managed to pass by the astonished police officers, running towards the plane.

Cukurs stopped at the end of the runway, turned the plane around, and began his slow return until finally stopping right in front of us and turning off the engine. People were already crowding around the wing before he could even open the cockpit, waving their hats and cheering. I stood close to the rear side of the wing. I had a clear view of the cockpit.

After a few moments, Cukurs himself emerged. He was wearing a dark coat, a leather cap covering his head, ears, and chin, and flying goggles strapped to his forehead with a bright band. He placed his hands on the sides of the cockpit, leaped out onto the wing, and straightened up. I saw that his hands were covered with dark gloves and his feet with tall leather boots.

He stood right above me, towering to an endless height, smiling at the large crowd and waving. Then, he turned his back and began walking down the wing until his feet stood on the ground right in front of me.

At that moment, I felt a crowd pushing me aside. I fell on the wet grass and my pants got dirty. By the time I managed to get up, Cukurs and the large crowd surrounding him had already moved away back to the enclosed area with the rest of the spectators.

I ran back and managed to see a young girl in a white shirt handing him a bouquet of flowers, and the crowd continuing to cheer for him.

As I stood there, enchanted by the event, I suddenly felt a strong pull on my left arm. Grandpa stood over me with an angry and worried look on his face.

"Where were you? Where did you disappear to? You worried me sick!"

I don't remember answering; I was in euphoria. Mikhail's words, "a metal bird among real birds," echoed in my mind.

I'm getting excited again just writing this entry. The plane, the pilot, even the clothes he wore, the whole atmosphere around there today — I've never felt like this before. I now know something I didn't know this morning. What I want to do in life is to fly. I want to be a pilot.

# Chapter 6

"Did you hear that, Daniel? He was a pilot too," David tapped his brother on the shoulder.

"We don't know that yet," Mark replied sternly. "We can't keep having all these interruptions. There's still a lot left to read."

"It's okay, Mark. Rubin needs to catch his breath every now and then too. It's actually interesting so far, isn't it?"

"No, Lilly, I still don't understand why this whole ceremony was so important to Dad."

"Let's continue," Rubin turned his head towards Lilly, "and thank you for your consideration. Things will become clearer as we move forward."

### Riga, Latvia, Wednesday, August 22, 1934

I've started taking an interest in aviation and following all the news related to it, but the news isn't very good. Every month there are accidents and pilots get killed. The whole thing seems very dangerous.

It's a really bad time to bring up the idea of taking flying lessons to Dad or Grandpa. I also need to figure out how to talk to them about it, how to tell them that I don't want to continue in their footsteps at the factory as they've decided for me.

I'll have to wait for a better time.

## Riga, Latvia, Monday, September 3, 1934

The school year at "Erich-German" has begun. According to the new law, everyone has to attend school according to their religion or nationality. Even private schools, which were independent before, are now subject to the Latvian Ministry of Education, and this law applies to them too. I really didn't fancy the idea of transferring to a new school, but since this is my last year anyway, they didn't force me to. I'll be able to finish my studies at the private school. What luck!

## Riga, Latvia, Monday, October 1, 1934

Time flies quickly, and I haven't done anything yet to realize my new dream of learning how to fly. I've been feeling my dream slipping away and wanted to experience that aviation atmosphere again, so I decided to ride my bike to Spilve, hoping I might get lucky and see the planes in the hangars up close.

It was the longest ride I had ever done, but I enjoyed it. I rode through some streets I know, parallel to Uzvaras Park. That's where I learned to ride a bike with Dad, and I have good memories from there. Some of the streets are narrow. I rode carefully along the winding Daugavgrivas Street, between the low houses on either side and, fortunately, it was completely free of cars and carts.

When I crossed Lilljas Street, I thought my luck had run out. A car appeared from my left, and its driver didn't see me at all. If I hadn't stopped, he would have run me over. It took me a moment to calm down and catch my breath. I continued pedaling at a moderate pace along Daugavgrivas Street until I reached the tree-lined avenue leading to Spilve's entrance. From there, the road to the office building at the gate to the aerodrome was short.

The place had changed a bit. I saw they had started building new hangars; there was a sign near one of them that read 'National Guard Air Force'[8] and another sign next to that said, 'Latvian Aviation Club.'[9]

A group of people was standing near one of the hangars, talking animatedly with their hands. I got close enough to hear snippets of their conversation.

They were talking about the crash of a plane called 'Blue Bird'[10] during aerobatic exercises and said that a pilot named Pullins managed to escape safely, against all odds. That name sounded familiar. Grandpa mentioned him on the day we went to see Cukurs land at Spilve; he tried to fly to Gambia and failed. This pilot had crashed twice and survived. He must be very lucky.

I returned home even more determined. The visit to Spilve strengthened my resolve to finally tell Dad about my intention to learn how to fly.

### Riga, Latvia, Sunday, October 7, 1934

Today I was brave enough and talked with Dad. He asked me during dinner if I had started thinking about what I want to do when the year is over. He talked about the various faculties and wanted to know which one I wanted to enroll in and what I wanted to study, because we needed to submit the applications for admission soon.

"My plan is to study mechanical engineering and aeronautics at the University of Latvia,"[11] I told him.

"I don't know what you'll do with aeronautics, but mechanical engineering is definitely a useful profession for the factory. You can work at the factory while studying and use the knowledge you gain to improve our machines."

Dad was clearly pleased with my intention to study mechanical engineering.

"I intend to combine my studies with flight lessons at Spilve." My throat dried up all at once. I waited for his reaction.

"Where did this come from? Since when are you interested in flying? Is that why you said you wanted to study aeronautics too?"

"I've been thinking about it for a long time. I want to move forward and be part of the new world, the future."

"Where do you even take these flight lessons?"

"You can study at the Spilve Aerodrome, at the Aviation Club."

"Can anyone learn to fly? Do you need your own plane for that?"

"I intend to find out all the details in the coming days."

Dad didn't say no! He didn't say yes either, but the fact that he showed some interest and didn't tell me he disagreed is already very encouraging. I think I have a chance to fulfill my dream.

"So what does that mean? Did he become a pilot or not?" David asked Daniel.

"I hope so. It would be interesting to hear how they taught flying back in 1934. Also, this pilot he mentioned, Zekurs, I think I've heard that name, but I don't remember exactly."

"Cukurs," Rubin corrected, "I also find that name familiar. Maybe he explains more about him later." He turned the page and continued.

# Chapter 7

### Riga, Latvia, Saturday, October 13, 1934

It rained all week. Today, the weather finally cleared up to allow for a ride to Spilve. I left at eight in the morning.

When I arrived, I didn't see anyone in the administration area. I knew that the Aviation Club was located near the end of the runway, in a kind of wooden hangar. I hoped someone would be there at such an early hour. I walked in its direction, and as I got closer, I heard noises from inside. I stood near the entrance and waited. I didn't dare enter uninvited.

After about fifteen minutes, someone came, but from outside. I didn't know who it was. He gave me a stern look, "Why are you standing here? What do you want?"

"I'm looking to inquire about flying lessons. I thought someone here might be able to give me information."

"Are you sure you want to learn how to fly? How old are you, anyway?"

"I'm almost eighteen," I said with open pride. I lied a little because I was afraid that he would send me away if I admitted I was only seventeen and a half.

"Wait here and I'll see if there's anyone in the club who can talk to you. But don't stand near the entrance—you're in the way here."

I moved away a bit and waited about twenty minutes, pacing back and forth until the door opened and a tall man stepped out, wearing a long coat. He had a wool scarf, a leather fedora, and a pipe like Grandpa's. He glanced in my direction and then approached.

"You're the kid who wants to fly?"

"Yes."

"How old are you?"

This time I didn't dare lie, "I turned seventeen on the day Officer Cukurs landed in Spilve after returning from Gambia."

"You were here when he arrived?"

"Yes, I was with my grandpa. I've wanted to learn to fly ever since."

"Have you ever flown? Do you even know anything about it?"

"No, but I want to learn. Ever since I saw Cukurs, I've been reading about planes all the time, and that's what I want to be. A pilot. That's my dream."

"Where do you live?"

"In Riga, on Antonias Street."

"So, you're a rich kid, huh?" he noted. "What exactly do you want to know?" he asked, giving me a piercing look.

"I was hoping to get information about the possibility of studying how to fly here, at Spilve."

"You want me to teach you how to fly?"

I didn't really know how to answer. I didn't know who he was, his name, or what his experience was, but there was something very pleasant and easygoing about his face and his look, exuding confidence.

"Yes."

"Well, I just wanted to see how you would react when faced with sudden discomfort; after all, you don't know me at all. You handled it well. My name is Edvins Ozols, and yours?"

I told him and felt my embarrassed smile as he continued, "Let's go to the offices and restart our conversation there, okay?"

"Yes, of course, certainly."

I choked up. Something that moments ago had just been a vague idea, was beginning to take a tangible and practical form.

We walked in silence.

Mr. Ozols led me to a side room with a small wooden table and three chairs. He sat down on one of them and motioned with his hand, so I sat opposite him. He took off his scarf and hat. He had blue eyes and his hair was short and light, like mine. I waited silently until he spoke.

"First, I'll introduce myself. As I said earlier, my name is Edvins Ozols. I'm 37 years old. I used to be a fighter pilot in the Imperial Russian Air Force, then flew in the Air Division, the Naval Aviation Division, and in the National Guard Air Force. Currently, I work as a test pilot for VEF[12] Company, and I'm also a member of the Latvian Aviation Club. Additionally, on weekends, I teach civil aviation as part of the club. I'll explain a bit about the lessons later, but first, I want to know who I'm dealing with here."

He pulled a small notebook from his pocket, and a pen appeared in his hand as if by magic. He placed them on the table.

"So, I understand you're seventeen, right?"

"A little more, I turned seventeen on May 24th."

"That doesn't matter; the main point is you're over. So, as far as age is concerned, I don't see a problem. And what about your health? I see you're not wearing glasses, that's also good. Do you have any health issues? Have you had any surgeries in the past?"

"No, not at all, I'm completely healthy."

Mr. Ozols wrote in his notebook.

"Have you ever sailed a boat?"

"Yes, of course. I've sailed many times on the Daugava River and along the coast when we used to sail to Jurmala."[13]

Why did he ask me about that?

"And how did you feel on the boat? Did you feel nauseous?"

"No, of course not. I felt completely fine."

Mr. Ozols wrote again in his notebook.

"You'll need to bring a certificate from your family doctor confirming you're healthy and fit, but we'll leave that aside for the time being. Now let's move on to your desire to fly and your knowledge of aviation. What do you know about it?"

"Not a lot, actually. As I told you earlier, I was only first exposed to it at the ceremony for Cukurs. I follow the topic in the newspapers, so I also know there have been a few accidents recently."

"You saved me the next question. You understand that it's a dangerous activity, that you could get killed? You're a young guy, you're not afraid of anything at your age, and that's a problem sometimes. Are you sure you're not afraid to fly at great heights and be completely dependent on an engine that could breakdown?"

I paused to consider my response. It's not that I don't think about the dangers; I know it's quite risky. But despite that, I want to learn and become a pilot. I tried to figure out from deep within what the best answer to give him would be. It was important that he knew I always tell the truth so he could trust me.

After a few seconds, I replied, "Yes, I'm afraid, but on the other hand, I know I can overcome it. It's no different from any other fear I've felt before and overcome. At least that's what I think."

"Well, we'll see that on your first flight, but I like your answer. I'm not sure everyone would admit it."

I felt relieved; I had passed another test. It's probably best to trust your inner instinct and act accordingly.

At this point, I felt secure enough to ask a question of my own.

"But I have a question about that. Don't pilots have parachutes for emergencies?" I remembered that one of the pilots had recently managed to save himself by parachuting from his plane.

Mr. Ozols looked at me and, for the first time, smiled broadly. "You think you're in America? Here, either you land or..." He looked at me to make sure I understood his meaning.

I understood, of course I understood, and it made me even more determined to be the best pilot possible. I wouldn't need a parachute. I would know how to handle any malfunction. Obviously, I didn't tell him all that. I just waited for him to continue.

# Chapter 8

"I don't get it. The man flat out tells him there's no protection, no safety net, that you get on a plane and there's no escape?" Daniel looked at Attorney Rubin.

"What did you think," his father replied, "that back then it was like it is today? I don't know much about aviation history, but it seems about right for the period. And if we've paused from reading, I have to say that I also recognize that name, Herberts Cukurs. Isn't he the one the Mossad took out in South America in the 60s?" he continued. "I remember it being mentioned a lot in the news a few years ago; they said he was a pilot before World War II. Yes, Herberts Cukurs, it's definitely him."

He turned to Lilly, "These names – Martin, Ernst, Hilda – do they mean anything to you?"

"No, I've never heard them before."

"Well, they're not related to Dad's parents or the rest of his family; this is Miku's diary. I guess it's yet another mystery we'll have to solve. What time is it? I'm starting to get hungry."

"Maybe I'll make you some coffee? There's probably a cookie somewhere around here for you," Lilly said.

"The food I ordered should be arriving any moment," Miriam said. "Shall we continue in the meantime?"

"Thanks, Lilly, I'll wait." Mark motioned for the attorney to proceed

"Now, there's one more important matter. Learning to

fly privately costs a lot of money. If I had to pay for it I wouldn't be a pilot today. I was lucky to learn how to fly in the military. How do you intend to finance these lessons?"

Mr. Ozols caught me completely by surprise on this matter. It hadn't occurred to me that I'd need to pay for it somehow. I improvised an answer, "I suppose my father will help me. I also plan to work at his factory to finance part of the lessons. That's my plan, at least."

Mr. Ozols didn't respond immediately. He looked at me for a long moment and then asked, "Do your father or mother even know about your intentions and your visit here today?"

"My mom died when I was a baby, and my father knows about my plan to learn to fly, but I haven't had the chance to talk to him about the money yet."

"Well, we'll need to address that as well. In any case, you'll have to bring written consent from him. I'll remind you that this whole thing is dangerous, and you're not yet eighteen. He has to agree to all this."

Then Mr. Ozols moved on to topics I felt more confident about. He asked me to tell him about myself, which school I attended, and was interested in my grades in mathematics and physics.

"Before you even get anywhere near a plane, you'll have to go through a series of exams that cover, among other things, meteorology, the structure of the aircraft, and the principles of flight. These require a good understanding of physics and mathematics," he said.

I told him about myself and our family's factory, that I'm an excellent student in physics and mathematics, that I have a great memory, and that I intend to start studying mechanical engineering and aeronautics at university next year. It seemed he was pleased with that, just like my father.

Mr. Ozols wrote it all down in his notebook, then looked at his watch. He leapt out of his chair and said something about having to rush to a lesson with a student and not wanting to be late.

"Precise adherence to schedules is one of the most important principles of flight, remember that. You just got your first lesson."

I hurried to get up after him and asked what I should do now.

"Bring a doctor's certificate, bring your father for a chat with me, and then we'll see what's next," he said while walking quickly. Just as he was about to exit the building, he turned to me and asked, "Why do you want to be a pilot, anyway?"

But he left the building and disappeared towards one of the hangars before I had a chance to think of an answer.

I have no doubt about my desire, but why? I couldn't form a clear answer for myself. Maybe because it seems like a unique and challenging task? Maybe because the thought of it sparks my imagination? Mr. Ozols's question remained unanswered, even for me.

So, my dream of flying took off. I got on my bike and spent the entire ride back thinking about this conversation and how to talk to Dad about it so he would agree. I know this is what I want to learn and do more than anything. It seems talking to Mr. Ozols was the easy part. Convincing Dad will be much harder.

# Chapter 9

### Riga, Latvia, Sunday, October 14, 1934

"I was at Spilve this morning and inquired about flight lessons," I told Dad. Grandpa and Grandma, who had come to eat with us, stopped eating and looked at me.

A knock on the door interrupted the reading. Attorney Rubin raised his head. "Yes?" Miriam called out loudly. One of the office employees opened the door. "We've arranged the food for you in the next room so as not to disturb you here. It's 10:20 already."

"Very good," said Mark, rising from his seat. "It's about time."

"We'll take a short break and come back right after; we still have a lot to read and I'd like to get through at least a third of this booklet today," remarked Rubin.

Mark was already out of the room and didn't hear any of this. By the time everyone entered the next room, he was already enjoying an avocado sandwich.

Twenty minutes later, the attorney repeated the two sentences Mark had missed before the break and continued reading.

"This isn't the time to talk about it," Dad replied.

"Why not? Let's hear what the boy has to say," Grandpa insisted.

"Grandpa, I'm not a boy anymore, and yes, I intend to learn how to fly. I was at Spilve this morning and even met with a flight instructor," I began, but seeing Dad's angry eyes, I quickly added, "but Dad's right, this isn't the time to talk about it."

Surprisingly, Grandpa didn't press the matter. After they left, I approached Dad and asked if now was a good time to talk to him.

"Now is certainly better than in the presence of your grandparents. Why don't you use your brain? Do you think they'll agree to this? They'll do everything to stop you from even thinking about it, both because it's dangerous and because they'll fear you won't take over the factory in the future. Now you can tell me what this is all about."

I described my meeting with Mr. Ozols.

"He asked to meet with you."

"And how exactly do you intend to finance these lessons? Did Mr. Ozols tell you how much it costs?"

"He said he'd talk to you about it, but I plan to work at the factory and pay you back every penny for the lessons."

When Grandpa was young, he established a factory for manufacturing pots, household goods, and custom metal products, and Dad has been managing it for years. The factory is located in a large five-story building on Gaizina Street,[14] right in the center of the market.[15]
The building is made of red bricks, and its front, facing Spikeru Street,[16] has two tall wooden doors that allow for the intake and outflow of raw materials and goods. The first floor stores raw materials, and the second floor houses the production machines. There's also a crane there for lifting the packaged goods and loading them

onto trucks for distribution. The other floors contain offices.

Mark straightened up involuntarily when he heard the description of the factory. Was it a coincidence? When he was in high school, his father forced him to work at a knife manufacturing plant in the developing industrial zone of Petah Tikva during summer vacations.

"If you want to be an industrialist, you must know this world well from the bottom up. Working in this factory, with the heat and the grime of the production lines, will thoroughly acquaint you with it. There will be no idlers or people with clean hands in my house, only strong, hard-working people."

His father, of course, never bothered to ask if he was even at all interested in becoming an industrialist. In his father's view, the only option was always whatever he'd decided or chosen.

Fortunately, the factory owner was a completely different person. Mark enjoyed working on the production floor, watching the metal melt in the furnaces and then flow into special molds. He also loved the sound of the cutting machines and the hustle of the workers around him.

He simply hated the fact that his father was dictating all this to him. Still, despite all the difficulties, deep down, he knew his father was right and that the experience of factory work helped him when he became a manager himself.

I find it hard to believe that this was a random choice, he thought. The feeling of discomfort from the whole situation only grew.

He refocused on Rubin's voice, who continued reading from the diary.

# Chapter 10

Dad used to take me to the factory every school holiday. He and Grandpa explained and taught me everything about production and management. Sometimes they let me play with various machine parts I found.

I hope Dad likes the idea of me working for pay. It'll prove to him that I'm responsible and am really ready to do whatever it takes to learn to fly. Nothing will stand between it and me.

"Did he tell you when I'm supposed to meet him? Should it be at Spilve?"

Again, I was caught off guard. I thought Dad would oppose my plans and refuse to meet Mr. Ozols. I wasn't prepared for him to simply ask when he should meet him.

"I'll check and let you know," I said, "and thank you, thank you."

"Don't get too excited, Miku. I haven't agreed yet. I know the future is heading in that direction and it's my responsibility to prepare you for it as best as possible, but that path isn't easy. That's why I want to understand what this is all about first," Dad tempered my enthusiasm.

## Riga, Latvia, Sunday, October 21, 1934

Yesterday was an important day for global aviation. The air race from London, England, to Melbourne, Australia, a distance of 18,200 kilometers, began. And today was an important day for realizing my dream.

The participants in the race are required to land at several mandatory stops, but beyond that, the pilots can choose any route they wish. The rules are very interesting; there's no restriction on the size of the plane or the number of crew members but, from the moment of takeoff from England, no one can join the starting crew.

I dream of participating in such a race. I learned about it when I heard a conversation between two pilots while visiting Spilve yesterday.

I rode my bike there like the last time but, this time, I knew who I was looking for. I patiently waited by the entrance door of the Aviation Club, and when someone came out, I asked to call Mr. Ozols.

"You again?" he said when he came out, but I thought I saw a glint of satisfaction in his eyes.

"Yes, I spoke with my father and he agreed to meet you. He wants to know when and where we can have the meeting." I shifted my weight from one foot to the other, holding myself back from asking again and again when we could have it. When?

"As far as I'm concerned, we can meet here tomorrow starting at nine AM I'll be here all day. If I'm in the air for a lesson with a trainee, just wait here until I land. You'll have to wait an hour at most. Is that okay?"

"That's perfect, thank you, thank you!"

I told Dad, and he agreed.

I could hardly sleep that night. I waited for morning to come. The clock simply refused to move.

Early in the morning, I was fully ready and waiting

for Dad to finish his business. Although it wasn't even nine o'clock yet, I felt he was dragging his feet. He drank his coffee slowly and took the time reading the entire newspaper.

We drove in his Ford Junior. It's only a matter of time before I can drive myself. I'm already learning from one of the factory drivers. Just a few more lessons and that's it.

When we set off, I started directing Dad on where to go, but he raised his hand and said it wasn't necessary. In fact, he drove all the way to Spilve without asking me for directions even once.

When we arrived, he parked the car in the lot next to the office building, turned off the engine, and got out.

I approached the club and asked if Mr. Ozols was there. I was told he was in a flight lesson but would finish soon.

Dad didn't want to wait for him at the club entrance, so we waited in the area near the office building. Ten minutes later, we saw Mr. Ozols landing with a trainee on the long grass runway and taxiing towards the Aviation Club hangar. When he looked in our direction, I waved to let him know we were waiting for him, and he signaled that he saw me. I envied the trainee who was with him. I want my time to fly to come already. I've never wanted or waited for something as much as I am for this.

---

"Almost like you, Daniel," said Tom. "Do you remember the stretch from when you were accepted into military flight school until it started? You were on edge the entire time."

"Yes, I remember that," added Hannah. "You couldn't stop smiling, and it was literally the only thing you could talk about."

"That's right," David joined in. "Even Mom and Dad were in on it; you were pretty insufferable at that time."

"Kids!" Lilly scolded them as if they were teenagers and not people over thirty. "Reminisce later, please."

They fell silent, smiling. Rubin finished cleaning his glasses and continued.

# Chapter 11

About fifteen minutes later, he came to us and introduced himself to Dad. They shook hands and walked side by side, talking. I walked a bit behind them and couldn't hear what they were saying.

The meeting took place in the same room where he had met with me.

"We're always happy to meet young people who want to join. The problem is not everyone who applies is suitable; these youngsters are impatient," he looked in my direction, "and since the path to getting a pilot's license is long and hard, many of those who start don't persist and don't get it in the end. On the other hand, it does have its advantages. It's easier to learn to fly at his age, and it's a career for life."

"I promise to persist, put in all my effort, and not give up until I get my pilot's license," I said immediately.

"What does all this entail?" Dad asked in his usual businesslike manner.

"It's complicated," replied Mr. Ozols, "but I'll try to give you a general description of the training phases to help clarify what's involved."

Dad took a sheet of paper from the corner of the table and pulled a pen out of his coat. "I'd like to write it down so it's neat and clear in front of me."

"The course begins with ground studies," Mr. Ozols began detailing the different subjects, "then we move on to the phase of getting to know the aircraft and learning its systems. Additionally, we teach the principles of aerial navigation and the identification of other aircraft."

"You think the diary details exactly what he learned?" Daniel asked his father. "I'm dying to know if he learned the same way I did."

"Stay quiet and you'll probably find out soon."

"Identification of other aircraft? Why is that necessary?" Dad asked.

Mr. Ozols laughed, "Honestly, I don't know; it's probably a remnant from military flight training, but it's part of the requirements. I suppose it can't hurt."

A loud engine noise was heard from outside. Mr. Ozols waited until the plane had passed and continued, "At the end of each ground study chapter, the trainee must pass an exam and, in general, he must successfully pass all these exams. From my experience, at least half of the trainees who start the flight course don't last to the end of this theoretical phase."

Mr. Ozols paused, looked at me, and remarked, "I assume that if you're good with the sciences, you won't have a problem passing the tests. The question is whether you'll have enough patience to learn everything. That depends solely on you and your maturity."

He didn't wait for an answer, turned to Dad again, and continued, "After the trainee successfully passes the ground study exams, we move on to the practical flight course."

"See, see? that's exactly how it is even today. Or at least it was fifteen years ago. Of course the theoretical studies come first, then the practical," Daniel couldn't hold back.

"Oh, come on, really. How many times do I need to ask for silence?" It was Lilly this time who, although smiling, was serious. "We have a lot of information to get through. Daniel, switch to airplane mode, please."

Everyone smiled, and Rubin continued.

"The practical course is done on the plane itself; 'dry runs' at first, without taking off, and later, naturally, the lessons and exercises are done in the air."

"How long does this phase last?" Dad asked.

"The pace depends on the trainee's abilities, of course. Some progress quickly at first and then slow down, while others improve steadily. I can't know in advance."

"I understand," Dad replied, "it makes sense."

"In the next phase, they practice performing various maneuvers and maybe even a bit of aerobatics."

"At what point do trainees start flying alone?" I butted in.

"We call it solo flight. It also depends on the trainee. On average, it happens after about fifteen hours of flight," replied Mr. Ozols.

"And that's the end of it?" Dad asked.

"No, no, in fact, the real course only begins at this stage. The trainee has to do more and more solo flights while simultaneously completing flights with the instructor. During joint flights, he learns things like practical aerial navigation and performs navigation flights.

Only once the instructor feels the trainee is ready does he invite another pilot, who is himself an experienced instructor in the National Guard Air Force, to test him. If the trainee passes, he prepares to take the state's official exam. After passing that, he receives his pilot's license."

"How many flight hours are generally required to reach this phase?" Dad asked.

"Again, it depends on the trainee's pace but, on average, between thirty-five and forty flight hours."

"And how long does the flight course last from start to finish?"

"There aren't many days suitable for flying in winter, and it's very cold because the plane is open. You can start the ground studies now, pass the exams, and be ready for practical lessons by May. I'm the only instructor here who teaches civilians, and the lessons are only held on weekends. Not every weekend is suitable for flying due to weather, so in the best case, it takes between a year to a year and a half."

"I see. Now, we need to talk about an equally important issue, the costs. I assume it's calculated per flight lesson, correct?"

"Yes, when it comes to practical flight lessons. Additionally, you have to pay for ground studies, and that payment is calculated differently." Mr. Ozols paused for a moment and looked directly into Dad's eyes.

Dad understood something I didn't, as he immediately asked me to leave the room and wait outside.

# Chapter 12

I walked toward the runway to watch the planes. I had a good feeling that Dad would say yes, but until I heard it from him, I wouldn't know for sure.

There was non-stop activity at the aerodrome; planes taking off and landing. The pilots flying them all looked much older than me. They were probably National Guard pilots.

I could see people in gray overalls approaching some of the pilots who had landed and stopped outside the hangars. I tried to see if Mikhail was there but didn't spot him. Not knowing when Dad and Mr. Ozols would be done, I didn't stray too far from the office building.

Suddenly, I heard voices behind me. I turned around and saw them shaking hands, with Mr. Ozols placing a friendly hand on Dad's shoulder as if they had known each other for a long time. Dad signaled me to come and headed towards our car.

He started driving immediately.

"What did you think of Mr. Ozols?" I asked.

"He seems like a serious and professional man."

I thought he would continue the sentence, but he fell silent. I waited a few more minutes until I realized he wasn't going to elaborate on the matter. "So, did you agree on anything?"

"He answered all my questions, and now I need to

decide what to do next."

I realized my best course of action was to wait. When Dad has something to say, he says it. "Be patient," or "show restraint and patience," Grandpa and Martha always tell me. It seemed like the right moment to apply their advice.

Dad was silent the whole way. He drove along the Daugava River and crossed the Pilsētas Canal. I thought he meant to head straight to the factory, but he stopped at the entrance of the market.

"Come on, let's go have breakfast at Daiga's."

Daiga's Buffet is in the middle of the market, across from the flower stalls. There are almost no people on Sundays, but she opens anyway. When we came in, Daiga stood behind the long counter attached to the left wall, always laden with cakes and pies. "Look who's graced us with his presence," she said, uttering the phrase I've been hearing for as long as I can remember.

The smell of the smoked fish dish she makes, the one Dad calls Liepāja style fish,[17] filled the air and stirred my appetite. Daiga continued, "He won't stop growing; soon, he'll be taller than his father."

I smiled at her, embarrassed, and we sat in Dad's usual spot. When she came to take our order, she wrapped her large arms around my head and pulled it close to her ample bosom.

"Soon you'll be a man and won't let me hug you anymore, eh?"

"I'm a grown up already, Mrs. Daiga, and you can keep hugging me. But please, stop with the announcements when I come in. Everyone looks at me and it's embarrassing."

"I make the rules here, Miku, but let's see what we can do about that." She winked at Dad and asked what he wanted to order so late in the morning.

"Please bring us two portions of Liepāja fish, the smell is killing me, and a few slices of rye bread." Dad turned to me and asked if it was okay with me.

"I'd prefer a potato pancake,[18] if that's okay." That's my favorite dish of hers. Daiga fries the pancake with a spicy, golden batter and tops it with sour cream, a piece of red salmon, and dill leaves. It's a real delicacy.

"And bring me a serving of your beetroot soup[19] too. Do you want some as well?"

"Yes, sure."

I remembered I hadn't eaten much since yesterday, being so anxious about today's meeting.

"What time is it?" Mark glanced at his watch. "When did you say they're bringing us lunch?"

David and Daniel began to laugh. "Dad, it's barely been an hour since breakfast. What's up?"

"It's Attorney Rubin's fault," Lilly said. "He's reading this so authentically; I also want a taste of that Liepāja."

"Anyway," Miriam intervened, "I didn't order you anything like that for lunch, so put your imaginations aside and let's continue?"

Mark sipped from his glass of water, as if trying to wash away the craving for beetroot soup that had suddenly struck him.

Rubin continued.

We gobbled up the dishes and didn't leave a single crumb on our plates. I hoped that maybe Dad would finally tell me what he'd decided about my flight lessons. It was really hard to show restraint and not ask him about it.

Dad ordered a cup of coffee too, and a slice of cheesecake with raisins for each of us. As he sipped, he relaxed, stretched out his legs, and asked, "So?

What do you think?"

"That was a really good breakfast. I didn't realize how hungry I was."

"That's how it is when you're excited; you'll learn. But it's best to make decisions on a full stomach, never when you're hungry, if possible."

I wasn't quite sure what he meant, and stayed silent. I was hoping we were finally going to discuss what I was actually interested in.

# Chapter 13

"Do you think you'll be able to simultaneously study for your final exams at school in May as well as the ground studies for the flight course? Under no circumstances are these lessons allowed to affect your high school exam results."

My heart was racing. This was the moment.

"I'm absolutely sure I can study for both and achieve good grades. Mr. Ozols said the material is based on a lot of math and physics, and you know I have no problem with those subjects."

"And when will you have the time to come to the factory and help me there? You'll be studying all day, won't you?"

"My studies have to be the first priority so I can get good results on my exams. I'll dedicate all remaining time to work at the factory, to do whatever you ask."

I was willing to promise absolutely anything, just to get his consent.

Dad hesitated. I could see in his eyes that he was considering it. I hoped my gamble would pay off.

"Alright, I'm willing to let you begin flight lessons, but I have a few conditions..."

It was really hard to concentrate. I was struggling to listen to him. He asked for regular updates on my progress and demanded a promise that I would always prioritize school assignments and later, university assignments as well.

There were two more conditions Dad insisted on: The first was that I speak to Grandpa and get his consent, which had to be done before I start. The second condition was that I commit to working at the factory for at least five years after completing my engineering studies.

"I agree," I answered instantly. All I wanted was to fly; I had no other plans for the future anyway. "And what about payment for Mr. Ozols?"

"Your salary from the factory work will cover the payments for the flight lessons; whatever you're short on, I'll give you as a loan. You will repay me through work after finishing the flight course."

I couldn't sleep again that night, this time from excitement rather than stress. I tossed and turned, imagining the lessons and the flights. I even thought about the flying gear I would wear. Finally, just before my eyes closed, I remembered I forgot to ask Dad when, if Grandpa agrees, I was to start the ground studies and where it would take place. I decided to ask him the next day.

### Riga, Latvia, Sunday, November 18, 1934

I finally managed to have the conversation with Grandpa today, and I still don't know what the outcome is. I'll need the help of Our Lord Jesus Christ.

I slept at Grandpa and Grandma's house last night. When I got up in the morning, I asked where Grandpa was, and Grandma said he'd gone to the Dome Cathedral.[20]

"Since when does Grandpa go to church on Sundays?"

"Good question. Yesterday, he told me he wanted

to go because there would be an organ concert with a choir; he's there now. Why are you asking?"

"I wanted to ask him something," I answered cautiously.

Grandma looked at me with suspicion and said, "You can join him there if you think you'd enjoy it."

I liked the idea and, after a quick breakfast, I wrapped myself in a coat and scarf and left. I walked, hunched against the cold wind, until I reached the large square outside the cathedral just as the crowd of worshippers began to leave.

A few minutes later, I spotted Grandpa, buttoning his coat as he was walking out. I approached him, but he only noticed me once I was standing right next to him. He looked at me with surprise.

"Miku, what are you doing here?"

"Grandma said you were here, so I decided to join you."

"A little late for that, aren't we? Shall we go?"

The moment of truth had arrived. I took a deep breath and said, "The truth is, I also wanted to talk to you, but without Grandma around."

"I figured there was a better reason than the excuse you just gave me; you're not exactly an avid churchgoer. Let's go sit at Kuze."[21] It's his favorite café.

"So, what did you want to talk to me about?" Grandpa asked after we sat down at a small table. "Is it about your new obsession?"

That start didn't bode well, but I had no choice. Dad had been very clear on the matter.

"Grandpa, it's not an obsession, it's really what I want to do. I can't stop thinking about it ever since our visit to Spilve."

"We can't get everything we want—"

"But I can," I couldn't help but interrupt him. He gave

me a stern look. "I promised Dad that I wouldn't neglect my studies and I'd work in the factory in the coming years, even while studying at university alongside flight training. I can do it, Grandpa, I really can, and the factory won't suffer."

"It's not the impact on the factory that concerns me," Grandpa said, "it's the impact on *you* that worries me. Do you have any idea how dangerous this is? What if something happened to you? You're almost eighteen and about to enter the adult world. You should already understand what I'm talking about."

I trembled a little. I'd never heard Grandpa speak like that before.

"I understand, Grandpa, and I'm not trying to avoid responsibility. The opposite, in fact. But I have the right to shape my life the way I want to and not just according to what you all expect of me. I don't know if I can become a pilot, it's probably very complicated, but I at least want to try."

Grandpa returned to his usual tone, "So what do you want from me?"

"I want your consent, your blessing. It's important to me, and I feel it will even protect me," I said quietly, looking straight into his eyes.

He was silent, and I could see his inner conflict.

"We'll discuss it with Grandma; she needs to know too," he decided firmly. "We'll talk to her about it over lunch," and seeing my expression, he added, "Don't give me that look; do you prefer I say 'no' outright?" He gulped down the rest of his coffee and signaled that it was time to go.

Grandma, of course, was strongly opposed. "We promised your mother we'd take care of you, and that's what we've been doing ever since. We won't agree to you risking your future for this fresh childish obsession."

"But it's my life. I'll be eighteen soon and have the right to live as I want to."

"That's a childish response. If you were truly mature, you'd understand that you have a responsibility and an obligation to fulfill your destiny, and I hope I don't need to explain *that* to you, at least," Grandma retorted angrily, muttering, "Christ help me get these ideas out of this child's head."

I'd never seen her so angry. The idea that I could have my own ideas about my future seemed inconceivable to her.

"What do you say, Hilda? Maybe we should ask our Archbishop? If he gives Miku his blessing, that comes from above. We don't know what our Inga would've done in this situation. If it's really his dream, maybe she wouldn't have stopped him. Let's agree," he turned to me, "that if the Archbishop opposes this, then no. He will decide."

His eyes welled up, and he blew his nose with a handkerchief while looking at Grandma. I'd never felt so close to him as I did at that moment.

"Alright, Grandpa, and I promise you and Grandma that I'll respect any decision the Archbishop makes," I quickly agreed. Not that I had a choice. But the way I see it, the more I agree with them now, the more they'll agree with me later.

I hope we'll be able to visit the Archbishop this coming week.

# Chapter 14

## Riga, Latvia, Sunday, January 13, 1935

This week, I passed the first test in the flight course. It was in meteorology. Other than that, it was also an important week for pilots around the world. An American woman named Amelia Earhart completed the first solo flight in history between the Hawaiian Islands in the Pacific Ocean and the city of Oakland in the state of California. According to the article in the newspaper, the flight took eighteen hours and sixteen minutes.

"Listen, this is a real piece of history Miku wrote here. We learned about this Pacific flight. What do you plan to do with this booklet after we're done?" Daniel asked, and Lilly felt that Attorney Rubin seemed pleased with the forced break.

"I don't precisely know yet. I assume there are instructions at the end on what to do with all this material," he replied and asked Miriam for a cup of tea, "I'd love to warm my throat a little. It's not easy to read out so much."

"I want it," Daniel said, "if there are no specific instructions against it, and if none of you mind."

"Take it," Tom said, "you're the only one interested in this whole thing anyway." The other family members gave their silent consent.

Miriam glanced at her watch. "We break for lunch in ten minutes. Let's stop now and continue at 2:30. What do you think?"

"What do you want with an old thing some stranger wrote?" Hannah asked her cousin.

"It's a historical account in real time. I love these things, especially when it's about flying and aviation," Daniel replied as everyone left the conference room.

Attorney Rubin looked refreshed after the break. He picked up the booklet, cleared his throat, and continued.

> It has been over a month since the Archbishop praised my courage and gave his consent. He also told Grandpa that the country needs young people like me. I met all the conditions. Grandma isn't pleased, but Dad and Grandpa support me. I'm sure that once she sees me in a pilot's uniform, she'll be proud of me.
>
> I met Mr. Ozols only once. It was in a small classroom at the Civil Aviation Administration offices in the city center. He said that I would be doing the ground studies there, and only after passing all the exams would we move to the practical part, which would of course take place in Spilve.
>
> "And then we'll meet again, if I'm still alive," he smiled at me. His humor is still strange to me; maybe they're pilot jokes. I smiled back.
>
> In the first lesson, I met Janis Dibovski, the meteorology teacher. He's very thin and his hair partially covers his eyes. The room we were in looked like a regular classroom, with one desk for the teacher at the front and several desks arranged facing it. I was the only student, which felt strange.
>
> Mr. Dibovski sat at his desk, placed a thin booklet before him, and began, "The first lesson will cover the layers of the atmosphere. The troposphere is the

lowest layer..." he started reading from the booklet in a monotone voice, sitting in his chair the whole time, barely ever looking up at me.

It was tough! I fought to stay awake. I've studied boring things before, but never when I was alone with the teacher. I wrote, stretched, and forced myself to concentrate. I do hope not all ground lessons look and sound like this. I thought it'd be far more interesting.

Once a week, we would meet in the classroom for a lesson that Mr. Dibovski delivered in exhausting dryness. On the other hand, the study material itself was quite varied. I learned about types of clouds and winds, temperature effects, weather forecasting, etc.

One time, a girl joined the class and sat at the back. She reminded me of the girl who gave flowers to Cukurs when he landed at Spilve.

Today, I finally took the meteorology exam, and I'm glad to say I already got the results. That's probably the only advantage of being the sole student. Mr. Dibovski informed me that I passed and told me the next course would be on technical knowledge and principles of flight.

I hope I don't have to see him again. With all due respect, I've never met anyone as boring as him.

# Chapter 15

### Riga, Latvia, Wednesday, February 27, 1935

This month has been stormy and cold. There's a lot of snow, and I can't ride my bike to the factory. The walk is difficult and wet. Grandpa and Dad invited me to participate in their monthly meeting for the first time.

When I arrived, Dad made me a cup of tea, and the three of us went into the office. Grandpa said something bad is happening in Germany and that he was worried about the situation. I didn't understand what Germany has to do with us.

"If this continues or, God forbid, worsens, it will affect our sales. I've noticed a drop in orders for pressure cookers from Heinz's office in Hamburg recently. Last week, I talked to him about it, and he hinted that it might be related to restrictions on metal products. He didn't want to elaborate, but if the situation continues, it could hurt us too."

Dad nodded, "We'll check on it next month and see what to do."

But Grandpa persisted, "Just last week, Adolf Hitler gave a speech in Munich at an event celebrating the anniversary of the Nazi Party. It was a militant speech with declarations of how Germany wouldn't sign any document that would damage its honor, as if the war hadn't ended. Martin, note that the atmosphere there is becoming very militaristic. This week, the German Minister of the Interior also announced that Hitler's birthday would be a national holiday, as if he were the emperor of Germany, no less. You need to keep a close watch on all payments from Germany."

Dad didn't seem worried, "I'll check with Heinz."

In fact, Germany seems to be quite active in the field of aviation too. Yesterday's newspaper said the Germans had conducted the first flight of the Heinkel 111. It's supposed to be a civilian aircraft but, according to the newspaper, it's actually a military bomber disguised as a civilian plane due to the military restrictions on Germany.

This worried me; if the factory doesn't earn enough, Dad won't be able to pay for my flight training.

"Remind me, how old is Miku?" Tom asked.

"Just under eighteen, why?" Hannah replied.

"Because there's about to be a war, the world is on the brink of an earthquake, and all he cares about is his flight lessons," he replied.

"You've always been a warrior for justice," Lilly smiled at her son. "Don't forget, he didn't know; no one knew what was going to happen."

"I want to know what happens later on in this diary. We need to keep going," Mark suppressed any conversation that might have arisen.

Rubin continued.

## Riga, Latvia, Sunday, March 3, 1935

This month, I started the course on flight principles. I was disappointed to see Mr. Dibovski walking in, as I realized I'd be studying with him again. I really hoped for someone less boring. It quickly turned out that he was actually an aeronautics student and had taught the meteorology course out of necessity, as a substitute teacher.

When he talked about flying and the physics behind it, he was a completely different person. Our bond grew stronger when I told him about my plans to study at the same faculty next year. Now we have an excellent relationship, and I think he's a great teacher.

The lessons were fascinating from the very start. He taught me about the airflow around the wing and how lift is generated to keep the plane in the air. He also drew a wing cross section on the board and enthusiastically demonstrated how it moved. Each lesson turned into an experience, as if we were both flying a plane in the air, moving our hands, heads tilting side to side, leaning one way or the other while learning the principles of physics behind flight. Everything is learned through the body as much as through the mind. If someone had walked into the classroom during the lesson, they might have thought we were two actors rehearsing for a play.

Mr. Dibovski's eyes shone during the lessons. He was interesting and full of energy. I looked forward to these lessons and found a way to get to class even when the weather was really stormy.

He taught me the principles of aeronautics and many other topics that affect the plane and its flight.

"Do you know all these things?" This time, it was Mark interrupting the reading as he turned to his son.

"Of course," Daniel replied, "It's really interesting. I didn't think they taught this in 1935."

"You're lucky you're enjoying it because I'm about to fall asleep here," David complained.

"I want to continue," said Rubin, glancing at the clock on the wall in front of him, "the day is growing short, and there's a lot to cover."

Mr. Dibovski enthusiastically drew graphs on the board to illustrate his explanations. In one lesson, he brought a small model of a biplane and used it to demonstrate the material he was teaching. We grew very close during these lessons, which only helped me understand everything better.

I asked him about the plane I would be learning to fly; it'll probably be a 'Flamingo.' I don't know it at all, but I can already imagine myself in a biplane.

He's helping me prepare for the exam. I feel confident, studying at home and any spare moment. This exam will be a big step toward the practical phase.

### Riga, Latvia, Sunday, April 7, 1935

I passed!!! I knew I was ready, but there's always a fear, especially since the course started three months ago, and they might've asked about something I don't remember anymore. Anyway, I went there yesterday; I was very tense. The girl I saw once before was there too. Apparently, she's also learning to fly.

Mr. Dibovski reassured me before the exam. He told me he had seen it and that although it wasn't easy, we'd covered all the material. When I came out, and he asked me how it went, I said I felt good about it.

They asked me to wait in the classroom for the results again. The girl and I sat there quietly. I didn't feel comfortable starting a conversation with her. She sat behind me and didn't say a word. Half an hour later, Mr.

Dibovski came in and congratulated me. Then he called her name, Juliana Bergs. She had also passed.

Lilly turned to Mark, "Bergs? Like Dad's orchard. We were talking about it just this morning. Could it be that Dad knew this Juliana Bergs?"

"Yes, it seems so."

Mr. Mirkin leaned toward the translator and whispered something in his ear.

"What did he say?" Mark asked.

"He asked me to tell you that his grandmother's name was Juliana, but the name Bergs doesn't ring a bell," the translator replied.

Mr. Mirkin leaned toward the translator again and continued.

"He wants to add that his father's name was 'Mishka,' which is actually a nickname for someone named Mihails, just like the one who wrote the diary," said the translator.

"There are too many 'Michail' here," Mark commented cynically. Nothing good can come of this. He was beginning to fear more and more that his father had prepared an unpleasant surprise for him.

# Chapter 16

It turned out this Yuliana got the highest score ever on the technical knowledge and flight principles exam. Ninety-five. Despite the relief I felt from passing the test, it stung a little. I'm used to being top of my class.

"Congratulations," I told her. "My name is Mihails, but everyone calls me Miku."

"Hello Miku, I'm Yuliana." She has thick black hair and there's a certain calmness about her. She speaks quietly and politely; I like her.

"Your next course will be aircraft and engine familiarization," Mr. Dibovski told me. "I won't be teaching it, but the lessons will still be here, every week, on the same day and at the same time."

He then turned to Yuliana, who was just passing him on her way to the door, and added, "You're also welcome to attend this course at the same time and day."

"Thank you," she said, noting that she wasn't sure yet if the time would work for her, and left the room.

On one hand, it'd be nice to study with someone else, especially her, but on the other hand, she's a top student. I'm not sure I want to compete with her for grades.

Anyway, I'm happy. I took another big step forward, and I'm sure Dad and Grandpa are proud of me.

## Riga, Latvia, Sunday, April 21, 1935

I started learning about the plane I'll be flying two weeks ago.

BFW U Bachmann Flamingo.[22]

And who showed up to teach me about it? Mr. Ozols, in the flesh. What a surprise!

---

"Wow, the Flamingo. That's not a plane; it's a kite," Daniel chuckled. "Remind me when we finish; I'll show you a video of it on YouTube. I'm surprised that's the one they chose to teach him on."

"Okay," replied Hannah, "Now let the man read. He was just talking about a surprise, and you interrupted him."

---

It wasn't even the first surprise, because when I got to the classroom for the first lesson on aircraft structure, I saw Yuliana Bergs there. She had arrived before me and was sitting in her 'usual' seat at the back.

I offered her to sit next to me in the front row, and she agreed. We've been side by side in every lesson ever since, and it's nice. I wanted to ask her where she was from and why she was learning to fly, but Mr. Ozols walked in before I had a chance.

"Hello, Miku and Yuliana. I see you already know each other and are sitting very, very close together. That's good, that's good."

Yuliana blushed, and I probably did too, because Mr. Ozols immediately added that we look like two ripe tomatoes. He really does have a strange sense of humor.

He took a model out of his bag and presented it. "This is the Flamingo training aircraft. You'll be learning on it, so let's start by getting to know it."

We learned everything possible about the Flamingo. I

could write a lot about it, but I'll just mention a few things. Firstly, it's made of wood. It has two wings, one above the other. Though it's originally German, this model is manufactured in Latvia and used for flight training, even for National Guard pilots. It's considered stable in the air and suitable for flight trainees. It has an open cockpit with two seats. The pilot or flight trainee sits in the back seat, and the instructor or passenger sits in the front.

"Well, there's your answer for why they chose to teach him that plane," Hannah said quietly.

Attorney Rubin looked up from the document. "I'm asking you, please, it's not easy reading this much text, and these frequent interruptions are very disruptive."

"What time do you expect us to finish today?" Mark took advantage of the break, "and regardless, I need to go to the bathroom."

"It's 3:30. I think we'll finish at 5 today. Tomorrow, we'll start at 8 AM We need to keep going with this."

"Fine," Mark grumbled. "I'm going to the bathroom; you can continue when I get back." Lilly accompanied him, and the younger ones took the time to check their phones. None of them dared to do so in Mark's presence. Ten minutes later, the two returned.

I wrote down the Flamingo's flight range, speed, and maximum altitude from memory, to test myself. I then checked and found all the data I wrote down was correct! I also reviewed the rundown of flight limitations and other details Mr. Ozols taught us. I feel ready for the test tomorrow.

## Riga, Latvia, Monday, April 22, 1935

Yuli and I waited together for the results.

"How did you do on the test?" I asked her.

"Great, I think. Other than one question, I think I knew the answers to all of them."

Would she get a higher score than me again? I didn't want that to happen.

"I did great too. Which question didn't you know the answer to?"

We talked about it a bit more, even though I actually wanted to ask her about herself. Somehow, I didn't manage to bring it up until Mr. Ozols arrived.

He updated us on our scores. This time, mine was higher than hers, and I'm very pleased. It didn't seem to matter to her.

I have two more exams to complete: one on navigation principles, which we know is going to be a difficult subject, and the other a sort of training in identifying other aircraft. The thought that I could start the practical lessons after passing these two exams made the flight course suddenly feel a lot more real.

On the other hand, I know it'll take me some time because I have to dedicate the next month to my finals at school. I promised Dad that flight studies wouldn't come at the expense of regular studies, and I won't do anything to jeopardize his agreement to pay for the flight course.

I told Mr. Ozols about this because he mentioned he would be instructing us in both subjects.

"The last exam is at the end of May, so I can resume studying with you in June," I said.

"I have no problem with that," Mr. Ozols replied, "May is already very busy for me with training Aviation Club and National Guard trainees. But what about you,

Yuliana? Are you okay to wait until Miku is ready to continue?"

"I need to study for my finals too, like Miku, so that works for me."

"Then we'll meet at the beginning of June, and good luck to you both," he said and left.

I wanted to invite her to eat a cake with me at a café, but I didn't have the courage. I decided I would do it next time.

# Chapter 17

**Riga, Latvia, Monday, April 29, 1935**

Today, Dad and I went to the Faculty of Engineering and Aeronautics to submit my application to study there.

"Send in your final exam grades as soon as you receive them," said the secretary. "Only then can we give you the final answer."

She glanced over my previous years' grades. "If your final grades will be similar to these, your chances of being accepted are very high."

"I'm sure they will be," Dad replied.

As we were about to leave the admissions office, she asked, "Are you Latvians?"

"Of course," Dad answered.

"Then I think there really shouldn't be any problem," she said.

For a moment, I froze in place. I remembered what Mikhail had told me at Cukurs' reception. Now I knew how it was being done.

Dad was completely indifferent to the secretary's comment and walked out.

"Did you hear her? Do you realize why she asked if we're Latvians?"

"What's the problem? Aren't we Latvians?"

"Obviously, but what would've happened if we said we weren't? What if we said, for instance, that we're Jews?"
"Why would we say such a thing?"

"I'm sorry, I don't get this," Tom's voice stopped the Attorney. "What's the difference between being Latvians and being Jews? Aren't the Jews and the Christians all Latvians?"
"What wasn't clear?" Hannah responded. "For hundreds of years, we isolated and segregated ourselves in Europe from the Christian gentiles around us who didn't particularly like us and would beat the shit out of us left and right. They got so used to seeing us as outsiders that when the Enlightenment movement began in the 18th century and we gained emancipation in the 19th century, the local gentiles still didn't see Jews as an integral part of their people. It was probably the same in Latvia: there were Latvians, and there were Jews. Did you get that, Tommy?"
"Suddenly you're a professor for Jewish Studies?"
"You'd be surprised; I studied this at university, and I finally have the opportunity to use that knowledge so Mom can see her investment in my education paid off," she said happily.
"Is that it? Is everything clear now? Can I continue?" Rubin asked. "Just so you know, I intend to get to page 100 of this diary today, even if it means we stay here past five."
"Continue, continue," Mark urged. "From now and until he's done – not a word out of any of you. Understood?"

"But I have Jewish friends I studied with in class, they're not Latvians," I insisted. "Do you realize that their chances of getting into the Polytechnic are lower because of this?"
Dad replied, "That's not our problem," and quickly descended the stairs out of the building.
I don't understand his answer. It doesn't seem like he

gives any importance to this issue of discrimination against Jews. I'll ask him why some other time.

## Riga, Latvia, Monday, May 6, 1935

Yesterday, we won the first European Basketball Championship. The championship was held in Geneva, Switzerland, with ten teams participating. We defeated Hungary in the first round, then, in the semi-finals, we beat Switzerland, and in the finals, we faced Spain, a massive country. Our team won against all odds and was crowned the first champion of this competition. I'm so proud. There was a lot of talk about it at school today. Everyone suddenly became a big basketball expert.

## Riga, Latvia, Sunday, June 2, 1935

I finally finished my exams. We haven't received the results yet. I hope they'll be high enough for me to get accepted to the faculty.

There were two important events in aviation last month. The first was at the beginning of May, when the American aviator Amelia Earhart flew for fourteen hours, twenty-two minutes, and fifty seconds from Mexico City to New York City. She became the first pilot ever to complete a nonstop flight between these cities. Another impressive achievement for her. When I read this article in the newspaper, I imagined myself sitting with her in the cockpit.

The second event occurred in mid-May. There was a major aviation disaster in Russia, when a Tupolev collided in mid-air over Moscow with a stunt plane, exploding and killing about fifty people.

I passed all the medical tests and received certification stating that I'm fit for flight lessons. I'll give it to Mr. Ozols the next time I see him.

We celebrated my eighteenth birthday today, a little late. Martha and Grandma prepared a special, festive meal.

Dad insisted I wear a white shirt, a tie and the new jacket we bought together. He also dressed up formally, but it wasn't until we arrived at Grandpa and Grandma's house that I understood why.

An unfamiliar woman dressed in a white shirt and black skirt with an apron and a server's headband stood in the corner of the large room.

The dining table was set in a particularly celebratory manner, with the tableware Grandma always kept in the glass cabinet in the guest room.

Grandpa and Grandma were also dressed in nice clothes, and even Martha wore a fancy long dress with floral decorations on the shoulders, and her hair was gathered and held by a colorful clip. I'd never seen her like this before.

She sat with us like one of the family. She basically *is* like family to me.

Grandpa stood up and waited for everyone to quiet down. He congratulated me, on behalf of Grandma as well, and finally added:

"I assume you'll soon finish not only high school but your driving lessons as well. So, Grandma and I have decided that when you get your driver's license, we will help you finance the purchase of your own car. That's our gift for your birthday. You must promise us that you will drive carefully and won't go flying off into the sky with it."

I know Grandma isn't happy with my flight lessons, so

I was very surprised by the last sentence.

They haven't gotten over their worries. Even though they're proud of my high grades and achievements, I realize it must be hard for them to stop worrying that something might happen to me. I'm glad they at least don't comment on it anymore and aren't waiting for me to change my mind about flying anymore.

# Chapter 18

### Riga, Latvia, Sunday, June 9, 1935

Last week, I finally went back to ground studies for the flight course and met Yuli in the classroom. It had been a long time since we last saw each other.

Mr. Ozols surprised us by saying that we would start with studying aircraft identification. He showed us pictures of various planes, explaining the characteristics of each and how to identify them and their national affiliation. At the end of the lesson, he asked if we were ready to take the exam right then and there.

Yuli and I looked at each other. I could see in her eyes that she was thinking the same thing, and we both answered yes simultaneously. I liked that it happened.

Each of us took the test quickly and were immediately certified as completing this training and passing the required exam. We only had the navigation principles course left.

Mr. Ozols handed each of us a thick booklet and told us to read it for the next lesson.

After he left the room, I gathered my courage and asked Yuli if she'd like to come with me for some cake.

"Where?"

"At Café Kuze."

"What? The rich people's café?" she said almost in alarm.

For a moment, I froze. Just as I finally dared to ask her, and it seemed she was about to agree—did I frighten her?

"It's not for rich people at all, just completely ordinary people. I'll treat you. What do you say?"

"Are you sure? I've never been there, only heard about it."

"Yes, yes, I'm sure." My heart was pounding. This was the first time I asked a girl out, and I wasn't sure if I did it right or if she would even agree. "It's just a short walk from here."

"Alright, sure," Yuli smiled at me, and I relaxed a bit, "but I can't stay long. My parents will worry if I'm very late."

The days are longer now, and it was still light outside. We walked through the old town, and after a short walk side by side, we arrived at the café. We sat by a small wooden table right at the entrance and placed our booklets on it. When the cakes and coffee we ordered arrived, Yuli suggested we share, and I was happy to do so.

"Today's exam was my fourth one, was it yours too?" I asked.

"Yes, meteorology, technical knowledge, aircraft familiarization, and identification, right?"

"So, where did you study? I've only seen you in Dibovski's classes once."

"At the same place, just on a different day and with a different instructor—not a very good one."

"And when did you realize you wanted to learn how to fly?"

"I've wanted to be a pilot ever since I was little, and it was clear to my whole family that as soon as I reached the age I could learn to fly, I'd do it."

"Really, they agreed to let you do it just like that? It

wasn't easy for me."

She told me about the process she went through until her parents had agreed. It turns out all adults worry the same way.

"How big is your family? Do you have brothers and sisters? Actually, I don't even know where you live."

Yuli giggled shyly and gently brushed a lock of hair from her eyes. "I live at 20 Stabu Street, and I have an older brother. And what about you? Other than learning how to fly, what are you going to do after school?"

I told her a bit about myself and the factory. "I realized I wanted to learn to fly after I attended the reception at Spilve for Officer Cukurs, and I also enrolled in engineering and aeronautics studies," I said proudly.

"Really, you were at that reception?'

"Yes, my grandfather had tickets."

"How did he manage to get them? I heard only people with connections managed to get any."

"I have no idea. Actually, I didn't even think about it until now. But your question reminds me that when I told Mr. Ozols about it, he was surprised too."

"I'm not surprised." There was a hint of cynicism in her voice. She ate some cake, and I took the opportunity to look at her. Her eyes were large and round, and their color was a vibrant green; they really stood out against her fair face. She was very beautiful.

When we were done, I walked her home. We talked about our studies, and everything she said seemed interesting to me. I was really disappointed we had to part when we reached her address.

## Riga, Latvia, Sunday, June 23, 1935

I've been studying the principles of navigation for two

weeks now. It's really hard. There are so many concepts and definitions to know. For example, 'distances.' There are many definitions and ways of measuring distances, not just in kilometers.

Mr. Ozols said we have to know every definition and the relationship between them to a T, that confusing them with each other could cause a pilot to lose their way in the air. I mixed them up a lot at first and had to constantly recalculate and check myself.

Even 'direction' is a complicated concept. Reading a compass isn't enough. It's even more complicated than the distance issue.

And that was the *easy* part.

We have to add meteorological effects on the flight to all these concepts, and more. Everything I learned in previous courses became practical now.

Each lesson, Mr. Ozols presented exercises where we had to calculate the plane's deviation according to various wind data, and it's hard, very hard. Even though I'm very good at math, I still struggled with these calculation exercises. At the end of the lesson, Mr. Ozols would show Yuli and I how we should've solved them.

He also gave us homework exercises.

I invited Yuli to do the homework together. It was a good opportunity to invite her over to my home. Not to my grandparents' house, obviously. We sat next to each other and tried to figure out how to solve the complex exercises. Every now and then, I'd sneak a glance at her. She was very focused and made faces at the paper when the numbers didn't add up. It was really cute. Sometimes we'd manage to solve a complex exercise together, and when that happened, her smile made my mouth go dry.

Yuli came several times during the week, and we've already developed a tradition. After two hours of intense study, we go for ice cream or cake at Café Kuze.

You could say we even have a regular table. Today, we celebrated the summer festival there together.

Last Thursday, the high school finals grades started coming in. So far, everything's awesome.

# Chapter 19

**Riga, Latvia, Sunday, July 14, 1935**

This week, I passed the navigation exam. That nightmare is over. The exam was difficult and confusing, lasting three and a half hours, and by the end of it, I wasn't sure if I'd answered any of the questions correctly or not. I was completely in the dark until Mr. Ozols entered the room and informed Yuli and I that we had passed.

It was a huge relief. For both of us. We even hugged spontaneously. Although it was a really short hug, it was very pleasant.

With this, we've finally completed the ground studies phase. Mr. Ozols announced that on the first weekend of August, he would give us a tour of Spilve to familiarize us with the aerodrome and the Flamingo. I am eagerly looking forward to it.

When we left, there was no need to ask Yuli what to do. We went to Café Kuze to celebrate the end of ground studies.

Alongside my school successes and progress in flight training, I'm also very worried about what's happening in Europe and the implications it has on the factory's sales. Ever since I heard the conversation between Dad and Grandpa, I've been more aware of what the newspapers say about it. The situation is getting worse.

Recently, talks between the British Prime Minister and Mussolini regarding Italy's military activity in Ethiopia have collapsed. The Polish parliament has been dissolved, and in Germany, compulsory six-month labor service has been announced for eighteen to twenty-five-year-olds. The newspaper also reported on a new law in Germany requiring anyone seeking university admission to prove they are of 'Aryan' descent. I wondered if I would've been accepted to study engineering in Germany and what Dad would've said if he had discovered that this is indeed 'our problem.' Europe is restless and uneasy, a terrible atmosphere for business.

I shared my feelings with Yuli.

"Have you noticed that we're starting to feel it here too?" she asked. "I saw that several shops suddenly have a sign saying they are a 'Latvian store.' You know what they mean by that, right?"

Of course I knew. I assumed it was because we have many citizens originally from Germany, like us.

"It reminds me of the university's decision to impose quotas on the number of Jews who can study there. But as my father told me, it's not really our problem. It's not that I'm against Jews; after all, I studied with Jews at 'Erich-German,' and some of them are my friends. But if there aren't enough places for everyone at the university, why should they be given more spots? There's logic in that, isn't there?"

"How can you even think like that!?" Yuli responded, frowning.

Her reaction surprised me. I didn't really understand what was wrong with what I had said.

"It doesn't mean I agree with that logic," I tried to correct myself, "but you can't ignore that many people think that way."

"So we should agree with them? There'll always be

people who want to hurt Jews, like what's happening in Germany. But we need to prevent that here."

"We?"

"Yes, we, you and I, and our friends. How do you not get that? Never mind. I don't want to talk about it. I need to go home anyway."

The atmosphere soured. She got up and prepared to leave. I stood up with visible reluctance, and we both went home separately.

## Riga, Latvia, Sunday, August 4, 1935

Good news, even better news, and not-so-good news.

The good news is that I was accepted into the Faculty of Engineering and Aeronautics. Next year, I'll already be a full-fledged university student.

The even better news is that we finally arrived at Spilve, and my head is already in the clouds. Well, not literally in the clouds, but it feels like it.

This morning, we had the tour of Spilve with Mr. Ozols to familiarize ourselves with the Flamingo. I was a bit hesitant about meeting Yuli. We hadn't met since the conversation that upset her, but when we saw each other, she smiled her charming smile at me.

Mr. Ozols showed us the buildings and the Pilots' club from the outside. He said it would be a while before we could enter. Something to aspire to. Then he took us to a hangar with several planes. One of them was the Flamingo. He showed it to us only briefly before we moved on.

The tour ended in the same small room where I'd previously met with Mr. Ozols. Yuli and I sat across from him. He explained what the first lesson would include and said that if we had time, we might do a familiarization flight.

I want to sit in the cockpit so badly, to breathe the air at high altitude. I wish we could have that introductory flight, I thought. I looked at Yuli and tried to figure out if she felt the same, but I couldn't tell; she was focused on Mr. Ozols.

He scheduled the first lesson for next Sunday at 8 AM Then he turned to Yuli and said he hadn't yet received her medical certificate, and without it, she wouldn't be able to start. Yuli replied that she was working on it and hoped to provide it soon.

After that, we rode our bikes home. I imagined that riding to Spilve and back on Sunday mornings would probably become our new custom in the coming months.

We rode side by side, and Yuli told me she had also been accepted to university but hadn't decided what she wanted to study yet. She didn't tell me which faculty she had been accepted to.

"I might devote most of my time to flight training at first, because I want to speed it up and become a professional pilot as quickly as possible. It means I'll probably progress in these lessons faster than you," she explained.

She'll progress ahead of me in flight training? I hadn't considered that. For some reason, I thought we'd learn together, even though there wasn't any real reason to think that.

"Well, then you can end up teaching me," I struggled to hide my disappointment.

"Yes, of course." She patted me affectionately on the shoulder as we rode.

"Can I ask you something a bit personal?" I asked.

"Personal?" she laughed. "Ask and we'll see."

"Have you heard about the recent accidents in Switzerland and Egypt?"

"I read in the newspaper about the Dutch plane crash on a mountain in Switzerland. It's terrible that all the passengers and crew were killed, but what happened in Egypt?"

"A plane crashed there too, killing seven people."

In fact, there hasn't been a week without such an accident. Reports of these events appeared in the back pages of the newspaper, and I hoped Dad wasn't aware of them. I feared he would notice them and cancel my flight training.

"Don't these accidents scare you?" I asked.

"Why do you ask? Are you scared?"

"It's a bit worrying, isn't it?"

"I just ignore it, so no. I'm more scared of what's happening outside, in Germany and Italy. You must've heard that Germany announced the cancellation of its trade agreement with the United States and that Jews won't be representing Germany at the Berlin Olympics next year. And recently, Goering ordered actions to be taken against Catholic priests, claiming they were acting against the state. What's happening there is really frightening."

"And what about the Ethiopian king's speech?" I said. "Two weeks ago, he gave a speech in their parliament preparing for war with Italy. What do the Italians even want in Ethiopia? It seems like the global atmosphere is really getting worse."

Everything really does hint at a bad atmosphere. It's not a good sign for what's to come. And even if there's something about Jews that might annoy the Germans and even people here, it's not right to hurt them, because they're good at business, and in the end, it'll harm Germany and our factory. I didn't dare say that to Yuli.

"And with that, ladies and gentlemen, we will conclude for today," said Attorney Rubin as he closed the diary, but not before marking the page he reached.

"Guys, it's really fascinating," said Daniel as he pushed his chair back and stood up.

"Maybe for you, because you understand and probably relate to him, but I'm dying over here," complained Tom. "Mom, are you sure I have to be here?"

"It was your grandfather's request," said Rubin. Everyone was already standing, stretching their arms, turning their heads from side to side, trying to release the tension in their muscles after the lengthy sitting.

"We finished a third, and bear in mind that we started today at around 10. We'll get more done tomorrow. I must say this is the first time in my career that I have to read an entire diary at a will reading. God knows what he was thinking, your grandfather; that we'd be done with it in a flash?"

"My father didn't think. My father did," commented Lilly. "If he decided that we need to hear this, then that's what we'll do."

David and Daniel kissed her cheek, shook their father's hand, and left the room. Daniel already had his phone in his hand, the word 'Flamingo' rising from its speaker.

"Do you need a ride home?" asked Mark.

"No, thanks. The kids are coming over; I'll go with one of them."

Everyone left, including the translator. Only Mirkin remained, standing in front of the large windows, looking towards the wide sea. Rubin glanced in his direction. He must be wondering what he's doing here. Damn, I wonder the same.

He called Miriam and asked her to ensure Mr. Mirkin had a hotel reservation and to assist him in getting to it.

# Chapter 20

"Did you rest well?" Lilly asked her nephews, who were the last to enter the conference room. Mark was seated at the table with a steaming cup of tea before him. Mirkin and the translator also had similarly steaming cups. "Very well, Lilly, thank you. And you?" David looked at his father.

Mark glanced at the clock on the wall. "Rubin will be here in two minutes. I ask you all to minimize interruptions, okay? There are two breaks; save your questions for then. As you can see, Grandpa is still running the show."

"It's hard to believe it's already been a month since he passed. I thought he'd be with us forever," Lilly remarked.

"He's still with us, Lilly. Don't be sad," Mark hugged her, and for a moment, Lilly rested her head on his shoulder.

"It's okay, Dad," Daniel said, "I'm actually curious to hear the rest."

"Good to know," said Attorney Rubin, entering the room accompanied by Miriam and carrying the large box in his hands.

"This whole thing is so official," muttered Hannah. Her brother smiled at her.

Everyone took their seats, and at 2 minutes past 8, Rubin began reading.

### Riga, Latvia, Sunday, August 11, 1935

This morning, Yuli and I arrived in Spilve for our first lesson on the plane. I started the day excited, but the closer I got to the plane, the less impressed I felt about the Flamingo.

Its Siemens engine juts forward as if it had been glued on artificially. It's round, with nine cylinders on all sides connecting to many cables and pipes. The bottom of the engine has the exhaust pipe, and a wooden two-bladed propeller decorates its front.

The body looks like an elongated box with two seating compartments in the first third, one behind the other. The tail is comprised of a large stabilizer and a small elevator. Each side of the Flamingo has two short wings, one at the bottom and one above the seating compartments. The upper wing is attached to the fuselage with narrow struts — two before the front seat and two more between the seats. There are also struts connecting the upper and lower wings. The whole setup isn't much to look at...

Beneath the engine are two medium-sized wheels and a similar-sized tail wheel, partially hidden by the fuselage.

"Look!" Daniel handed his phone to David, "You can continue; I'm just showing them a picture of the plane. He describes it so accurately. We can look and listen at the same time, right?"

The phone was passed around, and Rubin resumed reading.

"The plane is manufactured in Latvia at a factory named Kristina Backman,[23] except for a few parts like the engine and some other components imported from Germany or produced in other Latvian factories," Mr.

Ozols reminded us.

The name 'Kristina Backman' sounded familiar; for a second, I thought I'd heard it in a conversation between Dad and Grandpa.

Mr. Ozols led us around the plane, showing us the pre-flight checks.

"Remember, these checks are very important. They can save your life if you discover a fault while still on the ground. So, to ensure you don't forget any checks, always perform them in the same order. Start inside the cockpit and make sure the power switch is off. Then continue with external checks around the plane, clockwise."

He continued explaining a detailed series of checks starting from the wing connections on one side, moving through the front and engine, then the other side, checking the tail, and back to the starting point.

"After that, check the passenger and pilot compartments."

Mr. Ozols sounded very serious about this whole matter. Yuli and I wrote everything down exactly as he instructed us.

"You must bring the checklist you just prepared to every lesson and never skip a single check. Each one is crucial and lifesaving."

Some of the planes in the hangar, including the Flamingo, had a Fire Cross[24] painted on them, identical to the swastika used by the Nazis in Germany. When I asked Mr. Ozols about it, he explained that it was actually a positive cultural symbol representing thunder, adopted by the Latvian Air Force back in 1919, long before the Nazis in Germany appropriated it.

By the end of the tour, the Flamingo didn't seem so ugly to me anymore.

Mr. Ozols explained that next week we would start actual flying. Finally. It would be an introductory flight to give us a feel for what flying is like and to see if it actually suits us.

"Additionally, it will give me the first opportunity to assess your reactions in the air," he explained. "And you must come dressed warm but comfortable; it's cold up there, even in summer."

Just before he dismissed us, Mr. Ozols reminded Yuli to bring her medical certificate to the next lesson.

She was quieter than usual today. I couldn't talk to her, as Mr. Ozols was with us the entire time. When we walked to our bikes, I asked if she was okay.

To my surprise, she burst into tears.

"Yuli, what's wrong? Are you still angry?"

"It's not about you at all."

"Then why are you crying?"

She didn't answer and covered her face with her hands. Without thinking too much, I just hugged her. I don't know what I would've done if she'd pulled away, but she didn't. She leaned into me lightly. I kept holding her in silence until I felt she was no longer trembling. This was my first time being so close to her and actually feeling the warmth of her body.

Once she calmed down, I invited her to breakfast. I thought Daiga's food would comfort her, no matter what was making her cry. Yuli agreed, and we rode side by side in silence to the market.

This time, Daiga didn't embarrass me. She just winked at me when Yuli wasn't looking, probably to signal her approval of my choice.

It was a good idea to go there as, after a bowl of beetroot soup, Yuli calmed down and even smiled.

"Can I ask what happened now? Just don't start crying again."

"I'm fine. I mean, nothing is fine, but right now there's

nothing I can do about it."

"I don't understand. What isn't fine?"

"I'll never be a pilot, that's what isn't fine!" Tears welled up again, but she quickly wiped them away and smiled in embarrassment. "I just didn't pass the medical exams."

"What!? Are you serious? You look perfectly healthy to me."

"Yeah, I think so too. But when I was little, I had tuberculosis, and the doctors won't give me a medical certificate. They claim my lungs won't withstand the air pressure during flight, but I feel great and I'm sure nothing'll happen to me."

She paused for a moment and added, "I was just afraid to tell Mr. Ozols in case he'd stop me from attending the lesson today. And I still hope I can eventually convince the doctors to give me the certificate."

"I'm really sorry," I said to her. "I hope you do manage to get it, but more than that, what's most important is that it doesn't hurt you. Maybe the doctors are right? You don't know how your body will react when we're up there in the sky."

Yuli smiled sadly. "True, but it's my dream. I don't want to give up on it."

We left the restaurant and walked side by side, leading our bikes along with us.

"Let me know, okay? I'm worried about you," I said.

"Thanks," she replied. We had just arrived at her house, and she went inside. I really regret not giving her a kiss on the cheek. It was a missed opportunity. Given all this new information, I'm not sure if Yuli will be with me in the lessons, and that's really disappointing.

# Chapter 21

### Riga, Latvia, Friday, August 16, 1935

This morning, a photo of airplane wreckage in the newspaper caught my eye. Another aviation accident, this time in Alaska. A famous American pilot named Wiley Post was killed. He was the first pilot to fly solo around the world. His plane crashed during takeoff. I hid the newspaper to make sure Dad didn't see this article.

### Riga, Latvia, Sunday, August 18, 1935

It's very late now, and even though I barely slept last night, today was so exciting that I can't fall asleep.

The reason I didn't sleep last night was that I was anticipating flying for the first time today. What I didn't know was what would happen later with Yuli.

I hadn't heard from her all week. I waited for her at our usual spot at 7 AM, by the right turn onto Slokas Street, right after crossing the bridge. I stood there for fifteen minutes, looking in the direction she was supposed to come from. Eventually, I got on my bike and rode as fast as I could to Spilve. I didn't want to be late.

Mr. Ozols was already waiting for me at the entrance

to the office building. He was holding a leather cap in one hand, and a pair of flying goggles in the other.

He handed them to me. "These are for you until you get your own gear," he said. "I think the cap is your size. We'll adjust the goggle strap after you put the cap on."

"They didn't have a helmet with a fancy visor like you," Mark remarked. He looked at Daniel, and his voice carried more than a hint of pride.

Everyone nodded. Even the attorney and Miriam knew how proud Mark and Michael were. Michael had even attended Daniel's flight school graduation, which he completed with honors.

"Well, I'm glad they at least had a cap and goggles. Don't forget I only flew in enclosed planes. This Flamingo is basically nothing more than a sophisticated toy."

Rubin cleared his throat and continued.

I took them from him with excitement and couldn't stop smiling all the way to the hangar.

"I see you brought a thick coat. It's good enough for today's introductory flight, but if it's the only warm coat you have, we'll need to find another. It's too bulky and won't be comfortable in the cockpit. I'll try to find a more suitable coat for you for the next lesson."

We walked side by side, and he asked, "Are you excited?"

"Yes, extremely," I replied, debating whether to confess that I hadn't slept all night out of excitement, but decided against it.

"I made sure the plane is fueled and ready for our flight this time, but from next time on, it'll be your responsibility before the lesson. You'll need to come at least half an hour earlier."

Mr. Ozols must've read my thoughts because he continued, "Miku, this will be your reality every Sunday for a very long time. While your friends sleep in, you'll wake up very, very early to be ready for the flight. This'll be another challenge you'll have to face if you want to continue the course."

We reached the hangar we had visited last week. It was open, and the Flamingo plane we had inspected stood at the entrance. I knew it by the inscription on it, YL-ABZ. It seemed large and imposing this time.

Standing next to the plane was a mechanic in a thick work overall. He approached Mr. Ozols and shook his hand, then turned to me.

"So, you're the new trainee? Well, good luck. You have an excellent instructor and, for now, a great plane too," he said.

Mr. Ozols turned to me. "Miku, meet Mr. Kromins, the chief mechanic at Spilve." I shook his hand and remembered that Mikhail had told me he worked for the chief mechanic, so he must work for this man.

"Kurt, I want you to show Miku where you've recorded the checks you've performed, what he needs to check before each flight, where to refuel, and where to see if he needs more fuel."

"With great pleasure," replied Mr. Kromins. He pulled out a booklet from a flat leather bag he was carrying, displaying a drawing of a Flamingo plane on the cover. I saw the same code under the drawing as on the plane, YL-ABZ.

"This is the maintenance log, and I know it belongs to this specific plane by the code. It's the plane's tail number and its radio call sign." He opened it in front of me and showed me where to record the inspections and maintenance before each flight.

Mr. Kromins pointed to a large metal cabinet

standing at the edge of the hangar and explained that this is where the logs for all the aircraft are kept and that before each flight, I should pull out the relevant logbook and perform the check.

"I think that's enough for your first time. Now, let's go to the fuel tank."

He signaled for me to join him and pointed to the plane's fuel tank, the refueling port, and the scale showing the amount in the tank. "You don't take off before ensuring you have at least up to this line," he said, pointing to a blue line on the scale in the tank.

"Yes, I understand."

"Now show us the checks you need to perform before the flight."

Mr. Ozols instructed me to follow what we learned last week. I pulled out the paper from my coat pocket where I had written everything down, and started the checks with him standing next to me, occasionally commenting and correcting me. I felt sweat on my palms and slight shortness of breath, but as we progressed, my excitement level decreased.

The final two checks were the fuel quantity and the front wheels. I made sure the wheel chocks, intended to prevent the plane from moving forward after ignition, were in place.

Finally, I stood face-to-face with Mr. Ozols, and he said, "That's it, Miku, we're right before the introductory flight. You can still back out. Are you continuing or not?"

"I'm continuing," I replied, determined to start the flight. I felt my heartbeat pulsing in my temples.

"Fasten the flight cap I gave you, and let's adjust the goggles," he said. He pulled a pair of leather gloves from his coat pocket and handed them to me. "Put these on and get into the front seat. From the next flight on, you'll be sitting in the back. Because it's the first time, I'll be in the back today."

I put on the gloves that fit as if they were custom-made for me, climbed onto the back of the wing, and then moved to sit in the front. Mr. Ozols showed me a handle with which I adjusted the seat to fit the length of my legs. "Make sure you can see the top of the engine through the windshield." The small windshield was in front of me, and I hoped it could actually deflect the cold wind from my face.

Mr. Ozols connected a black cable hanging from my flight cap to a similar cable coming out of the plane's radio. "This is the intercom; you'll be able to hear me through it during the lesson," he said, pulling a kind of sleeve with a wide mouthpiece toward my mouth. "When you want to talk to me, you need to bring this mouthpiece close to your mouth so I can hear you."

He helped me fasten the seat belts and adjust them. Finally, he arranged the flying goggles over my eyes. "Always remember to make sure they're over your eyes, not on your forehead," he stressed.

After all the preparations that seemed to take forever, he said, "That's it; you're almost ready for your first flight."

I could barely breathe from excitement. After so much time, I was finally about to fulfill my dream, to fly.

Mr. Ozols took his seat in the back, and a slight tremor passed through the plane.

"Can you hear me?" he spoke into my flight cap.

"Yes, I can hear you perfectly," I replied immediately into the speaking sleeve.

"While on the ground, the pedals also serve as brakes. Push the right pedal forward, then the left one."

At first, I couldn't move the pedal. I thought it would be easy, but it wasn't. I had to exert a lot more effort to move the pedal forward. After a few tries, I got used to its resistance, and the pushing motion became smoother.

"Now hold the control rod, the stick, with your right hand, and move it to the right, then to the left."

The feel of the stick was also stiffer than I had imagined, but this time I was prepared. My hand trembled slightly, but I applied enough pressure to move it sideways.

Then Mr. Ozols instructed me to move the stick forward and backward to move the elevator on the tail.

"Excellent. Now let's go over the various instruments in the cockpit together. Just like the preflight checks outside, you start the cockpit checks from the left and go over all the instruments and levers clockwise."

"Got it," I replied.

# Chapter 22

We went over the cockpit together.
"This is the throttle," I heard him say. "Move it forward and backward and feel its motion." I did as he instructed. I knew this was how you increase or decrease the engine's power.

"Now let's check the instruments we have. The first instrument is the airspeed indicator. Right now, it should show zero speed. The next instrument is the altimeter, which shows the aircraft's altitude above, above what?" Mr. Ozols asked.

"Above sea level," I replied immediately.

"Correct. Right now, we need to set it to Spilve's known altitude above sea level. The next instrument is the tachometer, which shows the engine's revolutions per minute, it too should currently be at zero. We call this value by the abbreviated name RPM."

Mr. Ozols continued explaining the rest of the gauges and instruments on the panel.

"Now I'll show you how to start the engine. Don't touch anything. First, you check that there's no one around or near the propeller. Then you announce, 'start engine,' and wait a moment so that if there's someone you can't see, they'll hear you and move. Please make the announcement."

I lifted my gaze from the cockpit and only now noticed

that Mr. Kromins was standing at the front left of the plane, at a safe distance, looking at me.

"That's where the mechanic will always be standing before starting," explained Mr. Ozols.

"Start engine," I announced loudly.

"Excellent. Now we need to move the ignition switch, which we call the magneto, to the start position. It's the switch on the right side of your instrument panel. It has several positions. Move the switch to the 'both' position. That's our starting position."

I followed the instructions.

"Raise your left hand and signal to Mr. Kromins that you're ready to start and announce 'contact.' This means 'magneto connected.'"

I raised my left hand and announced with a slightly trembling voice, "Contact."

Mr. Kromins approached the nose of the plane and pushed the propeller down forcefully and quickly. The engine roared to life immediately, making a tremendous noise and emitting a strong smell. The propeller blades began spinning rapidly, and Mr. Kromins hurriedly stepped away from them. The plane shook as if it was eager to start moving forward, but the wheel chocks held it in place.

"Miku, I want you to place your hand on the throttle now and feel what I'm doing through it. Because of the loud noise, from now on and throughout the flight, you must repeat each of my instructions loudly. Understood?"

"Yes, Mr. Ozols, I'm placing my hand on the throttle to feel what you're doing," I replied.

"Good. You learn fast. Now notice that I'm pushing the throttle forward and feel the engine's response. Tell me what you see or feel."

"I see the propeller spinning faster, and the engine

noise is increasing."

"Look at the instrument panel in front of you. Notice the tachometer. Do you see the needle rising?"

"Yes."

"Right now, we want the engine to warm up and reach the required RPM for flight."

Mr. Ozols continued describing each of the instruments in front of me, and when the engine reached the desired temperature, I reported it to him.

"Alright then, everything is ready for takeoff. We only have one more thing to do. Do you see Mr. Kromins still waiting to the side?"

"Yes."

"Do you know why?"

"No."

"Because he needs to remove the chocks holding the wheels in place. It's a common mistake for pilots to rush to take off and forget to remove the chocks first. The plane won't move unless you remove them. Please signal Mr. Kromins with both thumbs, your right thumb pointing to the right and your left thumb pointing to the left, and he will remove the chocks. When we finish the flight and return here, your signal will be the opposite: both thumbs pointing toward each other, which will be the order in which he will insert the chocks. After he removes them, release the brakes so we can move forward."

I did as instructed, and Mr. Kromins approached and removed the wheel chocks. I immediately felt the wheels release, as the plane started rolling forward slowly.

"This is the time to firmly press the brakes, Miku," said Mr. Ozols. "We mustn't start moving forward. Not yet." I applied the brakes firmly, and the plane stopped moving.

"Now signal to Mr. Kromins with your left thumb pointing up that everything is fine, so he knows we're ready to go."

I raised my left hand and signaled. Mr. Kromins returned the same signal, turned, and walked away.

"That's it, Miku. We're ready to go. Are you ready?"

"I'm ready."

"Sit back, hold the stick, and place your feet on the pedals, but don't do anything on your own and don't resist my actions."

I repeated the instructions.

Mr. Ozols began gently pushing the throttle. My hand holding the stick stretched forward slightly, and we started rolling towards the runway. All I could see beyond the windscreen from my seat was the nose of the plane.

"The trick to taxiing is to use minimal engine power, just enough to move and make small turns," explained Mr. Ozols as the plane moved heavily until we reached the edge of the runway.

Mr. Ozols braked the plane's movement. "Before getting on the runway, we need to ensure no other planes are on it and none are coming in to land. Additionally, we need to announce over the radio that we're taxiing to the start of the runway. You should already know that each runway has two possible takeoff directions, opposite each other, and the takeoff direction is also the name of the runway. When the runway is facing north, its name will be three-six-zero, and if we take off facing south, its name will be one-eight-zero. When there's an air traffic control tower, it'll instruct us on which runway to take. Now, look to the right and tell me the wind direction."

Through the gap between the two right wings, I saw a tall pole with a colorful windsock. It hung limp by the pole and didn't point in any clear direction.

"It seems there's no wind at all."

"You're right, but every time you come here, before

getting on the runway, you need to check the wind direction to know your takeoff direction. You always take off – "

"Against the wind," I completed him.

"Correct. And when there's no wind, we prefer the runway used for the previous takeoff or landing. So, which way do we turn now?"

"Right."

"Correct. Now look to the right and tell me if it's clear or not."

"The runway is clear."

I heard Mr. Ozols reporting over the radio that he was taxiing to the start of the runway. The plane turned right and started rolling slowly until we reached the side of the runway, positioned at about a forty-five-degree angle to the takeoff direction.

"This is where we perform the final checks." He showed me how to perform them all.

"The most important check is the magneto check. It can only be done when the engine reaches its minimum flight temperature. Miku, please check if we've reached it."

"We have."

"If so, let's perform it."

I began pushing the throttle gently. The engine increased its power, and my hand holding the stick shook along with it. The needle on the tachometer started to climb, and when it reached the desired RPM, I stopped and reported it.

Mr. Ozols continued his explanations and finally said, "If the engine shuts off during these operations, don't worry, it happens sometimes. It's a matter of skill."

He continued giving instructions, and I executed them. I managed to do everything without the engine shutting off.

It was the very last check before takeoff. I was so focused on all the instructions that I forgot all my excitement. Now it was back, and I was eagerly awaiting takeoff again.

But it didn't happen.

"Now we'll practice taxiing on the runway," Mr. Ozols instructed.

We taxied along the runway, and Mr. Ozols demonstrated how to use the pedals to turn right and left and how to turn the plane around to retrace our steps.

It looked simple, but it wasn't. At first, I couldn't steer properly and the plane moved along the runway as if it had a mind of its own. Gradually, I learned to control the use of the pedals and taxi the plane in the direction Mr. Ozols instructed.

"Now we'll taxi to the start of the runway again, and this time we'll be taking off," I heard him say.

Finally!

---

"Finally indeed, I thought he'd never take off," said Daniel. "I think all the checks and everything he wrote are very necessary, but time passes much faster when you perform them than when you listen to someone read these instructions."

Mark stood up. "I'm sorry, I can't sit for so long. Please continue, I'll stand by the window for a bit and then sit back down."

"Great idea," said Lilly. "I'll get up soon too."

"We have a meal break in about forty-five minutes," said Rubin, sipping from the glass of water Miriam had placed before him when they entered the room. "I need a break too. Stand up; it doesn't bother me. Just keep quiet, okay?"

He returned to the booklet in his hand.

## Chapter 23

We reported it over the radio, and although no one responded, I taxied the plane to the start of the runway myself until it was again positioned properly at a forty-five-degree angle.

After completing the pre-takeoff checklist, Mr. Ozols increased the engine power, and we lined up in the correct direction. The runway stretched out before me, looking incredibly long. Without realizing it, I had managed to get used to seeing forward somehow, through and past the pistons protruding from the engine and the various pipes connected to it.

"Now, we'll push the throttle all the way forward to give the engine full power and start racing down the runway until we take off. Your feet on the pedals, one hand always on the stick, and the other on the throttle, got it?"

I repeated his instructions to confirm. My heartbeat sped up again, and a slight tremor passed through my whole body.

It was real. It was really happening.

Mr. Ozols pushed the throttle forward all the way. The engine's power increased significantly, the noise grew louder, and the plane began vibrating even more. We started gaining speed along the runway. The tail lifted, pushing my whole body forward. I could see the runway unobstructed. My gaze was focused entirely forward, sometimes on the runway and sometimes on the speedometer. Once we reached the necessary speed for takeoff, I announced it, and he gently pulled the stick back. My hand moved with his.

The plane responded immediately and began to lift off. A moment later, it shuddered slightly as it left the ground. Mr. Ozols increased the pull on the stick, and the climb angle grew. A quick glance to the sides allowed me to see the increasing distance between us and the ground. The landscape slid sideways and spread out before my eyes.

One year and three months after I stood there, watching Cukurs from the ground, and here I was — in the air! My dream had come true. The plane soared and so did my spirits. The wind pressed my coat against my body, and I smiled despite the cold air entering my throat. It happened. It was happening.

Once we were high enough up, Mr. Ozols stopped the climb and leveled us off relative to the ground.

We made a wide right turn toward the mouth of the Daugava River. It looked like we were flying over a living map painted with green, brown, and blue. It was incredible.

"How does it feel?" he asked.

"All good," I replied. I barely managed to get the words out. I'd never felt like this in my life.

"Excellent. Now I'll demonstrate the basic flight maneuvers, and then we'll see if you can replicate them yourself."

Mr. Ozols demonstrated a flight he called "straight and level." We flew like that for a few minutes. I noticed that the plane wasn't completely stable; it rose and fell slightly all the time, like a boat in restless waters.

Then he demonstrated a right turn. He tilted the stick while pressing the right pedal, and the plane turned as if rotating on an axis connecting its nose to its tail.

I panicked, released my grip on the stick and grabbed the sides of the cockpit with both hands so as not to fall out of the plane.

Mr. Ozols noticed immediately. "Put your hand back on the stick and your foot on the pedal," he instructed. "It's scary at first, but it's meant to make you understand the importance of fastening your seat belts before taking off. Can we continue?"

"Yes, we can," I replied weakly, my pulse racing. I didn't dare look to the sides, focusing my gaze on the plane's nose and the instrument panel.

Mr. Ozols returned us to "straight and level" flight and then demonstrated a left turn. This time, I was ready for it.

He went on to show me how to climb and descend.

As the lesson went on, I got more used to the movement in the air. Mr. Ozols let me hold the stick alone and feel the plane's response to slight and strong pulls, tilting it right and left.

At some point, he instructed me to gently pull the stick toward me more and more and watch the plane's nose gradually rise toward the sky.

"Notice the speed is dropping," I heard his voice in the headset. "You'll feel the controls becoming harder to manage." Mr. Ozols took over the stick again, and suddenly the nose turned sharply downward, and the ground started racing toward us. I stopped breathing.

"I'm keeping the wings level all the time; otherwise, we'll enter a spin, which is a situation we don't want to be in. This maneuver is called a 'Stall Recovery,' and we'll practice it again and again until you can do it yourself."

He then demonstrated a "Spin Recovery." You press

the pedal opposite to the spin direction and push the stick forward to stop it. Then, you increase the throttle to raise the engine RPM and gently pull the stick until you're back in level flight. It felt very scary, but also challenging.

Gradually, my tension levels decreased, and I began feeling more at ease. My grip on the stick also became softer.

Mr. Ozols probably sensed this. "Are you ready for an aerobatic maneuver?"

"I'm ready."

"We'll now perform a maneuver called a 'Loop.'"

We started with a gentle dive towards the ground and gained speed. Then, he pulled the stick and raised the nose of the plane towards the gray sky. The ground disappeared completely; All I could see was an endless expanse of sky and, for a moment, I didn't understand what was happening. It was so terrifying I couldn't stop my hands from leaving the stick and tightly gripping the sides of the cockpit.

After a few seconds, the horizon started approaching us, and I realized we were completely upside down. "Keep pulling all the time," I heard Mr. Ozols' calm voice. "Keep pulling."

The maneuver continued. "Keep pulling, keep pulling," I mumbled to myself.

The horizon disappeared somewhere beneath the plane's belly, and the nose pointed towards the ground as we dove, inverted, accelerating towards it. I saw the mouth of the Daugava pass beneath us quickly and disappear, making way for new passing scenery.

When will it end? I thought, just as I felt the plane recover from the dive and level off into a "straight and level" flight. The plane may have leveled off easily, but I wasn't at ease at all. What was that? We flew upside down? Why would anyone need to fly upside down? And how did we get back to normal flight? I took a deep breath, trying to calm down and regain focus.

"Don't worry, Miku," I heard Mr. Ozols reassure me as if he had read my thoughts. "What you felt just now is what every pilot experiences the first time they do a loop. With time, you'll learn to feel comfortable even when the plane is inverted, diving, and in a steep climb."

It was a bit too much for me; I felt nauseous. When Mr. Ozols asked if I wanted to end the lesson, I said yes, and he flew us back in silence until we landed.

He taxied along the runway and, when we reached the point where we had come from, we turned left and taxied back to the hangar. Mr. Kromins was already waiting and guided us until the plane was in place and the engine shut off.

I heard Mr. Ozols unbuckle his seatbelt and, out of the corner of my eye, I saw him get out and stand on the lower wing.

"Stay in your seat until I unbuckle you from the seatbelt and the intercom system," he said, and so I did. I was exhausted and wasn't sure I could get out of the seat by myself anyway.

He leaned toward me, showed me how to release myself, and signaled me to exit. He pulled me up and pointed to the spot at the base of the wing where I should place my feet. He then jumped to the ground, and I followed his example.

"So, Miku, how was your first flight?"

# Chapter 24

Attorney Rubin paused and looked up at the clock. There were ten minutes left until the break. He felt slightly dizzy. It wasn't easy to read for so long.

Mark had already returned to his seat, Miriam was typing something on her phone, and Lilly and her son, Tom, were standing by the window. Everyone was looking at him, waiting for him to continue.

"There's a slight delay with the food we ordered," Miriam whispered in his ear.

He took a deep breath, turned the page, and continued.

The first flight was more than I had expected. I was completely dizzy, my legs were shaking, and my thoughts were swirling in my head. I felt a little nauseous.

"I really enjoyed it," I finally managed to reply.

Mr. Ozols patted my shoulder. "Well, I see you're at a loss for words. Now we need to help push the plane into the hangar, and then we'll do the debrief for the first flight and prepare for the next. You can go on to the office; I'll join you shortly."

Just before I left the hangar area, I saw Mikhail. He had his back to me. I was relieved he didn't see me; I was in no state to talk.

I tried to catch my breath on the way to the office. I

touched my face and noticed it was cold.

We sat in Mr. Ozols' usual room. I'm going to call it the briefing room from now on. He reviewed everything we did during the lesson and told me again that next week I would be sitting in the rear seat and practicing everything he had taught me today.

"Use the time during the upcoming week to rehearse all we've done today in your mind. It'll help you when we start practicing again in the air. Ah, yes, there's one more thing. To commemorate your first flight, I have a gift for you."

He pulled a notebook with a leather cover from his desk drawer and placed it in front of me.

"This will be your flight logbook from now on. Every flight you make will be recorded here. This way, you'll know how many flight hours you've accumulated. It's how pilots measure each other's experience and seniority. Congratulations."

Mr. Ozols stood up. The debriefing was over.

I seized the opportunity and asked, "Can I ask what happened to Yuli? Do you know why she didn't come today?"

"I didn't want to upset you, Miku, but Yuliana won't be continuing her flight training with us."

"Oh no." I was disappointed. I knew it could happen, but I hoped she would manage somehow.

"Yuliana couldn't get a medical clearance. I'm sorry, but that's how it is for now," Mr. Ozols added and left the room.

I decided to ride straight to Yuli's house. I reached 20 Stabu Street and stood in front of the large building. Only then did I realize I didn't know which floor she lived on. There was a heavy door at the entrance.

Luckily, while I was contemplating what to do, an elderly woman opened the door and exited the building. I took the opportunity and quickly entered the lobby.

I found the name Bergs and the apartment number on the mailbox panel. I climbed the stairs until I reached the third floor, panting, and stood in front of the Bergs' family apartment.

I knocked and, after a brief moment, the door opened slightly, and Yuli peeked out. Her expression was somber. For a moment, we stood there without saying a word.

"Aren't you going to let me in?" I asked with a smile, but Yuli showed no sign of inviting me inside. "Mr. Ozols told me you didn't get the certificate. I was worried about you, so I came right away."

"Wait for me downstairs, I'll get dressed and come down." She closed the door in my face.

We went to the nearby Vermanes Park[25] and sat on one of the benches.

Yuli burst into tears. I put my hand on hers and held it. She didn't object. "Are you okay?" I asked cautiously.

"I'll never be a pilot. That dream has shattered. I'm not okay!" She smiled at me, embarrassed, tears streaming down her cheeks. "No doctor is willing to clear me to fly."

"I'm really sorry," I told her.

"I spent all morning thinking about how you're already in your flight lesson and I'm not. I'm so jealous of you."

She burst into tears again, and this time it took her a while to calm down. I promised her that if I completed my flight training, I would take her with me as a passenger, but it didn't improve her mood.

"Miku, I have a surprise for you," she said, wiping her eyes with her hand.

"What else could there be?"

"I was also accepted into the aeronautics program. Just like you. We'll study together. I hope you're not mad at me for not telling you that I applied to the same faculty."

I was so happy that I hugged her with both arms. Yuli hugged me back.

I turned my head towards her face and kissed her on the cheek. She shivered for a moment but didn't release me from her hug.

I think she might almost be my girlfriend.

I asked her if she wanted to go eat at the market again, but she said she preferred to go home and that we'd talk later in the week.

So many things in one day!

---

Rubin stopped. He looked up and saw one of his office employees approaching the conference room door. That was enough.

"Break," he announced and removed his glasses. He placed them on the booklet and stood up.

"I've never seen him move so fast," Lilly whispered to Mark as everyone stood up.

"I guess he's exhausted. And look, we've barely reached the middle of this thing. What do you think? Do you have any thoughts about Miku, Mirkin, and all these Latvians who have suddenly appeared in our lives?"

"Not really, but I must say I find the story interesting. It's also nice to see you and the kids day after day. That almost never happens."

"Come on, let's see what they brought us today," Mark took her arm, "and in that regard, yes, I'm also glad to be here with you."

# Chapter 25

"Well, we stopped at Miku's longest day and, I suppose, ours too," Rubin smiled, flipping back a few pages in the journal. "Yes, here we are. We're still on Sunday, August 18, 1935. Now that everyone is sated and satisfied, let's continue straight through until lunchtime. Ready?" He didn't wait for an answer and began reading aloud.

When I got home, I found Dad waiting for me at the dining table with a serious expression.

"Dad! You won't believe the day I've had. I flew today! For the first time. We were right above the Daugava, and I saw the whole city from above. It was amazing," I began, but he hushed me with his hand.

Only then did I notice the newspaper I had hidden, with the news about the crash in Alaska, spread out on the table in front of him.

"Wait, Miku. Sit down, please; I need to talk to you. It's important."

I panicked. "What happened?"

"Nothing has happened yet, thank God, but that's exactly what I want to talk about, and I need you to listen until the end." Dad fixed his gaze on me and continued, "There have been so many aviation accidents lately, Miku. It's simply too dangerous. I think you should stop your flight training.

You've barely started, so the damage won't be too great."

The happiest day turned into the worst in an instant.

"But Dad, you met Mr. Ozols, you know I'm in good hands. The Flamingo is very reliable; all those planes you read about in the paper are different. There's no need to jump to such extreme conclusions. There are car accidents too, but you haven't thought about not driving your car or preventing me from continuing my driving lessons."

"It's not the same, and you also have to consider that if, God forbid, something happened to you, there'd be no one to continue our family, and that's a consideration you're too young to understand."

"But Grandpa argued that too, and the archbishop approved. So you'd cancel everything just like that?"

I think it was the first time in my life that I raised my voice at my father like that. I saw the surprise in his eyes, but I was too angry to stop. "It's my life, and I refuse to give up what I want to do with it because of your fears."

I stood up; my chair fell backwards with a loud crash, and I didn't bother to pick it up. I just left. I didn't want to talk to him anymore at that moment. I went out of the house, took my bike, and started riding aimlessly until I found myself in front of Yuli's house.

Only she could understand me.

I stood there, but what did I actually want from her? She herself was devastated by the news that she couldn't continue her flight training, so what comfort could she offer me? What I thought of telling her would only add to her misery. I didn't know what to do.

I kept standing in the street, staring into space. For a moment, I thought about my mom and what would've happened if she were alive. Would she support me or agree with Dad? Maybe if I had a mom, I would've had brothers and sisters, and then this whole thing of having to continue their legacy in the factory would've been spared from me.

I didn't have an answer, but the thought helped me calm down and think clearly. After all, Dad wants what's best for me. He expressed concern for me, and instead of acting like a responsible adult and convincing him to change his mind, I threw a tantrum like a little kid. I was angry at myself and realized it would be better to go back home, apologize, and ask him to reconsider. He had to agree to let me continue. Now of all times, after finally feeling what it's really like to fly, I'm willing to fight for it.

But when I got home, Dad wasn't there.

### Riga, Latvia, Monday, August 19, 1935

I got up early today and managed to join Dad for breakfast.

"Good morning," I said, waiting for his reaction.

Dad nodded and continued reading the morning paper.

I sat down next to him.

"Dad, I behaved childishly and inappropriately last night. I apologize. I want to present my position to you," I said.

He folded the paper and focused on me. Our conversation lasted over an hour, until he glanced at his watch.

"I didn't realize it was so late," he said. "I have to run to a meeting. I am impressed by what you've said. I haven't made a final decision yet; maybe I'll speak with Mr. Ozols about it. In the meantime, continue as usual, and we'll talk about it again."

I wanted to jump out of my chair and hug him, but I didn't.

"Thank you, Dad. I promise to do my best to stay safe and respect any decision you make." I promised, though I wasn't sure I could keep it.

"My Miku, you're becoming a responsible adult," Dad said just as he left the house.

# Chapter 26

### Riga, Latvia, Sunday, September 8, 1935

I've had two more flight lessons since the conversation with my dad. Sitting in the rear seat is completely different from the front seat; you can see even less ahead of you. We practiced the different flight positions repeatedly, but thankfully, we didn't do the aerobatic loop again.

In the second lesson, we started practicing takeoffs too. By the end of the lesson, I managed to take off on my own, with Mr. Ozols only guiding me with his hand on the stick.

During the lesson, the plane responded strongly to the surrounding winds and showed a significant tendency to fly in a different direction from the one I wanted. Mr. Ozols explained that I needed to learn to control it. "Even if it seems like it has a mind of its own, you have to train it to fly according to your instructions, not the other way around. It's like riding a wild horse and taming it."

It wasn't easy. I had to constantly use the pedals with my feet and move the stick side to side.

"How am I doing so far?" I couldn't help but ask him at the end of the lesson.

"Your progress is reasonable, average," he replied briefly.

"I estimate that we will be able to start practicing landings in another lesson or two."

He explained the sequence of actions and preparations required for landing. I wrote everything down, and he instructed me to memorize it all by heart, "Because it'll be much more complicated in the air, and you won't be able to peek at your notebook."

Today, there was no lesson because there was an air show at Spilve called 'Flight Around Latvia' by the Aviation Club and the National Guard. The planes, most of which were biplanes like the Flamingo, were lined up side by side. At the tail section of each was a Fire Cross symbol, and some had the same symbol on the underside of the lower wing.

The pilots stood in military formation in front of the row of planes, waiting for the ceremony to start. I didn't see Mr. Ozols among them.

I stood in the crowd and watched. Military march music played in the background, and a light northern breeze waved the many flags set up on the sides.

The ceremony itself began when a group of officers marched toward the pilots in formation, some saluting. They wore military caps and tall, shiny leather boots.

Everyone watched, except for the younger children who were waiting for the carousel set up there. The weather was particularly nice; most people wore short sleeves and enjoyed the light breeze.

The person who interested me the most during the ceremony was the pilot Herbert Cukurs. The announcer introduced him while he stood beside a statue of a globe held by two birds of prey. He wore a uniform like the other officers, and a large medal hung on his chest. I couldn't see what was written on it from where I was standing. I still find it hard to believe that this man has influenced my life so much.

I was excited to see him again up close.

After the applause, the pilots dispersed to their planes, and the crowd sat down to watch the air show. The pilots began taxiing one by one, each with a mechanic in overalls running alongside the wing. I think one of them was Mikhail.

Cukurs stood in a spot where everyone could see him, explaining what the show would include and asking everyone to hold on tightly to the many balloons scattered around, so they wouldn't fly away and interfere with the takeoffs.

The planes took off one by one and began performing various maneuvers. The first approached us and dropped a parachute with a box. The children in the crowd ran toward the spot where the box landed.

The second plane flew very low over us. The next performed the aerobatic loop – the 360-degree vertical loop – like the one Mr. Ozols showed me in the first lesson. For a moment, I was afraid the pilot was going to fall out of his seat but, of course, nothing like that happened.

Then there was a formation flight of three planes that flew very close to each other, and at the end of the show, all the planes flew in formation, in groups of three. I counted eighteen.

I watched the planes maneuver and imagined myself sitting in the cockpit of one of them, looking through the canopy at the crowd, trying to spot Yuli in it, and then pulling the stick with all my might, performing stunts in the sky.

I'm eagerly waiting for the moment when I'll also know how to do these maneuvers. I know I have a lot to learn before I reach that level, but deep down, I feel that if they can do it, so can I.

"Excuse me," said the translator, "Mr. Mirkin needs to go to the bathroom."

Mr. Mirkin looked at the attorney with a questioning look. "Of course, we won't ask him to hold it in." Rubin gestured towards the door.

"Just tell him not to take too long," said Mark, taking advantage of the break to stand up again.

"Maybe we should all take a bathroom break and reconvene in ten minutes. What do you think?"

"I'm in favor," Hannah jumped up from her seat. "Come on, Mom, even if you don't need to go, take the opportunity."

"Is there a lot more left?" Mark asked Rubin.

"I think we're about halfway through."

"Well, I still don't understand the point of all this."

"We'll both be wiser tomorrow, I suppose," replied Rubin.

## Riga, Latvia, Sunday, September 15, 1935

This morning, Mr. Ozols asked me to recite the sequence of actions and checks required for landing by heart. He demonstrated how to do it one more time before we took off. I sat in the pilot's seat and he leaned in from outside, pointing and guiding me along the various handles and switches.

For the first time since I started learning, I managed not only to focus on the actual flying but also to look out at the landscape around us, even though the wings obscured part of it. We climbed to an altitude of 4,500 feet, and when I had a brief moment of free time, I managed to spot Kurpnieku Island[26] to my right, several ships that were docked at the north side of the Daugava, and where it flows out to sea. To my left, I saw the northern end of Jurmala and the mouth of the Lielupe River.

Towards the end of the lesson, when we saw Spilve from a distance, Mr. Ozols instructed me to start performing the sequence of actions for landing.

"Land by yourself, I'll guide you. It's important that you focus and keep your gaze constantly shifting between the speedometer, altimeter, and the runway."

It looked easy when he did the landing, but I couldn't manage it in any of my attempts. One time I came in too high, another time too low, and if he hadn't intervened at the last moment, we would've landed in the field before the runway. On my last attempt, I managed to come in at the correct height, but too fast, and Mr. Ozols had to save the situation again by pushing the throttle to maximum and taking off before we touched the ground.

By the time the lesson had ended, I was already exhausted and frustrated. At the debriefing after the flight, he reassured me and said that this happens to all the trainees.

"It takes time to get to know the plane well enough to land it successfully. You'll feel it in your butt."

"What do you mean?"

"You'll understand when you feel it."

# Chapter 27

### Riga, Latvia, Sunday, September 22, 1935

I was met with a real surprise this morning.

Mikhail was standing next to Mr. Kromins in the hangar. I was happy to see him and waved hello. A flicker of surprise crossed his face, and he returned the gesture. Mr. Kromins signaled me to go about my business, so I took the maintenance log from the cabinet and began preparing the plane for the lesson. We didn't get a chance to talk.

The sky began to darken, and it looked like it would start raining any minute. I remembered from ground studies that when it rains, the runway can become slippery and even muddy, making landings more dangerous. All my lessons had been in perfect weather until today. I wondered if Mr. Ozols would insist on holding the lesson anyway.

When he arrived, we stepped outside the hangar. Mr. Ozols gestured upwards and asked what I thought about the weather. By this point, black clouds had already covered the whole sky.

I didn't know how to respond. Was Mr. Ozols testing my determination? Or maybe he was testing my attention to flight safety, a topic he constantly emphasized?

"I think it's problematic weather for flying because of

the active clouds, and what worries me the most is that if it rains, the risk during landing increases," I tried to sound convincing.

"In that case, the lesson is canceled, and we'll meet next week," Mr. Ozols replied. It seemed he was actually pleased. He began walking away from me, then stopped, turned around, and said, "It's not easy to decide not to fly. It takes courage to make such a decision. Sometimes it can even save lives. So, even if we didn't fly today, you still learned something important." He turned away and left.

I returned to the hangar, hoping to catch Mikhail. I was glad the lesson was canceled. I'd prefer that he sees me landing without mistakes and mishaps.

I found him still talking with Mr. Kromins. I waited on the side for a few minutes until Mr. Kromins waved goodbye and left the hangar.

Mikhail was happy to see me again. It was raining heavily outside. Good thing we didn't take off and I came inside; otherwise, the rain would've caught me on my bike.

Mikhail and I moved to a corner with some chairs and sat down. There was no point in going out in the pouring rain anyway. I thought about my bike getting soaked and hoped the rain would stop in time for me to get home dry.

"Mr. Kromins told me you're Mr. Ozols' new trainee. So how many flight lessons have you had? What's it like being in the air?" he asked, continuing without waiting for an answer, "I told you you'd love it, remember? Anyway, I told Mr. Kromins we know each other, and he said that from now on, I'll be assisting you before and after every flight. So we'll be seeing a lot of each other."

"Good. It'll be nice to see a friendly face."

Mikhail laughed, "It will, it will. Just don't forget everything Mr. Kromins taught you."

"Say, Mikhail, could it be that I saw you at the air show here two weeks ago?"

"Yes! How did you spot me among everyone? It was my first time participating as a mechanic," he said excitedly. "One day, we'll both participate in an air show, me on the ground and you in the air."

We chatted until the rain stopped and then rode together to the Pilsētas Canal near the opera. From there, I rode home alone. I couldn't stop thinking about what made Mikhail choose to become an aircraft mechanic instead of studying engineering at the Polytechnic.

Last week, I heard that Germany passed new laws, mainly against Jews. It's truly awful. I wondered what would happen to Mikhail and his family if such laws were passed in Latvia too. It's one thing to think generally about Jews and these restrictions, but it's entirely different to know someone personally affected by them.

# Chapter 28

### Riga, Latvia, Sunday, November 10, 1935[27]

Flying has been impossible due to weather conditions for the past month. Today, however, was excellent, and the lesson was great. It was very cold, but the coat Mr. Ozols gave me protected me. The main issue was my face. The wind was so cold that it felt like it was piercing holes in my skin around the flight goggles. Mr. Ozols suggested applying a greasy ointment before each flight. I'll try that next lesson.

"Can you imagine it? Flying in the sky, in November, without a canopy? How much guts that must take," Tom said to Daniel.

Everyone turned to Daniel as the expert on planes.

"It sounds completely insane to me," David replied first.

"I have a feeling even crazier things are still hiding in this story," Lilly joined the conversation.

Attorney Rubin listened and didn't rush to stop them. He wondered if it would be appropriate to let Miriam continue in his place but decided against it. Michael Golber had requested that he do it, and he intended to honor that request.

He didn't hear Daniel's response, but it seemed the conversation had run its course because suddenly everyone fell silent and looked at him. He continued.

The lesson was particularly long because, for the first time, we navigated along the Daugava River until we reached the city of Ogre, and then flew back. Mr. Ozols explained how to determine our location and the direction of flight toward the destination.

"We're doing it without a map this time, but on future navigation flights, you'll need to check your location relative to the map."

This was the first time I saw how large the Daugava River is, with its many bends and surrounding lakes. Thanks to the beautiful weather, there were also many boats on the river.

I feel very confident flying the Flamingo. I pilot it myself most of the time now.

When we returned to Spilve, I also performed the landing and managed to do it on the first try.

"How did you determine the altitude and speed for landing?" Mr. Ozols asked after we landed.

"I felt it in my butt," I replied.

He laughed and patted me on the back.

I smiled from ear to ear. I climbed out of the cockpit and, for a moment, felt like Cukurs. In short, it was excellent.

As usual after every flight, we entered the briefing room and conducted a debriefing. Mr. Ozols told me everything he couldn't say while we were in the air and emphasized again the importance of orientation and familiarization with the terrain. At the end of the debriefing, I asked him about the Flamingo accident that happened last week. It had collided with a Bristol Bulldog and broke apart. Three people were killed.

"Did you know any of those who died?"

"All of them. They were my colleagues. Anyone who chooses our profession knows the risks. It's sad to lose good people this way. When I was in the army, we used to say that we part from life every morning before our first flight and give thanks for it every evening after our last landing." He looked at me intently and added sternly, "This is true here as well. This is the world you're entering, and these are the risks of our profession. It's not too late for you to reconsider."

Hearing those words frightened me a little, especially the tone in which they were said. I hoped he wouldn't tell my dad. So far, my dad hasn't contacted him or spoken to me again about my flight lessons.

Mikhail and I have a tradition by now: when I finish the debriefing, we sit together. So, after I parted from Mr. Ozols, I returned to the hangar.

He had just finished washing part of an engine and was wiping his hands. "Why so serious?" he smiled and asked.

"Did you hear about the accident between the Flamingo and the Bristol Bulldog?"

"Who hasn't? It's the talk of the day. I think I saw one of the pilots who died here before, but I'm not entirely sure. I guess Mr. Kromins knew them."

I told Mikhail what Mr. Ozols had said to me.

"He's right, but this isn't new to you. Okay, let's talk about nicer things."

"Like what?"

"Like the fact that you're getting better at flying, and I'm progressing too; Mr. Krumins really trusts me now. Last week he let me guide planes out for flights on my own. That's why I was the mechanic who assisted you this morning with the Flamingo's start-up. You did look surprised. They're all good things, aren't they?"

"It's a shame you were inside the hangar when we came back and didn't see my landing at the end of the lesson, because it was really good too," I boasted. My mood improved a bit.

"Say, Miku, when do I get to meet your Yuli?"

I had told him about her the last time we sat together.

"Funny! Yuli asked the same question when we were working on exercises from university. She's better than me at math and physics, so she helps me. Honestly, I don't know how others in the class manage without someone like Yuli to help them." Thinking about her already made me forget about the conversation with Mr. Ozols.

The three of us planned to meet during the week. We'll probably go to 'Otto Schwartz' Café in Hotel de Rome and rub shoulders with famous people. It was Yuli's suggestion. We agreed beforehand that meetings at Café Kuze is just between us, so we chose another café for this one.

# Chapter 29

## Riga, Latvia, Monday, November 18, 1935

Yesterday's lesson was awful. The weather was shit. Mr. Ozols didn't think the strong wind or the mud left on the runway were a problem, so we took to the air as usual.

The entire flight was turbulent due to the wind currents. Nothing went right, and I barely managed to control the plane. There wasn't a single maneuver I managed to perform properly. At some point, he must have given up because he took the controls and flew us back. I did manage to land, but it wasn't perfect. We came in too fast and bounced in the air quite a bit. It really scared me.

"I thought your skill level would allow you to fly in this kind of weather by now," he said during the debriefing. "We'll take off and practice it, otherwise we won't be able to fly all winter. You need to know how to handle difficult weather conditions."

Even Mikhail told me that from the ground it looked like I was constantly wobbling, and Mr. Kromins remarked that he hoped we'd manage to land safely. I suggested he join me for breakfast in town, but he had already arranged to meet some mechanics.

"So you prefer sitting with your mechanic friends?"

"That's how it is with us. We sit together and wait for you pilots, and after you go to rest, we start working. What cushy lives you have."

I thought Mikhail was offended by what I said.

"I didn't mean anything by it, I was just noting that you sit together. I don't have anyone to sit with here, except you, of course."

"At least here they still sit with me. Who knows how long it'll last with what's happening in Europe these days. Luckily there are still places in the world other than Europe."

How did he get to this topic so suddenly?

"There are other places in the world? I don't understand. What do you mean?"

"Places where they don't take away your rights because of your roots."

I knew this was a sensitive topic and saw no point in continuing to talk about it.

"When will you be done with them? Want to meet later for a beer?"

He told me he had plans with someone.

A faint feeling of jealousy washed over me. Does Mikhail already have a girlfriend?

"Someone I know? Something serious?"

"Serious? Why does it have to be serious? It needs to be good. In any case, it's not serious yet. We'll see how it goes today," he answered with a mischievous smile. "I'll update you tomorrow."

"Good luck," I wished him, and my gloomy mood stayed with me all day.

Today, however, was a great day. Mikhail, Yuli and I participated in the inauguration of the Freedom Monument[28] to commemorate our soldiers who died in the War of Independence. The monument was erected on Brivibas Street, a ten-minute walk from home. There were a lot of people, and we tried to find a spot from which we could see the ceremony. The monument is very tall and can be seen from everywhere. When we arrived, it was still covered with large fabric sheets.

Before the ceremony, we saw a convoy of official, open-top cars carrying important people along the city streets, with crowds cheering on either side. I also saw people saluting the convoy with a Nazi salute, like the Nazis in Germany. The first car carried President Kviesis, the Latvian flag fluttering on it. As it approached the monument site, it was accompanied by horse riders.

I glanced at Mikhail. He looked at me and muttered quietly, "We're Latvians, not Germans. What's with them and their nazi salute?"

Yuli replied before I could, "You're right, it's really out of place, but let's not talk about it now with all these people around us."

A group of soldiers was assembled in an impressive formation in the large plaza around the monument, with a row of flag bearers in front. One boring politician's speech followed another. Mikhail, Yuli and I waited until the monument was unveiled, and it was actually very impressive. At the top of the tall monument stands a statue of a woman raising both hands above her head towards the sky, holding three golden stars representing Latvia's three provinces.

Hannah pulled out her phone and, after typing something and tapping the screen, she passed the phone around. "Here, this is what it looks like even today. It really is very tall."

"I can practically imagine him, Yuli, and his friend standing there among the crowd," said Lilly.

"And I can imagine us finishing already," Mark said, reminding everyone that the day was short and there was still plenty to be done.

The monument and the statue at the top are so tall that I couldn't make out the facial features from where we were standing.

After the ceremony, we went to Otto Schwartz Café, like last week. Mikhail has a knack for connecting with people, and apparently charming women too. I wish I had a fraction of that talent.

Yuli and I had decided in advance to not talk about our studies so as not to make him feel left out, but he brought up the subject himself.

We talked a bit about university, and then Yuli showed interest in his work as a mechanic. I had stopped talking to her about my flight lessons. It made her sad, but with Mikhail, she didn't seem sad. I think it's because he's not a pilot, so it doesn't hurt her to talk to him about it.

"I'm constantly learning and advancing, getting more responsibility and compliments. At least over there, everyone is considered Latvian, even me, and what matters is your professionalism," he said enthusiastically.

"It seems like we Latvians aren't really sure about our nationality yet. It's probably new. I have no other explanation for the Nazi salutes we saw at the ceremony," Yuli remarked.

"What can you do, some people just don't like Jews. They just need to not mess with me, otherwise, it won't end well. Or I'll end up leaving here, maybe to America, maybe to Palestine."

Fortunately, the cakes we ordered arrived and we moved on to lighter matters, guided by Yuli.

Yuli and I have already kissed a few times, and we hug a lot, but nothing more than that. I'm sure I'm in love with her and hope she feels the same.

# Chapter 30

## Riga, Latvia, Saturday, November 23, 1935

As an esteemed member of the Chamber of Commerce and Industry, Grandpa Ernst received three tickets to the premiere of the opera "Lohengrin" at the opera house. Grandma suggested he give the tickets "to Miku and his new girlfriend, whom we haven't met yet but have already heard about. That way, she'll know Miku is cultured too."

I'll have to introduce them soon.

Yuli was delighted and said she had never been to such a premiere, with the mayor and other important people in attendance. She suggested bringing Mikhail along.

Grandpa informed me in advance about the dress code for such an event, so Mikhail and I wore black jackets, black pants, white shirts, and bowties. It was the first time I dressed this way for a public event.

Mikhail looked great, as always. He caught the attention of every woman that passed by.

And Yuli? Nothing I write down can do her justice. She was stunning, in a long burgundy evening gown, with her hair pulled up and her face glowing through light blush and delicate lipstick. It was the first time I saw her like this. She was the most beautiful woman there.

We mingled with the high-society crowd at the reception before the performance, and I'm sure everyone was looking at us. Maybe because we were the youngest there or because Mikhail made funny 'distinguished gentleman' faces as we enjoyed the free champagne glasses.

When we left after the performance, it was cold, and a light drizzle had started. Yuli and I shared an umbrella, and Mikhail walked closely with his own. We walked between the flowerbeds at the entrance to the opera house, humming the bridal chorus from the third act.[29]

We parted ways with Mikhail on Gertrudes Street, and I continued with Yuli to her house.

We stood under the umbrella at the entrance as the rain intensified and soaked the hems of our coats.

"Maybe you'll finally invite me inside this time?" I suggested with a smile.

She pressed her lips to mine and gave me a long, deep kiss, something we had never done before, and then, with her charming smile, said, "Good night, Miku."

She turned and disappeared into the building.

Now I'm certain she's in love with me too.

## Riga, Latvia, Sunday, December 15, 1935[30]

A wonderful day. That's it, I'm a pilot. Well, not quite, but on the right track.

The weather has been nice over the past month, and Mr. Ozols took advantage of it for navigation flights. Each flight lasted about two hours, and I had to prepare a detailed navigation map before each lesson, which I kept folded and strapped to my thigh with two rubber bands.

This morning, I arrived for another navigation flight,

but about fifteen minutes after we took off, Mr. Ozols asked me to turn back to land. I didn't suspect anything. I landed the plane and started taxiing towards the hangar. After we cleared the runway, he asked me to stop and leave the engine running.

He disconnected his intercom cable, unfastened his seatbelt, got out, and stood up on the lower wing.

"Miku, I think it's time for you to do a solo flight. I trust you. All you have to do is follow everything we've practiced. Fly for about fifteen minutes towards the flight area above the mouth of the Daugava, which you're already familiar with, circle there for a bit, and then return for landing. Land 'by the book.' I'll wait for you in the hangar."

I was so surprised that I didn't even have time to get scared or excited. I nodded, and after he got down and walked away, I taxied to the start of the runway, completed the checks, and took off.

For the first time, I was in the sky, alone.


"I'm really excited for him," Daniel noted. "That's a first time you never forget."
"Like any first time, really," David winked.
"Let him continue."


It's impossible to describe how I felt. The weather was nice, perfect actually. The engine sounded like soft music. The plane gently rose and fell in the air, as if happy about the opportunity to be just with me, alone. I turned right, and the mouth of the Daugava came into view in its full beauty. Barges were sailing on the river, carrying their cargo towards the Baltic Sea. I flew on until I saw Kundzinsala Island to my left, separating the Daugava from Sarkandaugava Canal. I also saw the edges of Lake Kisezers,[31] its waters calm and sparkling in the sunlight. If I had continued flying in this direction, I would've ended up over Riga, and I knew that was forbidden.

For a moment, I thought I'd fly straight towards Yuli's house, if only I could. I'd give anything for Yuli to stand outside, look up at the sky, and see me passing overhead, waving my wings in greeting. But I quickly dismissed that thought and refocused. On the way back, half an hour later, I really felt the plane in my butt, and the landing I made was smooth and precise. I taxied the Flamingo to the hangar and shut off the engine.

That was the moment I realized what had actually happened. I crossed a significant barrier and took a big step towards becoming a pilot. I was so excited that I just sat there for a few more minutes. When I finally got up and stood on the wing, I saw Mr. Ozols standing next to the plane, along with Mr. Kromins and Mikhail. They were all applauding me. What a great day!

---

"Think about it, a nineteen-year-old flying that thing alone. It's incredible," Daniel said, standing up to stretch.

"We're making good progress today," Rubin noted. "We'll be called for lunch soon."

Lilly intended to respond to Daniel but changed her mind. She would remind him later that he wasn't much older when he first flew a plane alone. But that wasn't important right now. She got up, stood next to him, and patted him on the back.

# Chapter 31

We have started a period of exams at the faculty, and Yuli and I are preparing for them together, usually at my house. Everyone in the family has already met her, and I'm convinced they like her. Why wouldn't they? Yuli is polite and friendly, and I feel like everyone's known each other for years.

After the meeting at my place, I walked her home as usual, and this time she asked me to come up and meet her parents. Thankfully, it all happened quickly, so I didn't have time to get nervous about it. When we walked in, I shook their hands and we talked a bit, mostly about our studies.

As far as I'm concerned, all the adults now know that we're a proper couple.

## Riga, Latvia, Sunday, January 5, 1936

I've flown solo several more times since my first solo flight. Each lesson is divided into two parts: the first part with Mr. Ozols, practicing drills, and the second part flying solo, repeating the exercises on my own. It seems that the Flamingo and I have gotten used to each other by now and understand one another.

After we finished the debriefing today, Mr. Ozols walked out of the office and asked me to come with him, but didn't say where.

It took me a moment to realize we were heading towards the Aviation Club at the edge of the Spilve runway. Mr. Ozols patted me on the shoulder and said, "This is in honor of your first solo flight, even if it's a bit late. Be polite and respectful."

The club is a sort of wooden hangar. The last time I was here, I could only peek inside; I wasn't allowed to enter.

Mr. Ozols signaled for me to go in ahead of him. I walked into a large, elongated space with several small tables and chairs scattered around. A large dark wooden table stood against the right wall, covered with magazines featuring pictures of airplanes. On the wall beside the entrance door was a framed photo of a stern-looking man with the name "Captain Janis Lindbergs." Next to it was another framed photo of another man with the name "Nikolas Sudmalis." Mr. Ozols saw me looking at the photos, approached, and whispered that Lindbergs was the first president of the Aviation Club and that Sudmalis succeeded him.

Further along was a bulletin board with papers pinned to it.

"These are the daily weather forecast reports. There's info here about Latvia as well as the surrounding countries," he explained.

He took me to the edge of the club and showed me where the pilots' dressing room is. Then, he opened a door I hadn't noticed before, and we entered another room.

"This is our map room. We bring every map we can get our hands on here. We already have a very impressive collection."

"Of Latvia?"

"Of course, but not just. Actually, we have maps of all flight areas up to the Mediterranean, excluding the area of the Soviet Union. We're not allowed to fly there, and we only have old maps from when my friends and I flew in the Imperial Russian Air Force."

When we left the map room, he walked over to a group of pilots standing by a raised counter on the other side of the club, chatting. They were dressed in flight uniforms, with tall leather boots, similar to Mr. Ozols, except one who was wearing a pilot's dress uniform. It consisted of black trousers and a black jacket with shiny metal buttons and rank insignias on its epaulets. Pilot wings were pinned to the upper left side and a dark leather strap stretched diagonally from the right epaulet of the jacket to the left waist.

They all looked about Mr. Ozols' age. Two of them held pipes emitting a sweet-smelling tobacco smoke. One of them patted him on the shoulder, and the rest shook his hand. I assumed they were all pilots from the days of the Imperial Russian Air Force and his friends ever since.

Mr. Ozols motioned for me to come closer and introduced me.

"This kid will be a serious pilot one day. He's already done several solo flights and is progressing well."

He had never praised me like that before. It was a bit embarrassing.

"That's a good reason to drink some pilot's fuel," said one of them, and a bottle of 95% Valsts Spirts shortly appeared, with a few glasses placed on the counter.

"You drink this in one gulp," said the pilot in the dress uniform. He handed me a small glass filled with this harsh spirit and, with the other hand, poured the contents of his own glass into his throat.

I did the same, and my throat burned. I immediately started coughing, to their roaring laughter. I sat down on one of the chairs next to them until the group began to disperse, and Mr. Ozols signaled that we were leaving too.

Attorney Rubin paused. "We'll take a fifteen-minute break. We have an hour and a half left until lunch." He stood up and noisily pushed his chair back.

This time, everyone stood up. Miriam hurried out after Rubin. Mark stood by the window, his sons by his side. "So what do you think, Dad? Do you know what Grandpa wants from us?"

"I don't know what to think; none of this story is familiar to me, and the time I'm spending here is worth money. I'm trying not to look at my phone. Yesterday, I had a lot of messages and missed calls from our executives. I told them to manage on their own for three days, but I can't stand the thought of things happening there without my knowledge."

"I don't think you have anything to worry about," said David. "I'm sure there are no crises."

"It's one thing to think everything is fine and another thing completely to be responsible for what's happening," Mark replied. "But positive thinking is always a good approach to life."

Rubin returned, accompanied by Miriam, who was holding a cup of tea on an elegant plate.

"Let's continue," he said, sitting down.

### Riga, Latvia, Sunday, January 12, 1936

Today we did a long navigation flight to Liepaja. I navigated using the map. We saw the Gulf of Riga and the coastline along the way. The trick was not to deviate from the route I had marked in advance. Overall, it was fine; the deviation was minimal, and I corrected it when I saw Liepaja from a distance.

We didn't land there. We circled the outskirts of the city and flew back, a total of about 400 kilometers. The longest flight I've done. We practiced low-altitude flight on the way back. The ground is very flat in this area, but it was still scary at first. You need to be very precise and focused during such a flight.

The lesson was exhausting, and I only got home in the afternoon. Yuli, Mikhail and I had planned to go ice skating, so I didn't really get to rest. I sat on the bench on the side for some time while Mikhail and Yuli skated without me. Occasionally, he'd spin her around and hold her so she wouldn't lose her balance, and they would skate holding each other. At times, it seemed like they forgot about my presence.

I don't mind. I think Yuli and I are 'properly' together. We never talked about it, but we spend time together both during and after school. Mostly after. Recently, when it's just the two of us alone, we lie on the bed, hugging all the time. I suggested we go to Jurmala for a weekend. I think she understands my intentions because she replied with a smile, "Maybe for my birthday in June. We'll see how it goes."

I hope it happens much sooner.

# Chapter 32

### Riga, Latvia, Sunday, February 9, 1936

The weather keeps disrupting my flying lessons. I haven't flown in two weeks. It's very cold outside. Meanwhile, the results of the first semester exams have arrived. My grades are reasonable. Overall, I'm satisfied. Yuli's grades, of course, are much better than mine.

I work at the factory three times a week. Sometimes they ask me to help in the office upstairs, but I usually work in packaging. The general impression is that there's a decline in activity due to reduced demand from Germany and Austria.

Last week, Mikhail and I met and talked a bit. "Have you seen the new planes that arrived here for the National Guard Air Force?" I asked him. "I heard they're called 'Kod-1.'"

"Not yet. They told me they're stored in the new hangar built especially for them, near the spot where they're building the National Guard administration building."

"We'll probably see them in the air a lot in the coming days and be able to get a better impression of them," I quickly replied. "And how's it going with the new girl you told me about?"

"Nothing. I ended it with her. She's not right for me." He sounded a bit gloomy.

Since renewing my friendship with Mikhail, I've been more aware of what's been happening in Germany regarding Jews. At the beginning of January, a law came into effect there prohibiting the employment of Jewish women under the age of thirty-five. As a result, 10,000 women lost their jobs. Jewish bookstore owners were required to obtain a license to operate their stores, and Jews were also prohibited from serving as tax advisors.

You can start feeling the influence of what's happening in Germany even here in Latvia. More and more shop owners are putting up signs in their windows indicating that theirs is a Latvian shop.

Mikhail is sensitive to anything I say on the subject of Jews, maybe even too sensitive. He told me that lately, he's been hearing more and more remarks about him being Jewish. He's very strong, so I'm sure no one would dare approach him and try to harm him physically. Although I don't like him bringing up this topic, I understand him, and it's clear that the atmosphere is very unpleasant.

I also had the opportunity to attend the premiere of the ballet "Don Quixote" at the opera house with Yuli, again with tickets Grandpa received. It's clear by now that he gladly passes them on to me. This time, Dad joined us, and it was very nice.

After the ballet, he invited us for coffee and cake at Otto Schwartz. As we sat down, he turned to Yuli, "I understand you're also studying at the university. How's it going for you?"

This was exactly what I was afraid would happen — that Dad would start grilling her. It made me uncomfortable and I wanted to stop it immediately, so I answered for her, "Dad, Yuli is doing great, but leave her alone."

"I'm sure Yuli can answer for herself," he replied seriously. Now I knew for sure that the invitation to the café wasn't innocent. I regretted agreeing to it.

"I have a knack for the exact sciences; I always have, so at least for now, I'm doing great," she said. I was glad she didn't add that she helps me with the assignments we get at the faculty.

Dad didn't let up, "Have you thought about what you want to do after you finish your studies?"

She remained completely calm. "I don't know if Miku told you, but I planned to learn to fly like him and work as a pilot, but because of doctors who mistakenly think I'm not fit enough, I couldn't get a medical certificate. I'll get it eventually. What I'll do until then, I don't know yet. It's still too early for me to make such a decision."

Dad asked her a few more general questions, and I felt she handled them well. I started to relax, but then he suddenly said, "You seem like a decent and sensible girl. Are you and Miku serious?"

It was very embarrassing and inappropriate. I intervened immediately.

"Dad, come on, that's really out of line. Leave her alone; let her enjoy her coffee. Enough."

Yuli placed her hand on mine, then smiled at Dad and said, "I try to be serious in everything I do."

Dad smiled with satisfaction. "Alright."

Yuli gave a small smile and remained silent.

Later, when I thought about the answer to Dad's question, I realized that, as I see it, until we've 'been to Jurmala together,' I won't really know her real answer.

---

"The boy's in heat," Hannah quietly commented.

"Look at that old-fashioned European education. Not like today – go on three dates and down to business," her mother replied.

"We don't know what it's like in Europe these days; they've progressed too," Tom smiled at his mother.

"Fifteen minutes until lunch break," Rubin noted. They fell silent.

### Riga, Latvia, Sunday, February 23, 1936

I'm finally back to flying. Because of the amount of time that had passed since the last flight, I flew with Mr. Ozols again and didn't fly solo. We practiced the usual drills and emergency landings. At the end of the lesson, he told me I needed to prepare for flights outside Latvia and that he plans to fly with me to Tallinn, Estonia.

"It's about a 270-kilometer flight each way, which means we'll need to land, maybe even stay overnight, and return the next day. You'll need to make sure you have a passport and prepare documents for crossing the border by air."

It's a significant step up in my training. I expect he'll soon talk to me about the test for obtaining the license.

After the lesson, I sat with Mikhail in the hangar. He told me he met a new girl, a nice one.

"She's not like Yuli," he said. "There's no one like Yuli, and you should appreciate having a girl like her as your girlfriend."

He also told me things were easy with this girl, and they'd already gone as far as you can; he winked at me.

I'm not there with Yuli yet.

### Riga, Latvia, Sunday, March 15, 1936

I didn't fly today because there was a cornerstone laying ceremony at Spilve for the National Guard Air Force headquarters being built there. The cornerstone was laid right next to the existing hangars. The building hasn't even been constructed yet, and it already has a nickname: Alcazars. I guess it's somehow related to the civil war happening in Spain right now.

## Riga, Latvia, Sunday, March 29, 1936

My flying lessons continued as usual until the training flight to Tallinn.

This time, the flight was over the Gulf of Riga, meaning over water and not land. It's a completely different kind of flight.

After about half an hour, we returned and landed. Mr. Ozols got out, and I continued to practice in the air for another hour.

There were a lot of planes in the sky that day, and I had to concentrate hard on what was happening around me so that I wouldn't collide with any of them. It took a lot of my attention and energy. In the debriefing, Mr. Ozols said that I need to get used to it because that's how it usually is. It's not like Sunday morning flying lessons.

Yesterday, I was in for a surprise. During dinner, I told Dad that at Spilve, I heard that our air force bought two Gloster Gladiators.

"With our money, Miku, with our money," he replied. "This purchase was funded by the Military Aviation Fund,[32] which was established at the beginning of the year precisely for this purpose. And who do you think contributed to this fund?"

"I don't know; I didn't know about it at all."

"Many good people donated to it, including your grandfather and your father, last year. You see, you're not the only one in the family interested in aviation. It's probably hereditary."

"How did you even come to donate?"

"We've had connections with the local aviation industry for a long time; we manufacture parts for several aircraft factories, including VEF Company. I haven't told you until now, but our factory also manufactures parts for Beckman Company, which makes the Flamingo you fly. So, sometimes, to maintain relationships with customers, you need to donate when they ask for it. On the other hand, sometimes there are honors, like the tickets we received to attend the reception for Cukurs when he returned from Gambia. You probably remember that."

"I didn't know that either."

"When I was with you at the meeting with Ozols, your instructor, he looked familiar to me. During the conversation, it turned out he works for VEF Company as a test pilot, and we probably met at some point. Pleasant man."

"He didn't tell me anything about that."

"True, because I agreed with him not to tell you so it wouldn't affect you in any way. In the meantime, you've progressed a lot in the course, and now, knowing all this is less significant. Still, it's better if Mr. Ozols doesn't know I told you, okay? At least until you get your pilot's license."

Now I understood why Dad knew the way to Spilve so well. The good news is that Dad no longer talks about stopping my flying lessons.

"That's it. Break time. There's food and refreshments in the next room; if you want to go out, that's also possible. I ask to be here at two-thirty. We made good progress, and I hope we'll cover a lot more today. Alright?"

"We're going downstairs," said David, and Daniel agreed.

"Don't be late, okay?" Mark signaled to his sons. "Two-thirty is two-thirty."

"Don't worry, Dad," David patted his shoulder. "Worrying all the time is unhealthy."

Daniel burst out into laughter, and they left the meeting room together.

# Chapter 33

## Riga, Latvia, Sunday, April 19, 1936

The final test is already on the horizon, and the lessons are dedicated to preparation. We practice the same things over and over, landings, and more landings. We also flew to distant places and practiced navigation. On one occasion, we landed in a small airfield with a short runway near the city of Jēkabpils, and then continued until we reached a similar airstrip adjacent to the military base in Daugavpils, a flight of about 200 kilometers each way.

## Riga, Latvia, Sunday, April 26, 1936

This week, I had a midterm flight test, but I had no idea I was being tested until it was finished.

I waited for the lesson by the plane as usual. Mr. Ozols arrived with someone else dressed in pilot's gear; he said he wouldn't be able to give me the lesson, and instead, the pilot with him would. He introduced him as Berzins.[33]

Berzins drilled me on all the topics I had practiced and shared various comments that were new to me. He was very businesslike and didn't talk to me about anything else during the flight. It was very different from my flights with Mr. Ozols.

When I parked at the end of the lesson in front of the hangar, I was surprised to see Mr. Ozols waiting there. Berzins got off first and approached him. They talked until I reached them and then parted ways. Berzins came over to me, said I flew very well, and left.

Only then did Mr. Ozols inform me that it had been a preliminary examination for the final test. It's a good thing I didn't know about it in advance.

It's still cold outside, but spring has arrived. The snow has disappeared, and the flowers are in full bloom. Yuli and I went for a picnic to celebrate my getting a driver's license. I was more nervous before the driving test than before a regular flight lesson.

After learning that I had passed a flight test without knowing it, we decided to celebrate that at the picnic as well. We took the tram and traveled to Mežaparks. A lot of people were walking there among the woods and open spaces. Yuli and I found a secluded spot, spread out a blanket, and placed a basket with a bottle of wine and cookies beside it.

We lay close together on the blanket, and Yuli asked me to pass her the bottle of wine.

"Already?" I asked, "We just got here!"

Yuli laughed, "Even if we open the bottle now, I'm not sure we'll be able to finish it. You know what, I'll get it myself. At my house, we don't wait long when there's a good bottle of wine around."

She rolled over me in an attempt to reach the basket. I stopped her just as she was on top of me. I hugged her, and we kissed for a long time. After a moment, Yuli completed the roll to my other side and pulled the bottle toward her.

"There, I have the bottle. Shall we drink?"

We sat side by side and I poured the wine. It really was good.

"Do you drink a lot of wine at home?" I asked.

"My father and brother know their wine and like to talk about it. So, we often have wine tastings."

I love hearing her talk. You can tell she's very smart. I was enchanted as she talked about the types of wine she had been exposed to, the differences between them, and the roles of their components. Her voice is confident and fluent, and her language is rich. I looked at her—she's stunning, simply perfect. After what I heard from Mikhail, I wanted to go as far as possible with Yuli already. I gently pulled her to me, and as she sat with her back to me, I placed my hands on her chest as if hugging her, and with my fingertips, I pressed the soft humps I felt through her shirt.

Yuli didn't say anything; I felt she was calm and relaxed. Afterwards, she curled up in my arms and we stayed cuddled there until it got dark and very cold.

When we got up to leave, she suddenly asked, "What about Mikhail? Does he have a girlfriend?"

"Yes, he does, but I don't know who she is," I replied quickly, but wondered why she was suddenly asking about Mikhail now.

"Then next time we meet him, we'll tell him to introduce us to her," Yuli declared loudly.

## Riga, Latvia, Sunday, May 3, 1936

I keep practicing for the test. The flight to Tallinn was canceled, and instead, we flew to Aleksotas Aerodrome in Lithuania, not far from the city of Kaunas, a flight of over 200 kilometers each way.

We made a lot of preparations for it. I had to take maps of Latvia and Lithuania with me. Mr. Ozols and I sat in the map room last week and marked the route. In addition, I had to take my new passport with me, of course.

Basically, we were supposed to submit a flight plan in advance to a representative of the Civil Aviation Authority, who had an office in Spilve's administrative building, and he was supposed to send it to the airport in Lithuania.

"But we're not doing that because it's a lot of bureaucracy that takes time we don't have," Mr. Ozols explained. "Instead, we simply prepare a 'flight plan' and take it with us. When we land there, we'll submit it to the aerodrome office, if they even ask us for it."

And so we did. The flight wasn't difficult and was good navigation practice, in an area I wasn't familiar with at all. I deviated a few times from the route we marked on the map, but corrected it in time. When we approached Aleksotas Aerodrome in Lithuania, I recognized it because of its proximity to the city of Kaunas. It's a big city, and you can't miss it from the air. When we landed, no one asked us for the flight plan or anything, maybe because it was a Sunday.

Mr. Ozols went to refuel from a fuel truck that stood there. He had prepared local money in advance, "But you can pay in British pounds," he explained. "They accept those everywhere."

The flight back went smoothly. The whole round trip took about four hours.

I assume the coming period will be very busy with both semester exams at university and preparations for the flight license test. I really hoped I'd pass everything successfully.

There's also the matter with Grandpa.

"Maybe we'll hear about his grandpa's matter tomorrow?" Mark stopped Rubin. "I'm really tired. We've been sitting for hours on end, and I can see it's hard on you too. You're reading slower."

"I'm sorry my pace isn't to your satisfaction," Attorney Rubin replied. He lowered his head slightly to look at Mark over his reading glasses. "However, we need to consider the limited time Mr. Mirkin has, as he needs to return home tomorrow night. Let's not forget we all have other things to do besides sitting here for hours. I suggest you stand as you did yesterday, maybe even walk back and forth in the room. It doesn't bother me. These interruptions in the reading do."

Mark examined Rubin's expression. Under other circumstances, he might've chosen to confront him, but now, with his father's spirit hanging over the room, he decided to back down.

"Good idea," he got up, "so please, continue."

Rubin nodded, adjusted his glasses, and resumed reading.

# Chapter 34

Grandpa is sick. He's been bedridden for two weeks and is having a hard time breathing. Grandma is by his side constantly, and Martha is pacing around restlessly with a worried look on her face.

The doctor we called examined him and then spoke quietly with Dad. When I joined them, I only caught the end of the conversation.

"...The problem is with his heart. His condition isn't good. I've given him some medicine to ease things a bit, but I think it's only a matter of time until—"

"That serious?" Dad interrupted.

"Yes. I could give you false hopes, but that's the sad truth. You'd better make the necessary preparations."

After the doctor left, I asked Dad what else he had said.

"What you heard was the main point. Grandpa's condition is really bad. It's a terrible time overall," Dad sighed.

"Why, what else happened?"

"Can't you see what's going on around us? The world is small, and what happens in other parts of Europe affects business all over the continent, including here in Latvia. The situation at the factory isn't as good as it was this time last year."

I went back to Grandpa's room and stood by the bed, facing Grandma. I assumed she understood the situation even without hearing the doctor's words. I held

Grandpa's hand and wondered what my life would look like without him. Another challenge I would have to face.

"Miku," Grandpa spoke softly, "you'll need to help at the factory more, at least until I can go back to work. You might have to change your plans a bit, and in any case, don't do anything stupid." He paused for a moment and then continued, "You know what I mean, don't you?"

Grandma lifted her eyes and looked at me with a sad, tired, yet piercing gaze. We both knew what Grandpa meant.

### Riga, Latvia, Sunday, May 10, 1936

The flight exam is approaching. I don't know when Mr. Ozols will schedule it but, from his comments during the last lesson, I have a feeling it'll be soon. My mood is pretty lousy, and that's really bad because this is exactly the time when I need to be at my peak concentration. This whole situation is really bothering me.

Even Mikhail noticed it, and when we met after the lesson, he asked me directly, "Miku, what's wrong with you?"

"Nothing serious, except that the grandpa who raised me is dying and our factory's situation is deteriorating because of what's happening in Germany," I replied with a dark cynicism that surprised even me.

"What do you mean?"

"Don't you read the papers?" I burst. "Don't you know the situation in Germany is getting worse? The Nazis are continuing to pass laws against Jews, and in the elections in Germany last month, their party won a landslide victory. It's hard to believe that the German people prefer that awful party. I read that 90 percent of young Germans are already members of a sort of military organization called the 'Hitler Youth,' and the government has announced that the parents of the rest should ensure their children join as well, or else special laws will be enacted to make it happen. Germany is becoming a military state; they're investing in weapons, cutting back on imports, and buying pots from here isn't exactly a priority for them."

"Miku, do you really think I don't know all that? Don't be so naive. What's happening in Germany is already affecting the whole world. Do you know that Austria has sent troops to its border with Germany, fearing an invasion? There's already a war in Ethiopia, and the Italians have captured their capital. There are riots in Spain, and the paper recently reported that in Palestine, local Arabs have started riots against the British Mandate officials and also against Jews living there. According to the paper, several dozen people have been killed. The world is going crazy, and not in a good way. Let me remind you that I wasn't accepted into the faculty because I'm Jewish, and I can't stop thinking about what'll happen if all this reaches here too."

"I don't think there's any chance of that happening," I replied.

"You have no idea what you're talking about, Miku. You really are blind," Mikhail raised his voice. "Do you remember a few months ago when you asked me how things were going with the girl I was seeing, and I told you I ended it with her?" He didn't wait for me to answer. "Well, I'll tell you why we broke up: because her parents didn't like that she was dating a Jew, that's why. They forbade her from seeing me, and the last time I came to visit her, her father came out and threatened me, saying if he hears I'm still seeing her, he'll make sure I get my arms and legs broken. And when my mother goes to

Vidzeme market on Matisa Street,[34] the vendors there make comments about how she has money because she's Jewish. So don't tell me it won't happen."

Mikhail's face reddened, and I could see he was really angry. He took a deep breath, and in a calmer tone, said, "As for your grandfather, I'm sorry to hear that, but that's nature's way, isn't it?"

I know Grandpa is old, and that that's the way of the world. That doesn't mean it's easy for me to accept it. As for Mikhail and his concern, I already agreed with him that what's happening in Germany affects all of us, regardless of whether or not he's Jewish. After all, Hitler wants to fight the entire world. All these restrictions on Jews don't make sense to me, and I understand it's uncomfortable for them to live like that, but he shouldn't be angry with me. I'm not the one who imposed them. I decided to change the subject.

"At least there's been one positive event recently. Did you know the airship Hindenburg completed its first transatlantic flight and reached Rio de Janeiro, Brazil?"

"No, I didn't know."

"After that, it successfully flew back to Germany. Later, it crossed the Atlantic again and reached New Jersey in a record time of 61 hours and 39 minutes."

"God help me, Miku. Do you really think that interests me right now?"

"He really is a bit clueless, that Miku," Tom remarked. "Sometimes I almost like him, and sometimes, like now, he's really annoying."

His cousins nodded in agreement while the others remained silent, and the reading continued.

## Riga, Latvia, Sunday, May 17, 1936

Today, Mr. Ozols told me he thinks I'm ready. "I'll try to schedule your test for next week, and in the meantime, come join me at the club today," he said, patting me on the back.

This was the second time he invited me to the Aviation Club, except for working with him in the map room, but that doesn't count. This time I felt more confident, almost like a pilot.

As I sat with him by the counter, I overheard some pilots talking about how Cukurs had completed building his new plane, and that lately, he's been conducting test flights with it. He named it the 'Three Stars.'[35]

I decided to sneak a peek into the hangar where he keeps it and try to take a look. I might need to ask for Mikhail's help with that.

# Chapter 35

## Riga, Latvia, Wednesday, May 27, 1936

I'm a pilot! I have a pilot's license! I'm the happiest man on earth!!!

It rained all last week, and flying was impossible. The weather finally improved on Saturday. I flew with Mr. Ozols on Sunday, Monday, and Tuesday in preparation. It was a good thing because there were a lot of planes in the sky, as well as on the taxiways and runways.

Mr. Ozols said the examiner could choose whether to take off with me or stay on the ground and evaluate my performance by giving me instructions via radio. My examiner was a pilot from VEF, and he decided to take off with me. This actually gave me a good feeling. Apparently, Mr. Ozols had told him that he felt confident in my abilities.

The test went smoothly. I made one mistake during one of the emergency landing drills. I hoped the examiner wouldn't fail me because of it. After we landed, even before I parked, he told me I passed and congratulated me on obtaining my pilot's license. Mr. Ozols, Mr. Kromins, and Mikhail were already waiting for me on the ground. The examiner gave them a thumbs-up to indicate I had passed, and they applauded me before I even had a chance to exit the plane.

Finally, two years after my visit here with Grandpa, I have my own pilot's license.

Everyone helped me push the Flamingo into its place in the hangar.

Afterward, Mr. Ozols asked me to recount the exam in detail. We sat in the corner of the hangar and I told him everything, as best as I could remember, despite my excitement.

He seemed very, very pleased with me and patted me on the back several times. When we finished, he invited me to join him for a toast at the club. "Miku, from now on, you're a pilot like all the other pilots, and you can call me by my first name, Edvins. We're friends now, not just instructor and trainee."

Mikhail approached and hugged me. He whispered in my ear, "I knew you'd make it." He's become my best friend by now.

The club was full of people. I already know everyone there, even if I hadn't really spoken to most of them. I managed to see all the pilots standing with a full glass in hand before Yuli jumped at me out of nowhere.

It turned out she and Dad were there as well. She hugged me, and everyone applauded. I was just as excited on the ground as I had been an hour earlier in the air.

"Okay, Yuli, that's enough hugs for now," said Mr. Ozols — or rather, Edvins (I'll have to get used to this change).

He raised his hand and said, "I invite everyone to raise a glass now in honor of our new pilot, the youngest pilot at Spilve at the moment. There's also some food and refreshments provided by Martin, Miku's dad."

Edvins handed me a full glass of *Valsts Degvīns Dzidrais*, which I knew was as terrible a pilot's fuel as the *Valsts Spirits 95%* I drank here after my solo flight.

Dad gave Yuli a glass after filling it with some luxurious *Lanson* champagne.

We all raised our glasses and drank the entire drink in one go. When everyone moved on to the refreshment table, Mikhail joined Yuli and Dad, and I introduced him. Yuli told me she had come to Spilve with Dad and that this was her first time here since she stopped her flight training. We hadn't discussed this subject since, and I think she's made peace with the situation.

But that wasn't all.

After the drinks, Dad and Edvins came over to me and handed me a large, heavy package wrapped in colorful paper. When I opened it, I saw a new dark-brown flight jacket with a gray wool collar, a black flight cap, matching dark-brown leather gloves, and brand-new aviator goggles.

"Try on the jacket," Edvins urged. "It cost your dad a lot of money. Let's see if it fits."

The jacket fit me perfectly. The leather was still stiff, but I'm sure it'll soften after a flight or two. The rest of the gear was also my size, which made me very happy.

Dad hugged me. "Miku, this is my birthday gift to you. Mr. Ozols helped me buy everything you need." I hugged him back.

So, I'm a pilot.

Two years ago, Grandpa brought me here as a birthday present, and today that gift has become the most significant thing I've done in my life. What an incredible day!

# PART TWO

# Chapter 36

**Riga, Latvia, Tuesday, June 2, 1936**

Grandpa passed away two days ago. In the past few weeks, his condition had steadily deteriorated. Grandma was by his side the entire time. I visited him almost every day. It was difficult and sad to see how much he was suffering. Dad and I were responsible for the oxygen tanks, making sure there was always an extra one at home.

The day before yesterday, he took his last breath. I stayed with Grandma at home while Martha and Dad made all the arrangements for the funeral, which took place yesterday.

Even though it's June and spring is in full swing, the weather was cold and gloomy when we—Grandma, Dad, Martha, and I—arrived at the church for the funeral service. The air was heavy with a sense of loss and grief that had descended upon us. Along the way, we were greeted by many familiar faces, all friends of Dad, Grandpa and Grandma, as well as people from the Chamber of Commerce, clients of the factory, and neighbors. They all came to pay their respects and offer their condolences.

As the service began, I took my place at the front pew next to Grandma and Dad. For some reason, Martha preferred to sit in the back row rather than in the front.

The pastor gave a touching eulogy, honoring Grandpa's life and legacy, and offering us words of comfort and hope. Then hymns were sung and a few prayers were recited, which gave me a sense of peace and even brought me to tears, even though I'm not at all a religious person. In contrast, Grandma maintained a stoic expression the entire time.

At the end, we stood up and kissed the coffin before it was taken out of the church. That's when I saw Mikhail and Yuli standing together among all the people. They seemed very close together, but it might have just seemed that way because of the large crowd.

As we stepped outside into the cold, gray day, I knew that Grandpa's memory would always stay with me. I hoped that the love and support of the community and friends would help Grandma get through this difficult time.

A group of men I wasn't familiar with lifted the coffin and carried it to the cemetery behind the church. The pastor led the way, and he also conducted the burial service. We threw a handful of soil on the coffin, and then we placed a wreath of white flowers on the grave.

When it was all over, we went to Grandma and Grandpa's house for the funeral repast that Martha and Grandma had prepared in advance. Many of Grandpa and Grandma's friends came. Yuli and Mikhail didn't come.

They did today. Together again. Yuli brought me her notebooks so I could copy what they covered yesterday at the faculty.

Mikhail looked very troubled. Before they left, I asked him if something had happened.

He hesitated for a moment before telling me, "When my dad and brothers arrived at the bakery two days ago, there was a Nazi swastika on the front door. I'm sure the ones who did it are the Perkonkrusts.[36] Now my family is marked by them, which makes things very dangerous for us."

I can understand him. It's truly disturbing.

## Riga, Latvia, Monday, June 22, 1936

So many things have happened since I got my pilot's license that I haven't had the time to write. It's evening now, and since the desk in my room is piled with books and is a complete mess, I'm sitting at the desk in Dad's room to write. He's not home. Today is the regular meeting of his group of businessmen.

About two weeks ago, I reminded Yuli about my suggestion that we go to Jūrmala for her birthday. "Will we be alone at the dacha, just you and me?" she asked.

"Yes, I think we're mature and in love enough to be there alone. We've been together for a long time. You know I'm serious about you, and you're serious about me, right?" I said to her. I felt like we were having a proper grown-up conversation.

---

"Excuse me, what's a da-cha? How did you pronounce that word?"

"I'm not sure I pronounced it correctly; I'm not familiar with it either," Rubin replied to Tom, removing his glasses.

"We have a translator right here," Mark remarked.

Mr. Mirkin lifted his head. Most of the time, he sat with his head slightly tilted toward the translator, listening.

"You barely feel them here, either of them," Lilly whispered to Hannah.

"Yes, they really blend in with the scenery," Hannah whispered back.

Mr. Mirkin said something, and the translator smiled. "It's a type of vacation home. It's suitable for spring or summer holidays," he explained to everyone.

"Well, maybe Miku will finally get to the point with her," Mark said. His sons erupted in laughter.

"Oh, Mark, you're so tactless sometimes," Lilly playfully pinched his hand.

Attorney Rubin put his glasses back on, and everyone fell silent.

"You know I am, but I've never..."

"Neither have I. And I want the first time to be with you. I feel like we're ready for this."

"I'm worried that if I agree, you won't respect me anymore."

"I promise I'll continue to respect you no matter what. I know who you are. It'll only bring us closer; I promise."

Yuli agreed.

# Chapter 37

I rented us a dacha and, last week, it finally happened. We spent five days in Bulduri, starting on Monday, one day before Yuli's birthday. We returned on Saturday evening.

Yuli was thrilled with the place — a small, single-story wooden cabin right in the middle of the forest, but not far from the beach. It was surrounded by trees that were much taller than the house, so it was completely enveloped by their leaves. There was abundant greenery and vegetation under the trees, including bushes with all kinds of berries — blue, red, and purple. Spring was everywhere, and the scent of flowers filled the air. There were also plenty of flies and mosquitoes.

"Look at the trail," she said as we walked along it together, "it seems like no one cleared the leaves from last winter. We're walking right through the actual forest." I could hear the excitement in her voice, and it made me love her even more. It was contagious.

The dacha was painted yellow and had a gray-tiled roof. It had elongated windows with wooden shutters, their slats tightly packed, so all you could see through them was the forest. There were no other houses nearby, so on one hand, we were as isolated as I wanted, but on the other hand, I knew the center of Bulduri wasn't far if we needed anything.

The dacha had everything we needed.

We arrived there on Monday morning by train. We sat close together, holding hands. It was the first time I'd gone away for several days far from home, and Yuli said she'd also only gone on vacations with her family — never alone, and certainly not with a guy. I felt special.

Each of us brought a small bag with clothes and, of course, a swimsuit. After settling in, we walked to the town center and bought groceries so we could prepare breakfast and sandwiches ourselves. In the afternoon, when it was warm enough outside, we put on our swimsuits and walked to the beach, just ten minutes from the dacha.

The beach was crowded, but very few people entered the water. I also tried to go in, up to my knees. It was too cold for me, and I didn't go further. Yuli, thinking I was going to swim, ran in. Just before reaching me, she slipped and found herself fully in the water. She jolted up because of the cold and hugged me to warm up, so in the end, I got completely wet too.

It was the first time I'd seen Yuli like that. Her wet swimsuit clung to her body and I could clearly see her breasts and nipples, which perked up from her meeting with the cold water. When she hugged me, I didn't feel the cold, only the excitement of being together as a man and woman. We ran out, laughing. I immediately wrapped a towel around her, and we kissed.

In the evening, we went to a restaurant in the center of Bulduri. We both had a glass of wine. Throughout the meal, we talked and mostly laughed about the cold water. We decided that we'd be brave the next day and go all the way in.

We returned to the dacha hand in hand. When we entered, I said, "I don't remember where the light switch is. Hold on, I'll find it."

But Yuli said, "I don't think there's any need. We both know the way to the bedroom anyway."

As usual, she was much more practical and energetic than I was.

"Wait outside until I call you."

I stood there in eager anticipation. For a moment, I even had trouble breathing.

After a few minutes, she said, "You can come in." The room was dark, with only a little starlight reflecting through the window.

Yuli was in bed, completely covered. She was waiting for me.

I quickly stripped and lay down beside her under the blanket. I reached out to her and discovered she was also naked. Her body was warm and inviting, and I eagerly accepted the invitation.

It was the first time for both of us, and I'm not going to go into detail beyond that. We've entered a new phase in our relationship.

The next morning, we woke up very early; I don't know why. It was her birthday. I got out of bed completely naked, but I felt comfortable and took out the gift I had bought — a pair of earrings. I hoped she'd like them.

I sang her a birthday song and handed her the small box, wrapped in a red ribbon. Yuli sat up, leaning against the back of the bed. She made sure to cover herself with the blanket.

"How beautiful! I wasn't expecting a gift. I thought this vacation was the gift."

"That too," I said, happy to see her eyes sparkling. I hoped she would like the earrings.

"They're lovely," she said, and I was glad I made a good choice.

As Yuli started putting them on, the blanket slipped off her, and for the first time, I saw her naked in the daylight. She didn't even try to pull the blanket back up. On the contrary – she pushed it off, got out of bed, and stood before me, as naked as I was.

"Well, how do the earrings look on me?"

I wasn't looking at the earrings at all. Her body was perfect. Her breasts were round and firm, and there was a tuft of curly black hair between her legs.

"Hey," she smiled at me, "the earrings are in my ears. How do they look?"

"I'm sure they look great," I said and hugged her. We went back to the bed, laughing and happy, and it took us a little more time before we managed to get out of it.

After getting dressed and having breakfast, we went for a walk in the forest. We made our way through the trees, bushes, and vines, as if we were in a jungle. There were a lot of different types of mosquitoes in the air. Luckily, we brought scarves and covered our faces with them, leaving only our eyes exposed. We walked through the forest until we reached the Lielupe River. There were a few sailboats and, not far from us, we saw some vacationers standing on the bank with fishing rods.

We went to the beach almost every day. Only now, as I write, do I realize that we never did go back inside the cold water. Every evening, we would eat at a restaurant, and the rest of the time, we were at the dacha, mostly in the bedroom. We were in bed, but we certainly weren't sleeping. It's a shame it ended so quickly.

"Well, the boy finally became a man." Everyone was surprised that it was Rubin who initiated the break. He placed the document on the table.

"It's 4:30 PM," he noted. "Let's take a short bathroom break and then finish this section and one more diary entry. Then, we'll wrap up for the day, alright?"

"No need to say it twice," said Lilly, pushing her chair back.

Lilly and Mark were the first to return to the meeting room. They were whispering to each other.

"The fact that Dad invited this Mr. Mirkin still really bothers me. What do you think?"

"I guess you're right," Lilly replied, "but there's no point in dwelling on it. Better to enjoy the story. I find it quite captivating. I'm going to make some coffee. Want some too?"

About fifteen minutes later, everyone was back, equipped with coffee cups.

Only Rubin had a cup of tea. He took a small sip and picked up the booklet. "So, where were we? Ah yes, he returned as a man from the weekend, and here's the rest."

---

Other than that, a few other events have occurred in the past few weeks.

The situation at the factory isn't good. Sales are constantly on the decline. Dad, who manages everything alone, has already laid off some of the workers on the production floor, keeping only the veterans – those I've known since I was a little boy. He told me he reached out to the government to inquire about producing metal products for our army, but so far, there's been no response.

He also contacted the economic attaché at the German embassy and offered to produce goods for them. They said they'd look into it but, so far, we haven't received any new orders from German clients.

I suggested we consider developing a new product line, but he dismissed the idea. I think he's starting to tire and doesn't have the energy to invest in further development. I believe there's no way around doing it. It's the call of the hour but, for now, I'm not the one making decisions. When I'll be the one running the factory, things will look different.

The next thing I want to write about is Grandpa's car, because it's connected to the factory's situation.

At the beginning of the year, Grandpa bought a new, large car, especially in comparison to Dad's Ford Junior. It was an ivory-white Mercedes-Benz convertible with a huge engine and a retractable roof. The car looked truly luxurious, especially with the Mercedes emblem on the hood.

Early in the year, I had overheard Dad and Grandpa arguing about whether it was the right time to buy such an expensive car, and Grandpa won. Shortly afterward, he fell ill and hardly drove it, so the car is practically brand new, 'right off the showroom floor.'

After Grandpa passed away, I thought that if Dad used Grandpa's car, he could pass down his Ford Junior to me, and I wouldn't have to buy a car myself. I don't have enough money for one anyway, even if Grandma helps me. When I asked him about it, I found he didn't like the idea. He claimed that the factory's situation was only getting worse and that he intended to sell Grandpa's car and put the money towards the factory's funds. So, I'm still without a car.

The last thing I want to write about is related to flying. A lot has happened during the time I didn't write, and my hand is already aching, but this is important.

In the days following the receipt of my pilot's license, I was euphoric, but when the first weekend after the exam came, I suddenly realized that I no longer had flying lessons and, in fact, had no way to continue flying. Only those who have their own plane can fly whenever they want. That's not my case.

So, on Sunday, the first one after I returned from Bulduri, I went to Spilve in the morning. I headed straight to the Aviation Club, hoping to find Edvins and consult with him about what to do in this regard. I'm still excited that I'm a pilot and can enter the club without needing special permission.

I met Berzins, the pilot who conducted my pre-exam, sitting alone at the counter. There were also two other pilots whom I had seen at the toast in my honor. They greeted me as if it was normal for me to be there. I approached Berzins because I knew he was a friend of Edvins and asked if he knew where Edvins was.

"He's in the air, teaching."

When he asked me what I wanted, I told him. After all, he could advise me just as well.

Berzins told me that I'm actually the first young person to complete the flight course, so they hadn't encountered this situation before. Others who finished the civilian course either bought a plane or already owned one beforehand. He suggested I ask Edvins to check if there's a possibility that I could continue flying the Flamingo as part of the National Guard. "They're always looking for pilots anyway," he said.

When Edvins arrived, he was surprised to see me there, but was very happy. He patted me on the back and sat down on one of the vacant chairs at the counter, next to me and Berzins, who told him what we had been discussing. Edvins nodded thoughtfully.

"I might have a solution," he said after some thought, "based on the fact that your father contributed to the Military Aviation Fund and that the slackers at the National Guard, who sit in their offices and have never risked their necks, actually know him. I'll check with them if there's a possibility for you to continue flying the Flamingo and be considered an adjunct pilot to the National Guard."

I don't know what an 'adjunct pilot' is, but I'm still waiting for an answer. Meanwhile, I'm not flying.

After leaving the club, I went to look for Mikhail. I hadn't seen him since I returned from Jurmala with Yuli.

Mikhail already has his own car. He bought one in poor condition and refurbished it with Mr. Kromins. Now he can drive anywhere. It has slightly improved his mood, which has been quite low lately.

Nothing else happened since the swastika was painted on the front door of their bakery. The area has been quiet, perhaps because they hired a Latvian guard for the night shifts, but the fear of what's to come remains.

When we met, I smiled at him, and it must have been a different kind of smile, because he immediately understood. He knew, of course, that Yuli and I had gone to Jurmala.

"About time, Miku. Congratulations!" He patted my back, smiling from ear to ear, and added, "Believe me, it'll be easier from now on." I'm not sure what he meant, but I didn't ask. There are things you don't talk about, even with a close friend.

"By the way, I re-enrolled in the engineering faculty at the Polytechnic," Mikhail continued. "I hope they accept me this time, and in the meantime, I'm continuing to work at Spilve."

"Are you happy with your job here?"

"Overall, yes. It's not like being a pilot like you, but I'm satisfied. Soon, I'll also take the exams to get a certified aircraft mechanic's license, but what's going on around us really bothers me. I honestly don't know what people want from us — from people like me. What do they have against us?"

"Not everyone is like that," I quickly replied, "but let's leave it for now. Be optimistic."

## Chapter 38

"Kids, you've got to see this." Mark handed them his phone. "The car his grandfather had is really something. While you were reading, I searched for a picture of it online, and here's what I found."

"Dad, maybe you should buy a car like that? You could drive around the city with the top down and everyone would stare at you," Daniel joked, but he quickly fell silent when Mark shot him a sharp look.

He definitely didn't appreciate that comment.

"Shall we continue?" Attorney Rubin asked and, without waiting for an answer, resumed the reading.

### Riga, Latvia, Tuesday, June 30, 1936

Last week, Edvins informed me that they agreed to consider me a kind of reservist for the National Guard, even though I'm not officially enlisted. "For emergency reconnaissance flights," as they put it.

This is important because it means I can fly their planes regularly and maintain my flight proficiency. From now on, in addition to having the privilege of entering the Aviation Club, I have a locker in the changing room at the back. Sometimes, I leave my gear there instead of taking it home. The only condition is that I must pay monthly membership fees to the National Guard.

It's a great arrangement and will also allow me to fly other planes if I become certified for them. I'll need to complete a few familiarization flights to do that, as well as a test, but not a full flight course.

So, today I used the opportunity of not having any lectures in the morning and finally flew the Flamingo for the first time since getting my license. It felt a bit strange because I was flying on a Tuesday, not a Sunday as I was used to, and there was a lot of activity at the aerodrome. This time, I didn't need to wait for a briefing from Mr. Ozols, I mean Edvins. The full responsibility for preparing the plane and checking it was mine, with no one double checking me afterwards.

Luckily, both Mr. Kromins and Mikhail were at the hangar, and they helped me get ready for the flight. Mr. Kromins congratulated me on my appointment as a pilot in the National Guard. News travels fast here.

I had been waiting for this moment – to be in the air again, without anyone checking on me or telling me what to do. I wasn't nervous; I was simply content. I flew, enjoyed the view, and thought about how things were finally falling into place for me. When I came in for landing, I was surprised to have to wait in the air until the runway cleared. I clearly remembered the instructions to circle at a distance in 360-degree turns until it was my turn. Although I had never encountered this situation before, I wasn't worried at all.

There was a lot of activity down at the aerodrome – constant engine noise, takeoffs and landings, and various planes taxiing between the runway and the hangars. Mechanics in overalls were walking or riding bicycles from place to place. As I taxied the Flamingo back to the hangar, I had to be very careful not to hit any of them.

Among the many planes, I recognized at least two Gloster Gladiators, which are biplanes like the Flamingo, two of the new KOD-1's used by our Air Force for training (also biplanes), and even Cukurs' new one, the 'Three Stars,' which was taking off for a test flight just as I cleared the runway after landing.

This new plane is nothing like my Flamingo. It looks like a long cigar with a lower wing positioned slightly ahead of the cockpit. The cockpit itself is fully enclosed and very elongated. Its front wheels are covered with windshields, the back of which are very narrow, like knives designed to cut through the air. Its engine is also huge and, at least from the outside, it looks particularly long. There's no doubt it's on a completely different level than my Flamingo or any of the other planes here.

In front of the new, large hangars of the Aviation Club stood two Flamingos and one plane with a top wing. When I asked Mr. Kromins about it, he told me it's a model of the 'Blue Bird.' Now I remember that one of those crashed just before I started my flight training.

Mikhail was very busy when I landed, but we found a few minutes to talk after we put the plane in the hangar.

"How's it going with the Polytechnic? Have you heard anything?"

"No. I think they only send responses in August. If I'm not accepted again this time, I'm getting out of here," he said suddenly. "If that happens, I have no future here. I'll emigrate to America or Palestine, but I won't stay here. I've passed the exams and I'm a certified aircraft mechanic now. I can make a living from that anywhere."

I was quite surprised by this statement. It seems things at home aren't going well for him.

I told him that from what I've read in the newspaper, things aren't good in Palestine either. There are many riots, new and strict laws, and Arab sniper shootings. "If you think it's safer over there, then you're probably mistaken," I told him. He didn't respond to that.

"And with that, ladies and gentlemen, as promised, we'll wrap up for today. We have less than a third of this booklet left and, as you can see, there's another envelope and some documents in the box, but nothing too thick; it shouldn't take long to go through them. I'd like to believe we can finish everything tomorrow," said Attorney Rubin.

"And finally get to the will itself," Mark added.

"Well, that's why we gathered here in the first place," Rubin smiled.

The younger folks left the room, eager to return to their lives. Miriam also left and returned a few minutes later, carrying a tray to collect all the cups on the table.

"Thank you, Miriam," Rubin said, watching her until she left. He remained seated, with Mark and Lilly beside him.

"So, what do you think?"

"I don't think anything. I still don't understand who the young man who wrote the diary is or how it's relevant to us. We'll be wiser tomorrow, and I hope happier too."

"You're happy either way," Mark said as he stood up, signaling Lilly to do the same. "Your future doesn't depend on this will."

"Neither does yours, really," Rubin replied. "Whatever your father had, if it goes to you, will add to what you already possess, which isn't inconsiderable, as far as I know."

"It's not about that," Lilly said. "Mark is part of this business. He should be the one to continue running it."

"We're not in disagreement there," Rubin said. He also stood up, putting his glasses into the front pocket of his shirt.

He walked them to the door of the office and returned to the conference room, where he put the booklet back in the box and locked it.

# Chapter 39

"Good morning," Attorney Rubin greeted everyone as they entered, "I'm glad you all arrived on time and without delays. Let's continue."

### Riga, Latvia, Tuesday, July 7, 1936

Today, I watched an airshow at Spilve, which was more like an air parade. All the planes were lined up in front of the hangars, and beside or in front of each one stood its owners and the designated pilots. The guests at the event walked by and inspected them, and then there was a brief aerobatic display.

### Riga, Latvia, Sunday, August 2, 1936

It's been a long time since I last wrote in the diary. I've finally gotten around to it.

Most days, I spend my mornings studying and my afternoons working at the factory. I find myself spending more and more time in the office rather than on the packing floor, helping Dad with ordering raw materials, sending letters to customers, and filing documents, almost as if I'm his personal assistant.

I visit Grandma at least twice a week and have dinner with her and Martha. No one dares sit in Grandpa's empty chair, but apart from that, there's no air of sadness. Grandma has been conveying that life goes on. Her questions are mainly about my studies and Yuli. She doesn't ask about my flying at all.

Sometimes I stay the night there and, if she goes to bed early, Martha and I chat in the dining room. It's developed into a routine by now.

As my own life goes on, the world is going crazy. Spain is now in a full-blown civil war after an attempted coup. Britain announced that it'll no longer allow German airships to fly over its territory, except in weather emergencies. From what I've read, they suspect that the Hindenburg used a return flight from America to spy on Britain. This means that tensions with Germany are increasing.

Additionally, last month, a Jewish journalist from Slovakia shot himself to death during a meeting of the League of Nations. He left a note explaining that he did it to draw attention to the plight of Jews in Germany.

Mikhail tells me about the treatment he and his family receive every time we meet. There's always tension in the air. The only things going well for me are Yuli and the fact that the Olympics began yesterday in Berlin.

## Riga, Latvia, Sunday, September 12, 1936

Yuli and I are almost living together now. Why almost? Because Dad isn't home during the day and only returns late in the evening, so we're here alone most of the day.

She told me that her parents don't like this arrangement, but as long as her grades are good and it probably saves them money, they might grit their teeth but don't really interfere. Besides, they need to understand that she's nineteen and can make her own decisions.

Yuli found a job at the VEF factory, in the department that handles drafting airplane wings. One of our professors recommended her, and she goes there three times a week in the afternoons, except during exam periods. On those days, after work, she comes to stay with me.

Mikhail wasn't accepted into the Polytechnic. Unbelievable. He was so disappointed that he hasn't been willing to meet with me for almost a month. Even when he took me out for a flight, he was purely businesslike and wasn't willing to talk about anything else, as if it's my fault that he's Jewish and that Jews aren't exactly loved around the world right now.

This really bothered me, and I told Yuli about it.

Thanks to her, he 'came back to us' today. She came to Spilve specifically for that purpose, as if to see me fly, and I took the opportunity to show her my locker at the club. While I was flying, she went to talk to him.

When I returned from the flight, I found them sitting on the couch that had recently been placed in the corner of the hangar.

"Mikhail is about to finish for the day, and we agreed to go for coffee at Otto Schwarz," Yuli said and quickly added, "I suggested to Mikhail that he bring his girlfriend, and afterward, we could all go to the Roma Hotel and dance a little." I wondered which girlfriend she meant because Mikhail changes them frequently. He has extraordinary success with women, even those older than him.

"Yeah, that's right," Mikhail confirmed, sounding a bit embarrassed.

He suggested that we all go together in his car, stop by to pick up his girlfriend, and continue to the café. We obviously agreed; it was better than walking to the bus station. A photographer I know appeared as we stood by the Spilve gate, right before the parking lot. He offered to take a picture of the three of us together.

We stood in front of him, Yuli between Mikhail and me. The entrance gate to Spilve was behind us. We looked at the camera, happy to be reunited. I held my coat and flight cap, with the goggles attached, in one hand, and with the other hand, I hugged Yuli. Mikhail also hugged her from the other side, and that's how we posed for the photograph.

## Riga, Latvia, Friday, October 2, 1936

Today, the construction of the Alcazars building was completed, and its inauguration ceremony took place. The building is three stories tall. The ground floor has offices, the second floor houses a large briefing room, and the third floor is the most important, because that's where the commander's office and those of other professionals are located.

There's an open terrace on the roof of the building where you can observe what's happening on the airfield.

The news coming from the world isn't encouraging. The Germans have really gone mad. Recently, they ordered all German churches to stop using the word 'Hallelujah' in prayers and hymns because it's originally a word in the language of the Jews – Hebrew. Where will all this end?

About ten days ago, the photographer brought me four copies of the photo he took of us at the entrance to Spilve. I gave one to Mikhail and took the rest home. One copy will go to Yuli, and I'll give another to Grandma. She loves putting framed pictures on her counter at home.

### Riga, Latvia, Wednesday, October 21, 1936

Today, Cukurs took off from Riga on a flight to Tokyo, Japan, in his new plane, the 'Three Stars.' The newspaper "Latest News"[37] will publish his travel journal. I'm looking forward to reading it.

"Cukurs again," Mark muttered with disgust. "This little Miku guy really idolized him. I suppose if he knew what was later claimed against Cukurs in the sixties regarding his actions during the Holocaust, he might not have admired him so much. Or maybe his little anti-Semitic side would've won out. Sorry, that annoyed me. Let's continue." He gestured for Attorney Rubin to proceed.

### Riga, Latvia, Thursday, December 31, 1936

I'm very sad. Grandma Hilda passed away suddenly on Christmas, last Friday. She went to bed and didn't wake up. Martha found her in the morning. She called to inform us and said, "God invited her to join Him for the holiday."
    Dad, Martha, and I cried at the funeral. Once again, there were plenty of people, not as many as for Grandpa, but still a lot. The pastor talked about what a strong woman she was and mentioned that despite the loss of her daughter — my mother — she raised me and supported Grandpa all her life. After the funeral, Dad invited Martha to move in with us. She said she'd think about it. Grandma's funeral was much harder for me than Grandpa's; I no longer have any grandparents.

## Riga, Latvia, Sunday, January 24, 1937

It's been three weeks since Grandma passed away. It feels strange to go to their house and not see them there. I think Martha will accept Dad's offer and move in with us. She hinted that it's hard for her to live alone. She has no one else left in the world besides us. Once, when I was rude to her, Dad told me that she gave up having her own family for *our* family, and especially for me, because she chose to raise me in place of Mom.

I had a strange conversation with Mikhail the last time we met.

"Are you capable of flying long distances and even crossing borders?" he asked.

"What do you mean? Why are you asking?" I didn't understand his intention.

"Just curious, that's all," he said. I have a feeling that's not true; he wasn't asking out of curiosity, but I let it go. When he wants to explain, he'll explain.

This reminds me that about a month ago, the American pilot Howard Hughes set a new transcontinental flight record. He flew from Los Angeles to New York City in seven hours, twenty-eight minutes, and twenty-five seconds. He covered a distance greater than the aerial distance from Riga to Tehran or Kazakhstan, and greater than the distance from Riga to Spain or England.

## Riga, Latvia, Sunday, March 14, 1937

I haven't written in two months, not because there was nothing to write about, but because time passes so quickly, and between Yuli and everything else I'm doing, I haven't had a moment's rest until now.

Last week, I was called to participate in a National Guard exercise for the first time. They even paid me for it. Honestly, I would've gladly participated even if they hadn't. Flying with our National Guard, with all the responsibility that comes with it, fills me with immense pride. I don't know anyone my age in the military, let alone as a pilot.

They gathered us in the large briefing room in the new building. I was the youngest there. I had seen most of the attendees at the club, but there were some I didn't recognize.

There were maps of different regions of Latvia on the walls in the room, with flight routes marked in various directions.

Most of the pilots sat down, and then an officer stood up and presented the exercise, the different missions, and the assignment of pilots to different planes. The Flamingo pilots were given reconnaissance missions.

After that, they gathered all the Flamingo pilots in one of the rooms, and each received their mission. My task was to fly along the border with Estonia. I was given a list of coordinates that I needed to pass through. Since this was my first time participating in such an exercise, they assigned an observer to accompany me so I could focus on the flying itself.

I was given a different Flamingo than the one I was used to, but that wasn't a problem. I took off heading north. The air was very cold, and I was glad I had enough sense to wear warm clothes under my flight jacket. The observer and I barely spoke. I don't even remember his name. The flight itself was completely ordinary, and we landed safely after about two and a half hours.

Martha has moved in with us. On the one hand, it's convenient — I get to eat what she cooks again, and the rooms are always clean and tidy — but on the other hand, Yuli comes over considerably less. She says she doesn't feel comfortable being with me when someone is at home all the time.

I have a feeling she's not telling me everything.

# Chapter 40

Yuli has been taking on extra shifts at the VEF factory, so we've been seeing less of each other in the past two months. When we do manage to meet, she talks a lot about Mikhail. I listen to her, but it seems strange that she knows so much about him. Could it be that she's been meeting him, and that's why she doesn't have time for me?

There's nothing new at the factory; the downsizing continues. Dad is very worried, and more than once, I've heard him say that we've stopped making a profit and are teetering on the edge of financial viability. He also hasn't been feeling well lately. Maybe the stress is affecting him.

Last night at dinner, he said, "I'm considering laying off more workers, including some of the long-timers. There's no choice. We have to cut to the bone and rethink the future of the factory. I've acted with sensitivity toward our veteran employees until now, but in situations like this, you can't mix emotions with business — only the tough survive."

To postpone the inevitable, I suggested renting out half of the first floor, where we store raw materials. It's mostly empty right now. I also suggested consolidating the production machines we bought last year on the second floor. The advantage there is that there's a

crane that can extend outward toward Gaizina Street.
Dad accepted my suggestions.

It took a little time, but all the spaces were rented out to merchants looking for storage close to the market.

It's a crucial source of income for the factory right now, and Dad likes to remind me that it was my idea. He seems pleased with it.

### Riga, Latvia, Wednesday, March 31, 1937

Recently, a delegation of pilots from Britain visited Spilve. When I entered the map room today, I found a new and impressive atlas of British spheres of influence, including maps of East Africa, India, and the Middle East. Each map had several copies for actual use. I wonder who could make use of this atlas.

### Riga, Latvia, Sunday, April 18, 1937

A few days ago, while I was deeply engrossed in working on a paper for university, there were loud knocks at the front door. By the time I got up and went to open it, the knocking had only intensified.

Standing at the entrance was Mikhail, out of breath, his hair disheveled, his face red and soot-covered, and the smell of smoke clinging to his clothes.

"Mikhail!" I exclaimed in surprise.

"Can I come in?" he asked before I could even gather myself.

"Yes, of course. What happened?"

"You won't believe it. Someone sprayed a swastika on the entrance of my dad's bakery again, and this time they also set the door on fire. Fortunately, the neighbors smelled the smoke in time and alerted us. We managed to put out the fire, but the wall is completely blackened now. I told you that what's happening in Germany would get here too. I'm fed up with this. They don't want me at the university, and now they're trying to burn down our business. I've received the message," he said loudly.

I couldn't calm him down.

"I want to leave Latvia. There's no future for me here. I want to emigrate to Palestine." This wasn't new, but what he said next left me stunned.

"Miku, I've heard from Mr. Kromins and Mr. Ozols that you're an excellent pilot, so I came here because I wanted to ask you a very important question."

"Me? What do I have to do with all this?"

"Listen carefully! Because I'm completely serious," Mikhail looked me in the eyes. "Would you be willing to fly me there? If Cukurs managed to fly from here to Japan, I'm sure you and I can do it together. Palestine is closer than Japan. The question is, are you willing to do this for me?"

The tone in which Mikhail said these things left no doubt in my mind. He was dead serious about this.

But it was utterly absurd. I'm not Cukurs, and just because he can fly vast distances to far-away countries doesn't mean I'm capable of doing the same.

"Have you lost your mind, Mikhail? Do you think flying is a game? That anyone can just fly wherever they want? Where would you get a plane? And fuel? What about your family? And mine? And saying goodbye to Yuli? Do you think you can just disappear to another country?"

Mikhail took half a step back.

"Look, it's not that—" I tried to explain myself, but he was already offended.

"Fine, thanks. I get it. I thought you might be interested, but I understand. It's dangerous and maybe too big of a risk for you," he cut me off before I could finish my sentence and walked out without saying another word. We didn't talk about it again. But since then, things have been rather cold between us. When he escorts me out for a flight—and it's almost always him who does—he's very professional, but much less friendly.

## Riga, Latvia, Sunday, May 9, 1937

Today, Mr. Kromins escorted me out for a flight instead of Mikhail. After the flight, I asked him where Mikhail was.

"About ten days ago, he suddenly left for a long vacation, without any prior notice. He explained that he had to travel abroad urgently for family matters and didn't elaborate. Honestly, I was upset with him for surprising me like that, but he's such a nice guy and an excellent mechanic that you can't really stay mad at him."

I was surprised. I didn't know he was planning to take such a long vacation.

"When is he coming back?" I asked. I wondered if Yuli knew anything about this.

"He'll be back in a month. At least that's what he told me."

I'll find out what happened when he comes back. I decided not to ask Yuli about it.

## Riga, Latvia, Thursday, June 3, 1937

Something strange and not at all good is happening between Yuli and me, especially after our conversation today at school. When we left the faculty building, I said to her, "Yuli, in the past three weeks, we haven't managed to meet outside of class even once."

"I'm working a lot, and the combination with school and exams is killing me," she replied, not looking in my direction.

"Maybe we can take advantage of the weekend to take a boat and sail in Kisezers?"

"I was thinking of using the weekend to catch up on the homework I haven't done yet."

"So, do you want to be with me at home? You can do your homework in my room," I said.

"I don't think so," she replied shortly. It seemed like she was avoiding me, but I didn't want to give up.

"So, what do you suggest?"

"Nothing right now. I'm tired."

"So when can we spend time together?"

"I don't know. Maybe next weekend. We'll see."

At least she reached out and stroked my shoulder. I have no idea what's happened to her.

"Look at that; he was so in love with her that he was content with a shoulder pat after they'd been far more intimate than that," Hannah said. She had been sitting with her elbow on the table, her head resting on it, facing Rubin.

"We don't know that yet," her mother responded. "Please sit properly."

Hannah lowered her elbow and leaned back in her chair, while her brother Tom smiled and whispered in her ear, "She'll make a proper lady out of you yet."

She gestured for him to shut up and looked at Rubin.

The attorney continued.

### Riga, Latvia, Sunday, June 20, 1937

I still haven't been able to meet Yuli outside of class hours. It's driving me crazy. I haven't even been able to hug or kiss her.

And Yuli? It seems she's not even trying to make it happen. It's depressing.

### Riga, Latvia, Friday, July 16, 1937

Cukurs returned from Tokyo. He completed the round-trip flight. Unbelievable!

They held a welcome ceremony for him again, just like they did last time when he returned from Gambia. It's been three years since then already; how time flies. This time, I received an invitation for myself and a guest. I asked Yuli to come with me, but she said she was busy. Again.

This time, her response really hurt me.

"Are we even still together? Because with the way I've been feeling lately, it doesn't seem that way," I said to her angrily.

"Possibly. You said it seems that way, didn't you? So maybe we should just draw some conclusions," she said coldly, grabbed her bag, and walked away from me.

I stood there, speechless. Did Yuli just tell me it's over between us?

By the time I recovered, she was already far away, and my pride, or what was left of it, kept me from running after her to find out what she meant.

I've tried to talk to her several times since then, without success. I mean, we've talked, but not like two people who love each other. I asked her what happened, what I did wrong, if I hurt her.

Nothing worked; she didn't want to talk about it.

It's clear that our relationship is over, but I have no idea why. I feel a deep sense of emptiness, as if I'm in mourning. I miss the scent of her hair and the warmth of her body every time I go to bed.

The welcome ceremony for Cukurs was a good distraction.

As I was about to leave, I caught sight of Mikhail out of the corner of my eye, after more than a month of not seeing him. I approached him. He smiled at me and waved. He looked tired.

"Mr. Kromins told me you went on a long vacation. What happened? Where did you go?"

"Not here," he said quietly and motioned me to follow him. Only after we were far from any people did he say in a low voice, "No vacation. I told you I wanted to get out of here. So, I tried and, as you can see, I failed. It's enough to drive you crazy."

"Are you serious? Where were you?"

"I heard that someone named Moishe Kribushein set up a camp near Vienna in Austria to organize groups of young people to board ships for Palestine, so I went there."

"And what happened?"

"There was no room left, so they turned me down," he said in frustration. "I also ran out of money, so I came back. But I'll find a way to get out of here." He looked me in the eyes, smiled wearily, and added, "Maybe by flying."

We both knew what he meant.

"Incredible. That's one hell of a trip. Did anyone know?"

"My parents, and I told Yuli about it."

Yuli? His comment caught me off guard. I couldn't help but ask, "You were in touch with Yuli? Did you talk to her recently, even after you got back?"

He started to vehemently deny that he had met her, maybe too vehemently.

Mikhail's reaction only worsened my mood, which was already terrible to begin with.

# Chapter 41

### Riga, Latvia, Friday, August 20, 1937

Dad informed me today that he has decided to lay off all the workers and close the factory at the end of the month. His attempts to find a partner over the past months have failed. The only income we've had is from those renting space from us, but it's not enough.

"It's better to cut this whole thing off now rather than continuing to operate and losing money. We'll live off the rent from the building. It's good income, without much work needed. We'll keep a small maintenance staff, and that's it," he told me.

Even though Dad is right, I'm sure Grandpa and Grandma are turning in their graves. I couldn't help but think how lucky I was to have finished the flight course on time.

This news only adds to the bitterness I've felt since Yuli left me. She also stopped helping me with my studies, so I'm forced to handle all the lessons and exams on my own. Not that I can't do it, but it was easier with her.

So, I've lost Yuli, we've lost the factory, and everything seems completely miserable.

The only things that slightly lift my spirits are the flights I'm doing all the time as part of the National Guard training. I feel like I'm getting better with every flight.

Sometimes, while in the air, I think about Mikhail's question and try to imagine such a long flight with the Flamingo. When he mentioned it, it seemed absurd. But now, I think it could be possible if properly planned. Not that I would ever do something crazy like that, but the more I think about it, the more possible it seems.

"Alright, folks, it's time for our morning break," Attorney Rubin announced.

"What do you think? Will he actually do it in the end?" David asked Daniel by the buffet table in the other room. They picked out a few sandwiches and headed towards the coffee machine.

"If he does, then it'll have been worth listening to this whole story. It's so bizarre that I can't even imagine it," Daniel replied.

"Come on, hurry up, kids. We've got to finish today," Mark said, taking a big bite of a bun. Avocado spread slipped off the other side and landed on the floor near his feet.

"Here," Lilly handed him a plate. "That stuff leaves stains that won't come out."

He looked at her appreciatively.

They returned to the meeting room sated and ready to finish the journey they had started three days earlier.

### Riga, Latvia, Thursday, September 16, 1937

A terrible day. A great disaster.

The morning started normally — I left for a training flight, and everything was fine. As I taxied the Flamingo back to the hangar, I saw a group of pilots gathered near the offices.

Mr. Kromins greeted me with a pale face. He motioned for me to come over. There was no sign of Mikhail, even though he was the one who escorted me this morning.

"Miku, I have some very bad, very sad news that just came in a few minutes ago," Mr. Kromins said.

I tensed up, fearing it was about Dad or Mikhail.

"Edvins was killed this morning during an approach to land in Liepaja," Mr. Kromins began, his voice breaking. "It was probably a test flight on a new plane."

Everything went dark around me. The world started spinning rapidly and my vision blurred. Mr. Kromins held me tightly and led me to the couch. He said no one knows exactly what happened yet, so there was no point in asking for more details.

The truth is, it didn't really matter anymore. Edvins Ozols was dead. My mind refused to process the bitter news. Tears began to flow from my eyes, even though I tried to hold them back. We hurried to the Aviation Club to see if there was any more information.

Many pilots were already crowding the entrance to the club, and there was no room to squeeze through. After a long wait, someone finally came out and read a statement that didn't reveal anything new. What I knew for certain was that I would never be able to consult with him again or enjoy his calming presence.

I remembered that, so long ago, he warned me that this was a dangerous profession and that on my first day of ground studies, he said we would meet again "if I'm still alive."

We won't meet again. So sad.

## Riga, Latvia, Saturday, September 18, 1937

Edvins' funeral was held yesterday, attended only by his family. Today, I participated in a memorial service for him at the club.

Six veteran pilots who knew him stood in a line along

the bar, each holding a full glass of 95% *Valsts Spirts*, pilot's fuel. Each one, in turn, shared a story they had with Edvins; they then declared, "To Edvins, who is in the sky," and all six drank in unison. Another pilot went around with the bottle, refilling their glasses and those of anyone in the audience who asked. One round was enough for me. After all six had shared their stories, they hung a framed photo of Edvins on the wall leading to the map room, saluted the picture, and everyone dispersed.

### Riga, Latvia, Wednesday, October 6, 1937

Dad's health is not good. It started a few months ago and is getting worse. He seems to have heart problems, and he's struggling to breathe. The doctor gave him pills to help him breathe easier, but day by day, his health is deteriorating, and it seems like he's lost the will to live.

Martha stays with him most of the time, making sure he takes his medicine and isn't left alone. Today, I stayed home to take her place. I sat by Dad's bed, and we talked. He slept part of the time, but I continued sitting next to him. From time to time, he woke up, and I held his hand to encourage him, but it's clear to both of us that the chances of his recovery are slim. The last time the doctor checked him, he made it clear to me that Dad probably wouldn't recover.

"Don't forget to collect the rent from the factory tenants," he said, struggling to breathe. Even in his weakened state, Dad remained practical. "And the car needs to go to the garage for service; it's a chance for you to drive it," he chuckled. "Everything's on your shoulders now," he added before falling asleep again.

I always knew Dad would get old one day; I never considered any other possibility. And now he's slowly fading away right before my eyes, and I can't do anything to stop it. It hurts, it's frustrating, but who can I complain to? It's probably his fate, and mine.

At his request, I've been handling the sale of Grandpa and Grandma's apartment over the past month. He asked me to clear it of all personal belongings and try to sell it with the furniture included. He also updated me that Grandpa had a safe and gave me the code to open it.

Inside the safe, I found a pistol, several boxes of bullets, and a cloth bag with stacks of British pound notes. For now, the gun, bullets, and money are in a drawer in my room.

This is a truly terrible time. I have no one to talk to about it. Yuli left me, Mikhail is preoccupied with his own issues, and my father is dying. I'm alone.

## Riga, Latvia, Tuesday, November 30, 1937

Dad passed away two days ago. In the span of a year and a half, I've lost everyone who was dear to me.

All the rituals surrounding the funeral and burial repeated once more, just like with Grandpa and Grandma.

As I stood by Dad's grave, I realized just how central he was to my life — a role model, a source of guidance and support. A deep, powerful sense of sorrow and loss struck me in the chest as I laid down the wreath of flowers I had brought with me.

I was surrounded by many people who came to say goodbye to him, and as I looked at them, I was also filled with pride and admiration for him. Even though I knew him as a hardworking and successful industrialist,

I had never fully appreciated the extent of his influence and connections.

When the pastor delivered the eulogy, I was astonished to learn about all the ways Dad had touched so many people's lives, and I couldn't help but feel a sense of awe and respect for the man he was.

Yuli and Mikhail came to the repast that Martha organized at our house. They arrived together.

Yuli approached me and hugged me tightly. I really needed that, to feel her warmth and support. Before we parted, I looked at her with a questioning gaze. I wanted to know why, why she chose to end our relationship.

"Miku, not everything you think you see or feel reflects reality," she said and then went her way. I have no idea what she meant.

I was very glad Mikhail came to visit me. I hadn't seen him since he escorted me out for a flight on the day Mr. Ozols died. We sat together in the kitchen and ate cookies that Martha had made.

He shifted uncomfortably in his seat and, eventually, he said, "I think I owe you an apology for not being there when you found out that Edvins was killed. I know what you've been going through this past year, and I just couldn't bring myself to be the one to tell you. So I just left. I'm sorry."

"It's okay, Mikhail. With everything that's happened since then, it really doesn't matter anymore. What else is new with you?"

"Nothing special, just everything being depressing here. We'll find time to talk about it. Now, with everything you're going through, isn't the right time. There'll be a better opportunity. For now, the most important thing is that you look ahead, think positive thoughts, and let me know what I can do to help you get through these terrible days more easily."

He got up to leave. I extended my hand to shake his, but he pulled me in by the shoulders and hugged me tightly for a long minute. Then he went on his way.

Only now did it occur to me that I should've asked him why he and Yuli arrived together. At least he didn't ask me anything about a flight to Palestine.

## Riga, Latvia, Saturday, December 25, 1937

This is the least festive Christmas I've ever had. Martha tried to cheer me up by baking a big chocolate cake, but it didn't really help. She's very sad too. She dedicated her whole life to my family and me, and now that I'm no longer a child, she's left completely alone. We were two sad people sitting alone in the kitchen, eating chocolate cake.

In moments like these, I can't stop thinking about Yuli. I miss her.

Since Dad passed away, I've been thinking a lot about the future. The rent from the factory in the market supports me well enough, and my studies are progressing well overall. I go to the faculty and return home to Martha. About once a week, I drive Dad's Ford Junior to Spilve and fly the Flamingo. I tried to explore the possibility of learning to fly another aircraft in the National Guard, but with Edvins gone, there's no one to help me, and nothing came of it. Nothing really satisfies me.

Mikhail and I meet at Spilve every time I'm there. He told me that his parents asked all the siblings to find a way to leave Latvia, to escape. They feel it's becoming more dangerous for them here by the day.

# Chapter 42

## Riga, Latvia, Monday, January 24, 1938

Today, work began on the construction of two new hangars at Spilve for the National Guard's air force. After the cornerstone-laying ceremony, all the pilots who attended the event flocked to the Aviation Club, and I joined them.

While the pilots leaned against the bar in the club, one of them announced that he had joined the Thunder Cross organization, and pulled out a flag bearing the organization's symbol—a fire cross set against a background of red crosses. The other pilots laughed, and some even clapped for him.

"From now on, no Jew enters our club," another pilot shouted amidst more applause.

"I don't trust Jews or Communists," said one of the pilots I had seen at the club before. He turned to me and added, "Miku, that includes your Jewish friend. Tell him not to dare touch my plane from now on."

Some of the pilots standing nearby turned their gazes toward me.

"But he's an excellent mechanic."

"Excellent or not, he's a Jew, and you, Miku, better decide whose side you're on," he replied, and turned back to the other pilots who patted him on the back and continued laughing.

I was in shock! I couldn't believe pilots would speak this way about Mikhail, who has been escorting them out to flights and maintaining their planes so professionally.

"Go to hell," I muttered and left the club.

So Mikhail was right all along! I thought as I walked toward the exit of Spilve. Now I understand what he was trying to tell me. He truly has no future here at Spilve, and maybe not even in Latvia in general. At this rate, what's happening to the Jews in Germany will happen here too, and Mikhail and his family are in great danger.

## Riga, Latvia, Sunday, January 30, 1938

I've been thinking all week about what happened at the club. It's simply awful! I'm seriously considering Mikhail's request to fly him to Palestine, even though he hasn't mentioned it again.

The situation for Jews is worsening, with new reports of harassment every day, and the news from Germany is just chilling. I can't help everyone, but I can help Mikhail, and myself, too, to get away from all the sorrow and troubles around here.

Such a journey will take me weeks, preparing for it and flying there and back. It's enough time to clear my head. I know that when I return, I'll have to face real life, finishing my studies and worrying about making a living. For now, though, this adventure, the more I think about it, seems possible. But where will we find a suitable plane?

I came to Spilve today specifically to tell Mikhail that I'm willing to consider his request. Who knows, maybe he's already given up on the idea? But I didn't see him. I'll tell him the next time I come to Spilve.

## Riga, Latvia, Wednesday, February 16, 1938

These days, I've been focusing on completing the preparations list for the flight to Palestine. This is the most important thing. Two weeks have passed since I spoke to Mikhail about it.

He was taken completely by surprise and asked several times whether I was serious or joking.

"I'm completely serious; I just don't know if it's even possible."

His eyes sparkled. "Then we'll make it possible."

Since then, we've been meeting almost every evening at my house, going over the various issues we'll need to address.

The plane I'm most familiar with is the Flamingo **YL-ABZ**, the one I've been training on. This means we'll have to take off in secret and not report it to anyone.

There are countless details we need to prepare in advance: flight and navigation equipment, spare parts for the engine and its systems, fuel, oils, inner tubes for the tires, and a pump. We'll need to stock up on foreign currency for the countries we'll stop to refuel and rest at. We'll need maps and weather forecast reports. We'll have to prepare a cover story in case we're stopped and questioned along the way, supported by official documents.

We have to think about the best time to make the flight. It'd better to wait until the end of winter, when the air warms up and stabilizes. The flight route must be as short as possible and has to consider that we cannot enter Soviet airspace, the mountain ranges we'll have to cross or bypass, and the preplanned landing spots. On the one hand, there must be fuel available at each spot, and on the other hand, the places shouldn't be too central for fear that local police might reach us.

Mikhail and I divided the tasks between us. He's handling the technical and professional side, while I'm responsible for preparing the plane, navigation, various flight documents, money, and the cover story.

In addition to all this, I need to plan my return to Riga. I obviously can't fly back alone, and I won't be able to give a reasonable explanation for reappearing with a plane that disappeared a few months earlier. I'll have to plan a different way back so that I'm not linked to its disappearance. I've started exploring the possibility of flying back on one of the regular flights operated by the Polish airline *LOT*, from Palestine to Warsaw via Romania and Greece, and taking a train from there to Riga. And there's another issue that's bothering me. Mikhail has never flown and doesn't know how to behave during a flight or in emergencies. He needs to train for it.

Surprisingly, ever since I've gotten involved in this crazy adventure, my mood has improved greatly. The only thing weighing on me is that Mikhail told me yesterday that he meets with Yuli from time to time, "but it's not really serious," he explained apologetically.

I didn't say anything to him about it. Yuli made it clear that things between us are over, so it really shouldn't bother me. But it still does. I still miss her a lot. If it were the other way around, I wouldn't even think of meeting with someone he loved.

"Then I don't understand why he's willing to help him," Daniel interrupted Rubin.

"You're taking this story too much to heart," Mark scolded him. "What do you care why this Miku did what he did? We've been listening to a stranger's diary for three days now, and I still don't understand how it's connected to us at all, and you're interested in why he helped him?"

"What's wrong, Mark? We're in the final stretch, and *now* you're losing your patience?" Lilly asked, surprised, like the others, by his outburst.

He stood up and walked over to the window. "I have a bad feeling," he muttered, almost to himself. He turned towards Attorney Rubin. "Go on, go on. I'll stand for a bit. My back is killing me."

### Riga, Latvia, Wednesday, April 6, 1938

Most of the preparations are complete. All that's left is to wait for the planned date and hope that the weather forecast remains true.

I informed Martha that I'm planning to go on a tour of Germany to explore a potential deal that could help me revive the factory, and that I'll be there for several weeks. She didn't ask me too many questions about it, just requested that I inform her in advance once I know the exact date of my trip.

From time to time, I take some of the excellent maps from the atlas the English pilots brought to the club. We now have maps for the entire flight route and the radio frequencies of every official aerodrome along the way. We're all sorted on that front.

The route I planned goes through Lithuania, Poland, Hungary, Romania, Serbia in Yugoslavia, Bulgaria, Greece, Turkey, the French Mandate in Syria and Lebanon, and Palestine. I exchanged money and have local banknotes and coins for nearly all the stops. I'm also taking the British pound notes I found in Grandpa's safe.

I decided to take the gun and bullets that were in the safe, despite the explicit ban on flying with weapons. There's no point in leaving it in the drawer, and we might need it.

Mikhail made a compartment that he'll install behind

my seat where we'll store our personal belongings. Additionally, he sewed a hidden pocket into the seat bottom where we'll put the money and the gun. He surprised me today when he said he exchanged the money he saved from working at Spilve for diamonds, and will bring those too. "You can always sell diamonds," he said.

Our cover story is ready too. If we're questioned, we'll claim that we're part of an international tour to explore the Middle East. We both speak German, so that's the language we'll use to make them think we're Latvians of German descent. The fire cross emblem on the plane will also help with that. I also instructed Mikhail not to bring a camera under any circumstances so that no one suspects we're spies.

The date is set for Monday morning, May 23.

I had learned that an aviation exhibition will be held in Helsinki between May 14th and 22nd. In recent days, I've heard that many pilots from Spilve, including Cukurs, plan to fly there with their planes and those of the National Guard.

Most of them will only return on Monday. Until then, Spilve will be fairly empty, and no one will be around the hangars. It's an excellent window of time for us to prepare for the flight to the Middle East. There will already be aircraft movements on the day of the flight, so I don't think we'll attract too much attention. A few days earlier, I'll submit a flight plan to the offices in the administration building for a "cross-border" training flight to Lithuania. It's a standard training flight, and I assume it won't raise any suspicions.

I'm going to miss the final exams at university. I'll have to make up for it when I return. Getting this degree is important to me.

I promised Dad, and I intend to keep my promise.

I updated Martha on the date like she requested, and will make sure to leave the Ford Junior in the factory's parking lot. As far as I'm concerned, everything is set. I hope I've thought of everything.

Mikhail arranged a passport for himself and also prepared a large bag with tools and mechanical parts. He'll place the bag under his seat and under his feet. It won't be comfortable, but he claims he'll manage. I weighed the bag to check that it wouldn't affect the plane's balance. It's borderline. Luckily, Mikhail doesn't weigh much.

He told me the only thing that worries him, for which he has no solution, is the fuel issue. The fuel suitable for the Flamingo's engine is high-octane. There's a certain risk that we might not find it everywhere along the way.

"Different fuel could cause blockages in the system," he explained. "I'm taking several critical parts with us so we can replace them in case that happens."

There's also the matter of his flight training. That part was easy. I told Mr. Kromins I felt something unclear during the flight and would like Mikhail to come up with me to check it out. The chief mechanic was very relieved I didn't ask him to fly with me and didn't wonder why I was the only one complaining. After that, we requested that Mikhail fly with me because I found that the additional weight he adds stabilizes the plane during flight. That excuse also worked.

I trained him in all flight conditions, including emergency landings on land, water, and trees. Additionally, he practiced navigation, since he's supposed to be the navigator. He told me that only now is he beginning to understand that this crazy adventure is far more complicated and dangerous than he thought.

In addition to all that, we decided to choose a name, just as Cukurs named his plane. We chose the name 'White Cloud.'[38]

We'll continue the preparations and hope for the best. It's hard to believe, but this crazy adventure is actually about to happen.

## Riga, Latvia, Wednesday, May 18, 1938

Yesterday, while Cukurs and his crew were at the exhibition in Helsinki, another disaster occurred during a demonstration flight of a new plane made by VEF, and the pilot, Karlis Lesinskis, was killed along with his passenger. From the few pilots left at the club, I heard that yesterday at four in the afternoon, Lesinskis took off with a passenger, and shortly afterward, a report came to the control tower that the plane had crashed about two and a half kilometers from the aerodrome. I think I know him. I've seen him a few times at Spilve. He was a National Guard pilot, quite thin and short, with a prominent chin and a constant smile on his face. These accidents are stressing me out. If such an experienced pilot was killed in a plane accident, what does that mean for me, a young pilot on the verge of such a long flight on a route I've never taken before?

## Riga, Latvia, Saturday, May 21, 1938

That's it; everything is ready. Yesterday, I got back the flight documents I submitted, and the flight plan was approved. As I thought, no one asked for any further details. I'm extremely excited. I'll be celebrating my birthday in three days in the skies, on the way to Palestine.

"...Tomorrow we set off. May God be with us!" Rubin read aloud, completing the diary entry from May 22, 1938.

"Well, you got your answer," Mark said, returning to his seat.

"Of course, the diary is here in the box. It had to get here somehow, right?" Tom replied.

Right, I hadn't thought about that, Mark thought to himself. Tom was always quiet and smart. It's a shame Dad banned employing family members in the company. This is a guy I'd want by my side. After I become the owner of Citrus, there will be some changes. That will be one of them.

"I'm continuing," announced Attorney Rubin.

# PART THREE

# Chapter 43

## Poland, Ulez, Monday, May 23, 1938

We're in the village of Ulez. We landed here about three hours ago after more than five hours of flying. I'm exhausted, and Mikhail also looks very tired. My lips are chapped, and my hands ache from gripping the stick for so long.

After refueling White Cloud and returning from a visit to the village, I found some time to write in the diary. There's still light outside. Mikhail is sitting not far from me. He's resting his head on his bag; maybe he's sleeping. I don't know. I can't sleep.

The departure from Spilve went smoothly. We reached the hangar at first light, in his car, which stayed there. He left the keys on Mr. Kromins' desk so he can do as he pleases with it when he realizes Mikhail isn't coming back.

We also left a letter I wrote to Yuli on his desk, explaining where Mikhail and I had disappeared to. I sealed the letter tightly in an envelope. I asked Mikhail to write in his own hand, *Please deliver to Mrs. Yuliana Bergs, 20 Stabu Street, Riga.*

Mr. Mirkin raised his head, looking at Rubin in surprise. The attorney, engrossed in reading, didn't notice and continued.

"You're leaving a letter for Yuli? You're still in contact with her?" he asked.

"Not really, but I still figured it would be best to leave something for her," I answered briefly. I didn't want to talk about her with Mikhail. The relationship between them still isn't clear to me.

Despite what happened between us, Yuli still means a lot to me. She'll read my letter and understand everything. That way, if I don't survive this journey, she can also explain to Martha that it was my free choice, for better or worse.

I wrote about how I feel about her. How I still feel. So she'd know.

Just before I sealed the envelope with the letter inside, I added the photograph of the three of us at the entrance to Spilve. She'll keep it for me until I return. If I return.

"And why don't you write her address yourself?"

"Because I don't want them to immediately link me to this mess. I don't want them to recognize my handwriting."

"Fine, give me the envelope and I'll write what you asked. Let's finish this and get out of here," Mikhail said and, after doing so, placed the envelope next to his car keys.

"I hope for your sake that Kromins actually delivers the letter after he finds out what happened here."

We dressed warmly, loaded up the remaining items, and I began performing the essential pre-flight checks. I placed my hand on the engine and patted the plane. "Do you understand the gravity of this mission?" I asked aloud, "I really hope you're ready, because Mikhail and I are counting on you wholeheartedly." Mikhail, who was standing behind me, chuckled when he heard me, but I was dead serious. White Cloud is completely dependent on us, just as we are on it.

We rolled the plane out and started it up. Mikhail sat in his seat, we did an internal communication check, and shortly after, we took off.

The weather was excellent, and White Cloud swayed gently, as if happy to be on the way. I was familiar with the first leg of the flight, so I didn't expect any problems. The map we had marked our planned flight path on was in Mikhail's hands.

The length of the first leg was about 260 kilometers (bearing one-eight-nine). The plan was to reach a landing strip in Lithuania that I had identified on the map, refuel there, and continue flying south to get as far away from Spilve as possible. I decided to fly at an average speed to conserve fuel. I estimated the first leg of the flight would take about two hours.

I turned south and climbed to about 4,000 feet (about 1,220 meters). I looked down at Riga, at our beautiful old city. I recognized the Dome Cathedral, St. Peter's Church, the square in front of St. John's Church, the Opera House and Pilsētas Canal, the strip of gardens alongside it, the market, and the round roofs of the pavilions. I felt a deep pang at the thought that this might be the last time I see this beautiful sight.

We kept on flying south. From time to time, I checked the compass to ensure our course was correct, as well as the terrain, to make sure Mikhail was navigating without errors.

After about half an hour of flying, I recognized the town of Bauska and realized we'd drifted slightly off course to the east due to a westerly wind. I pushed the pedals in the opposite direction so the rudder would compensate for the westerly wind and instructed Mikhail to be aware of it.

We crossed the border into Lithuania and, after about an hour and a half, I recognized the city of Kaunas. I continued south for another ten minutes, and then Mikhail told me he thought he saw the spot I had marked on the map as a landing strip. I had to descend to a fairly low altitude to properly identify the thin strip of compressed grass in the middle of a green field. If I hadn't noticed a pole with a windsock, I might not have recognized it as a landing strip. The windsock indicated a light westerly wind parallel to the runway.

The landing was easy and, after we got out of the plane, we stretched our legs. Then we approached a nearby building and, luckily, quickly located the person in charge. Mikhail spoke to him in Latvian and, when he indicated that he didn't understand, Mikhail switched to German and asked if we could refuel. I was glad Mikhail took the initiative and responsibility for that. The man in charge replied in broken German that there was a fuel tank behind the building and motioned with his hand that we should taxi White Cloud back there.

The fuel was suitable for our engine. We refueled quickly, but the wind had picked up, and there were some very strong gusts. Since we still had plenty of daylight left for the flight, I preferred to wait, hoping the wind would die down.

The person in charge invited us to drink coffee with him in his modest office. After about three hours, we decided to continue. I paid him for the fuel, coffee, and refreshments in local currency, and we took off for the next stop, Ulez, Poland.

This leg of the route was about 360 kilometers (bearing one-nine-eight), nearly three hours of flying. I chose to fly low because, from now on, we were flying without any legal permission, and I didn't want anyone to be able to spot us from afar. We had enough fuel, even considering the increase in fuel consumption during low-level flight.

The ground had warmed up, and we felt it in the air turbulence, but overall, the weather and visibility were good.

When Mikhail announced that he recognized the city of Marijampole,[39] I turned slightly east to avoid it. We skirted around it and returned to our predetermined course. Twenty minutes later, we crossed the border between Lithuania and Poland.

From this point on, we were in constant danger, without a reported flight plan, without any permission, and without a visa to enter Poland or any of the countries we would cross later. Poland has an excellent air force. I hoped that if I flew low, they wouldn't see us. If they identified us as a foreign aircraft, they might even shoot us down. I continued flying low, fully focused. To improve our chances of not being detected, I preferred to fly well east of Warsaw.

After about three and a quarter hours, Mikhail identified the Ulez airstrip. It's an agricultural landing strip with a clearly visible runway, but we didn't see any planes around. After circling around it once, we landed. I taxied White Cloud to a side spot and shut off the engine.

Shortly after, two men arrived to see who we were. To our relief, they weren't in uniform. They were the ones in charge of the airstrip. We used our cover story. I noticed they eyed the insignia of the Fire Cross, which they recognized as the swastika, and their looks weren't particularly friendly. Apparently, they don't like Germans here.

But they were polite, allowed us to refuel, and even

took us in an old car to the village of Ulez to buy supplies. We walked back to the airstrip. I breathed a sigh of relief when I found White Cloud just as we had left it. We'll sleep in a tent under the wing tonight and take off early tomorrow morning.

Mikhail and I sat at the entrance to the tent, watching the setting sun. I took the opportunity to ask a question I didn't get a chance to ask until now, "Why Palestine of all places? Why do you want to go there?"

"Because there are cities and settlements there where only Jews live. Everyone there is Jewish, and everyone is equal. There's no *numerus clausus* in Palestine, no one makes remarks just because you're Jewish, and you're not a minority among Christians. The Jews are the majority there. They're building a new world for themselves, even speaking a new language, Hebrew, and I want to be part of that..."

I felt his pain. For the first time in a long while, I sensed he was speaking to me with complete honesty, without hidden motives, without needing to be cautious with his words, and with no defenses. Simply from the heart and from a place of deep pain.

"...You can't understand it, Miku, but it's hard to be a Jew in Europe in general, and in Latvia too. Look at what's happening in Germany. You think it can't happen back home? It can happen in Riga too, and it's already happening. I'm no longer willing to wait to be accepted into the Polytechnic, when people less talented than I are accepted without issue, and I'm rejected just because I'm Jewish. We'll build our own country in Palestine, a country for Jews. That's what keeps me going all the time. That's my dream, and I'm about to fulfill it in a few days, even though I had to leave behind my parents and brothers, and I'm not sure I'll see them again. But I can't wait any longer."

I *could* understand. I had seen it with my own eyes at

the Aviation Club. I didn't tell Mikhail about it. I figured it might hurt him even more.

"Do you know anyone there?" I asked.

"My father has a friend who owns a factory that supplied wooden crates for packing oranges from Palestine to Europe. He told my father that the citrus industry there is in crisis. I assume you can buy orchards cheaply, so I thought of buying an orchard with the diamonds I brought with me and, at the same time, study engineering. Or at least give it a try."

"You'll be a farmer?" I laughed. "That's new to me. But if you buy an orchard, I'll join in on the purchase and be your partner from afar, from Latvia."

"You're serious? You'd want to do that?"

"If I know you're taking care of it and managing it, of course, yes."

The idea of a partnership in an orchard with Mikhail actually appeals to me.

## Hungary, Miskolc, Tuesday, May 24, 1938

Today, I turned twenty-one.

We flew over three countries today. We took off from Poland, crossed Slovakia, and landed in Hungary.

We took off at first light, heading southwest. I tried to continue flying low, but I climbed a bit in altitude when the landscape changed from flat farmland and rivers to hills and forests. I asked Mikhail to constantly think and look for a place for an emergency landing, because you can't land just anywhere on such terrain. As we approached the border with Slovakia, the hills turned into mountains. We had to fly in valleys along the ridges and cross them at valley junctions, so the flight was no longer straight but in zigzags.

At some sections, there was no choice but to climb to 9,800 feet (about 3,000 meters) to cross the mountains. I had never flown so high before, and it felt uncomfortable. I explained to Mikhail that there's less oxygen at this altitude so, if he started feeling a bit strange, he should let me know immediately. We didn't practice such prolonged flights in his training, and I had to make sure he was okay. That's why I also made sure to ask him some question or another every few minutes to make sure he was fine.

Mikhail has it easy. He's not worried about everything involved in flying the plane. He trusts me completely, but I have no one to rely on except myself and White Cloud. Everything rests on my shoulders, and at the end of every leg of flight, I feel the full weight of that responsibility.

When Mikhail told me he thought we had crossed the border into Slovakia, I felt relieved. I was glad we managed to leave Polish airspace without being intercepted. I knew this was only a temporary relief, but at least we managed to cross Poland safely.

I didn't have much time to enjoy it.

There was a massive jolt, and White Cloud veered sharply to the right, straight towards the mountain, as if the air had been sucked out from under the right wings.

My breath caught, the seat belts locked tightly, I felt dizzy, and for a moment, I couldn't see anything.

---

"Oh no," a voice of alarm escaped Hannah's lips. All eyes turned to her. "That really scared me," she apologized.

"You're really into it," Tom chuckled.

"As strange as it may sound, I think I was in that area," Rubin remarked. "When I think about it now, I remember that the landscape was really mountainous. I think it's pretty dangerous to fly there, between the mountains. Especially with such a small plane."

"They were very brave," Hannah commented.

"Or foolish," her brother Tom replied. "Mountains can be deadly."

I didn't have time to process exactly what happened. With my last shred of consciousness, I reacted as Edvins had taught me. I quickly moved the rudder to the opposite side and pushed the stick forward.

A strong shudder passed through White Cloud's fuselage and it began diving toward the ground, still leaning toward the mountainside. Out of the corner of my eye, I saw Mikhail gripping the sides tightly. Gradually, I managed to balance the wings. The haze lifted, and I returned to full focus. I powered the engine up to the maximum and carefully pulled the stick back until I managed to stabilize the plane.

In a single moment, we dropped 650 feet (about 200 meters) in the air. If I hadn't reacted like that, we would have crashed into the rock wall on our right.

"What was that?" Mikhail's voice came through the headphones. He was scared. I was scared, too. It was a terrifying event I hadn't experienced before. Mikhail was sitting up front, watching White Cloud hurtling toward the ground while I was busy stabilizing.

I added more power to the engine, and we started to regain altitude as I moved us away from the ridge. Only then did I manage to figure out what probably happened.

"I think we were too close to the ridge, and strong downdrafts from the ridge's edge hit us, knocking down our right wings," I replied, struggling to sound calm. A few more minutes of flying passed before I fully recovered and regained my focus.

From then on, I made sure not to get too close to the

ridges. The length of the leg I had planned was about 390 kilometers in a straight line (bearing one-nine-one). If it had been in a straight line, it would have taken only three hours. In practice, while flying along the valleys to avoid climbing too high, it took a little more than three and a half hours, and we were approaching the lower limit of our fuel gauge.

The landscape we flew past looked like a postcard: mountains covered in green forests. Here and there, we saw patches of snow still lingering on the peaks. Valleys lined with small villages stretched between the ridges, all similar to each other—a square in the center of the village and a church with a spire, from which two roads often branch out, the village houses built along them. You could almost always find cultivated fields between the villages. Most of the valleys had nice streams running through them. If I lived in one of these villages, I'd probably go fishing a lot.

Mikhail announced that he thought we were about to cross the Slovak border into Hungary. He said he recognized a large settlement that appeared on the map on the Slovak side, near the border. I knew the landing site was about 50 kilometers into Hungary, which is roughly 25 minutes of flying. I needed to prepare for that. The mountains had cleared, and a wide plain stretched out before us.

# Chapter 44

"The town of Boldva is on the right, and Miskolc is straight ahead."

This was the place where we planned to land at the end of this leg of the flight. It's about 150 kilometers from the capital, Budapest. About a month ago, I read in the newspaper that a Christian International Congress was expected to be held in Budapest today, with about 100,000 people attending. I assumed the police would be busy. The second reason I chose this airstrip was that it was far enough from the Ukrainian border. I hoped we wouldn't raise any suspicion by landing there.

The airstrip itself was a patch of green, trimmed vegetation that looked similar to the surrounding fields. What distinguished it was a lone hangar with a windsock on top. I circled once as usual and then made a perfect landing. As I taxied White Cloud toward the hangar, I saw a nearby fuel pump. I parked next to it, and Mikhail and I got out to stretch our legs. It seemed we were both relieved to feel solid ground under our feet.

A broad-shouldered man with round, red cheeks emerged from the hangar and walked toward us, swaying slightly. Mikhail turned to him in German and asked if he could refuel our plane.

We were both momentarily surprised when the man responded in perfect German, saying he would unlock the pump, but that we would have to refuel it ourselves. He didn't ask anything, and we didn't offer any information. After refueling and payment, he disappeared into the hangar and didn't come out again.

We're resting under the wing now, like we're White Cloud's chicks. The next planned leg will be similar in length to the one we just completed, about three hours of flying. It's 10:30 AM, and we have plenty of time to complete it, but based on yesterday's experience, the fatigue is accumulating and could lead to an accident. We need to make a decision.

"Will the flight be over mountainous terrain like what we just crossed, or is it easier terrain?" Mikhail asked.

"According to the map, the terrain looks pretty flat, but we'll have to cross the border from Hungary into Romania and, shortly after that, the border from Romania into Serbia. As far as I know, there are military planes stationed in border areas. It concerns me a bit, and it will require low-altitude flying. Beyond that, I don't foresee any problems," I replied.

It seemed the decision was made. We would continue the flight. We're getting ready to go soon.

## Serbia (Yugoslavia), Pancevo,[40] Tuesday, May 24, 1938

If I had known what still awaited us on the flight, I might've answered Mikhail differently, but I didn't know and hadn't really calmed down from what had happened to us earlier.

We took off southward toward the border between Hungary and Romania. We flew for about an hour and a half. Just before crossing the border, White Cloud's engine began to sputter, and the power dropped significantly. The plane seemed to stop in midair for a moment. I lowered the nose to gain speed, but I could barely keep it from dropping to a dangerous level where we would lose the ability to stay airborne.

To Mikhail's credit, he kept his cool and said nothing. He probably didn't need to. He realized what I realized. The engine was about to stop working at any moment.

I told him to look for a place to make an emergency landing. He chose a straight bank of a riverbed. I shut off the engine, which wasn't functioning anyway, closed the fuel valve and the electrical switch, and began descending toward the spot he pointed to.

The plane became uncooperative. It bucked from side to side, trying to roll the wings right or left, and I had to repeatedly adjust the stick and pedals. At one point, I thought we were on the verge of stalling and spinning. The sideways movement only worsened due to the hot air rising from the ground. Luckily, we managed to land before losing control.

I performed an emergency landing straight ahead, managing to keep the plane relatively level so that both front wheels touched down more or less simultaneously. White Cloud rolled quickly along the strip of grass we landed on and stopped just before a water channel that crossed our makeshift runway. White Cloud knew exactly where to stop.

I looked at my hands and saw that they were shaking.

After we got out of the plane, we checked it to see if any damage had been sustained. We were relieved to find none.

I ran my hands along White Cloud's fuselage. "Thank you for keeping us safe. What would we do without you?" I believe it can hear and understand.

"I suspect it's the fuel," Mikhail said, "After the engine cools down, I'll have to dismantle the carburetor and see what's going on there. Did you notice anything on your gauges before the engine stopped working?"

"No, nothing. It happened completely by surprise," my voice was still shaky.

We ate quietly while waiting for the engine to cool. We didn't talk. We both knew how close we had come to crashing. Again.

Mikhail took out the spare parts and tools bag he brought with him and worked for about two hours dismantling and inspecting the carburetor. He's a true professional, and my confidence in him only rises. "It was the fuel; it was really dirty. I had to replace the filter," he said finally. "Let's hope we can make it to our next stop with this fuel."

We hurried to take off before anyone in the area decided they wanted to find out what we were doing there. We crossed the border into Romania and flew in its airspace for only twenty minutes before crossing the border into Serbia.

For the next fifty minutes, we flew very low toward Pancevo. Even before we arrived, we had already spotted the converging Sava and Danube rivers, and the city of Belgrade on their other side. I hoped that despite the proximity to the city, luck would continue to be on our side and we wouldn't run into trouble with the authorities, but when I spotted the control tower, I realized the chances were slim.

Once we landed, even before we shut off the engine, a vehicle with a uniformed man appeared in front of us. The driver signaled for us to follow him, and we drove to a parking spot where a few other planes were already parked.

As soon as we were on the ground, the man approached me in German (he probably saw the Fire Cross and assumed we were Germans) and asked me to accompany him and bring the flight and plane documents. I took a seat in the vehicle, and the driver didn't say a word to me for the entire ride. I was very tense and tried to prepare myself, but I didn't really know what to prepare for. Mikhail stayed behind with White Cloud.

I was taken to an office at the base of the control tower and told to wait. The office was large. On the walls hung aerial photographs of the area and a map of Eastern Europe. Out of the corner of my eye, I tried to retrace the flight path we'd taken yesterday and today, when a man in his sixties entered the room, wearing the same uniform as the driver. He introduced himself as Jordán, the control tower manager, and invited me to sit across from him. He asked in German why we had landed in Pancevo.

I presented the aircraft logbook and used our cover story, speaking in German myself.

"Why didn't we receive an official flight plan?" Jordán asked.

"You should have received it a while ago; I wasn't handling it; it was the duty of the tour organizers from Berlin." I made every effort to remain calm.

"I see you have a Latvian tail number, so it's clear you're not pirates or anything like that."

Thank God I didn't listen to Mikhail's advice to erase our tail number; maybe it would save us now.

Jordán continued, "If you say it was sent a long time ago, it's quite possible that the flight plan is buried somewhere in the pile of papers with the flight coordination officer here. He's not a very organized person. I'll talk to him about it tomorrow."

I nodded in agreement and remained silent.

"When are you flying out of here, and what's your next destination?"

"Tomorrow at dawn, we'll continue southward, probably to Ihtiman in Bulgaria."

"Nice place. Keep in mind that if you land on runway 320, you must be careful with the approach due to the ridge southwest of the airfield, but if you don't have the flight plan paperwork, that's not good. I'd better prepare the proper paperwork for you so, at least within Serbia, you'll have that sorted."

I couldn't have asked for more. Jordán opened one of the drawers in his desk, pulled out some forms, and began filling them out. From time to time, he asked me for details about the plane and our passports.

After a short while, he looked proudly at the documents and remarked, "That's it; now you're all set. I'll keep the original, and you take the copy with you."

After we finished, he told me he studied air traffic control management in Germany and that he admired German orderliness.

I asked him if he could help us refuel, and he agreed. He called the driver who had brought me and exchanged a few words with him in their language. The driver nodded and signaled for me to join him. We drove back to the plane. Before I got off, I signaled to Mikhail that everything was okay because he looked very tense.

"I took the time to clean the carburetor again," he said after I told him about our good fortune.

Shortly after, an old truck arrived with a fuel tank attached to its rear, and after Mikhail confirmed that the fuel was suitable for White Cloud, we refilled our tank.

The sun began to set, and we wondered where we could find something to eat. I had forgotten to ask Jordán about that. While we were thinking about it, I saw him arrive in a vehicle with the driver.

I was afraid he had discovered our ruse, but he got out with a pleased look and didn't seem threatening at all.

"How about you come to my place for dinner tonight?

I even thought of calling the Latvian embassy in Belgrade to see if the ambassador would like to join you for dinner."

I was horrified. That was the last thing we needed.

I didn't want to offend him or raise his suspicion, so I explained that we planned to take off very early and if we went out to eat, we wouldn't have enough time to complete our flight preparations. It seemed Jordán was convinced, and he graciously offered to bring us food from a good restaurant he knew in Pancevo. He was shocked when he realized we planned to sleep in a tent under the wing and suggested we use the rest room next to his office in the control tower instead.

In the end, we refueled, received an official flight plan for the next leg, ate well, and now, once I finish writing, we'll go to sleep. I think Mikhail already is. He brought an alarm clock and set it for 5:30 AM By the time Jordán arrives tomorrow morning, we'll be long gone.

# Chapter 45

### Turkey, Canakkale,[41] Wednesday, May 25, 1938

There was no one around when we took off. From now on, we would be flying southeast the entire time.

Right at the start of the flight, I climbed to nearly 3,000 meters. The flight plan I had made gave me confidence, at least for this leg. I knew we would pass several high mountain ranges along the way and preferred to avoid them. It was very cold at that altitude, but we prepared for it and were dressed warmly.

I reminded Mikhail that there's less oxygen at such an altitude.

The first leg of the route was about 370 kilometers (bearing one-three-six) from Pancevo to Ihtiman in Bulgaria. We flew at an average speed, not too high, to conserve fuel. I estimated that the first leg would take about three hours.

At first, the landscape was flat farmland, divided into countless separate plots, creating a kind of patchwork quilt stretching to the horizon. Later, the landscape became mountainous, forested, and etched with small valleys.

"Take a look, at your two o'clock, there's a plane flying not far from us," I suddenly heard Mikhail's voice. He pointed in that direction. I strained my eyes and managed to see it, even the swastika marked on it. It was a German reconnaissance plane that I had seen in the photos Mr. Ozols had shown Yuli and I in the identification course. I silently thanked him for it. Any reminder of Yuli still hurt, as did the thought that Edvins was dead.

Thankfully, the German continued on his way. I assume it was in the area due to the cooperation between Serbia and Germany.

The border area between Serbia and Bulgaria wasn't clearly marked and didn't have any distinctive features, so we could only be sure we had crossed it once we saw a wide, flat valley that we identified on the map. In hindsight, I think the border was close to where we saw the German plane.

"Ihtiman is straight ahead," Mikhail announced. "It's in a kind of triangular valley between three ridges."

Now that I could see Ihtiman from the air, I understood Jordán's warning about the ridge during landing, but when I circled the airstrip and spotted the windsock, I realized that the landing would be in the opposite and more favorable direction.

We landed, refueled, and took off. Just like that. The second leg, from Ihtiman to Canakkale, was a completely different story.

"Ladies and gentlemen, it's lunchtime. We have a half-hour break, and then we'll continue to the end," Rubin lowered the booklet to the table. He stood up.

"Just a little longer," Lilly smiled at Mark.

"Yes," he replied, "just a little longer, and we'll find out what surprise he has in store for us."

"A good one. I have a good feeling," Lilly said.

"You know, Dad never surprised us in a good way. I really don't know what to expect."

"Dad loved us, Mark. In his tough and uncompromising way, he loved us. You know that."

Half an hour later, Rubin picked up the booklet again. "One last time," he smiled at everyone. "So, where were we? Yes, from Ihtiman to Canakkale. Here we go."

First of all, we entered a region with a completely different climate than what I'm used to. We flew over a sea much warmer than the Baltic, and therefore the weather around it is also different. Since I don't know what the weather forecasts are, I expected surprises.

Secondly, we have entered Turkish airspace.

From what I managed to hear about Cukurs' experiences, I know the Turks are very tough and militaristic. Entering their airspace without an approved flight plan could end very badly for us. I'm very worried about that and can't wait to leave, but it'll take time. We have at least three nights to spend in Turkey, and I hope we get through it safely.

The second leg we planned for today was about 340 kilometers (bearing one-three-eight). I estimated the flight would take about two hours and forty-five minutes, if there were no surprises.

At first, we flew over a landscape similar to what we saw in the first leg, so I made sure to maintain the same altitude. The further south we flew, the more humid the air became. The engine was working harder and its temperature rose. It was still within the acceptable range, but I realized I had to start monitoring that gauge more frequently.

Suddenly, we saw the Aegean Sea, a huge patch of bright blue. The sun was above us and the water sparkled like a giant mirror. It was beautiful.

Two mountain ranges led directly to the sea. The highest

point between them marked the border between Bulgaria and Greece. I began to descend and fly between the ridges rather than over them, hoping to stand out less this way. As we descended and got closer to the sea, we saw a strip of coastline between the mountains and the water, glistening in white.

We were about to fly over the sea for the first time. On the other side of the strait, 86 kilometers away, or forty-two minutes of flying, Turkey awaited. I set the flight altitude to 3,200 feet (about 1,000 meters) and went over the emergency water landing briefing with Mikhail again.

We crossed the coastline not far from a town named Petrota on the map. To our right, we saw the islands of Samothrace and Imbros (Gökçeada), which helped us navigate to the point where we wanted to cross the coastline on the other side, at the Gallipoli Peninsula in Turkey.

We crossed another strait and saw our destination, the city of Canakkale and its small aerodrome. In fact, we had no choice but to land there because the mountain ridges came right up to the Aegean coast, leaving no other place to land.

When we were still over Gallipoli, I tuned White Cloud's radio to the control tower frequency and reported my tail number and landing direction before anyone could respond. To my relief, there was no response at all, and I hoped no one was in the control tower. After circling once, we landed on a compacted dirt runway.

The unfamiliar heat and humidity overwhelmed me. I was sweating under the warm clothes and gloves. I taxied White Cloud to the parking area where two other biplanes were already stationed, and shut off the engine. I didn't know what to expect, but hoped for the best.

## Chapter 46

The control tower and the adjacent office building appeared empty and abandoned. Despite this, I preferred to approach them on my own initiative rather than wait for someone to come to us. I entered the ground-level office and approached the first person I saw.

A large window overlooked the airstrip, and I assume he saw me when I walked towards him. He was sitting behind a small office desk, dressed in a light-colored suit, and looked like he had been waiting for me. A map of Turkey hung on the wall behind him, and a black metal fan on the ceiling rotated slowly on its axis, creaking loudly and stirring the air. I didn't see anyone else, nor did I hear anyone in the adjacent room. The man's face was long and unshaven, with a mustache over his upper lip. I noticed a ring with a large ruby on one of his hands.

I addressed him in German, but he gestured that he didn't understand. He asked me something in English, and I stammered, "No, no," in response. I continued in German, but he stopped me and again motioned that he didn't understand.

I managed to make out that he was asking for the flight plan, so I handed him the one Jordán had prepared for us. I added in broken English that the rest of the flight plan was supposed to have been sent by the organizers of the international tour from Berlin.

Unlike what happened with Jordán, the man stood up and started shouting at me in Turkish, waving the flight plan in his hand. I didn't understand what he was saying, but I could guess.

When he realized I didn't understand a word, he repeated the words "flight plan" several times and gestured with his head and hands that the flight plan I had given him was not acceptable. Since I knew that relations between Germany and Turkey were supposed to be good, I kept repeating in German that the flight plan was supposed to have been sent directly from Berlin.

It was a dialogue of the deaf.

Eventually, as I stood there with sweat dripping from my forehead, despite the fan, the aggression in his voice subsided. He gestured for me to sit down and sat down himself. Then he asked for my passport. I presented my passport and the aircraft logbook to show him that I was from Latvia and that the plane also bore a Latvian tail number.

He flipped through the logbook, occasionally pointing to some detail and asking me what it was. The more I explained in a mix of English and German, the more it seemed to calm him down. After a few minutes, he told me in English that our entry into Turkey was illegal and that he would have to call the police. The word "police" is the same in every language and just as frightening. I struggled to maintain a calm demeanor.

He pulled a form from a document tray on his desk, written in both English and Turkish. I recognized the title: it was a request for a flight plan. Then he spread his hands out to the sides, holding my passport in one hand and the form in the other. When he moved the hand holding the passport, he said the word "police," and when he moved the hand holding the form, he said a word I didn't understand, but now I know was "baksheesh."

I realized he was asking for a bribe. He didn't relent until I asked him with my hands how much he wanted. He asked for ten pounds. He said, "British, British." That sounded like a lot. I had no choice, but if I was going to pay, I wanted to get the same from him as I got from Jordán.

I walked around the desk and approached the map of Turkey behind him. I tapped on various locations leading southward, and after each tap, I repeated the words "flight plan," "flight plan," while miming writing motions with one hand and pointing to the form he held with the other.

I saw a glimmer of understanding in his eyes. He asked me with his fingers how many flight plans I wanted, and I signaled five. His face fell, and he shook his head in refusal, repeating the word "no" in English. I asked him how many he was willing to provide, and he signaled two. I indicated that I wanted four. He hesitated for a moment, then smiled at me and said, "Okay," motioning for me to sit down again. He pulled three more blank flight plan forms from the tray on his desk and gestured for me to fill in the names of the places where I wanted to land.

I took a folded sheet of paper from my pocket, where I had written down the places I planned to land and the expected landing dates. He began reviewing the list, lightly nodding his head and muttering to himself in Turkish, marking a checkmark at the end of each line. When he reached the last airstrip I had listed, he started speaking rapidly in Turkish, trying to explain something to me. I signaled that I didn't understand, so he got up and went to the map. He read aloud the name of the last airstrip, pointed to it, and then marked an X over it. Instead, he pointed to another location, further south, and gave a thumbs up, indicating that it was a better place. The distance between them wasn't significant, and after I nodded in agreement, he proceeded to fill out the forms.

After he finished, he pulled out a stamp from a drawer, stamped all the forms, and signed them. Then he reached out towards me and repeated the words "ten pounds." He still held my passport in his hand.

I gestured that I needed to go to the plane and would return shortly. I walked quickly and retrieved two five-pound notes from the hidden pocket. Mikhail asked what was happening. "I'll explain in a moment," I told him, and hurried back to the Turk. At that point I wasn't sure if I was sweating from the heat or the pressure.

He waited for me in the exact position I had left him. I showed him the bills and requested the passport and forms. For a moment, we stood there, facing each other, without moving.

Finally, I placed one five-pound note on the desk, and he handed me my passport. Then I placed the second note down and received the stack of signed forms. The deal was successfully completed.

The Turk walked around the desk, hugged me by the shoulders, and introduced himself as Ahmet. "Miku," I said, adding the word "Petrol," to which he nodded in agreement. I then rubbed my stomach and said, "Hotel." Ahmet began to laugh and got up from his seat. He motioned for me to follow him and left the office. He led me to a fuel tanker on the other side of the building, gestured for me to get into the truck, and then got into the driver's seat. We drove towards the plane.

We found Mikhail leaning against one of the Flamingo's wheels, almost entirely undressed and dripping with sweat. Ahmet and Mikhail introduced themselves and shook hands. Afterward, Mikhail refueled. Ahmet wrote down the amount we needed to pay for the fuel and left with the tanker. I updated Mikhail. He patted me on the back, and it was clear that a huge weight had been lifted off his shoulders as well.

I returned to the office and paid for the fuel. Ahmet put the money in a cash register located in one of the office cabinets and even exchanged some of my sterling notes for Turkish currency.

He then grabbed my arm and said the word "food" in English. I nodded, even though I didn't fully understand what he was saying, and went back to Mikhail.

A short while later, Ahmet arrived in a private car and motioned for us to get in. We drove to the office, where he laid out a large spread of meats and side dishes on the table. He tied a large cloth napkin around his neck and began devouring everything in sight, gesturing for us to join him. It was one of the best meals of my life!

Tonight, we will sleep on mattresses that Ahmet laid out for us in the room adjacent to his office; after he left, we spread them out on the floor and stretched out on them. As I'm writing in the diary, Mikhail just turned to me and asked, in a completely indifferent tone, "Did Yuli ever give you a reason for why she broke up with you?"

I was completely surprised, and it took me a moment to gather myself.

"No. To this day, I have no idea. I still keep asking myself why. She just started distancing herself from me, and in the end, she made it clear that it was over between us."

I waited to see his reaction. Mikhail said nothing, so I added, "Did she tell you anything? You kept in touch with her, didn't you?" The thought of it still pains me.

"I didn't ask her, and she didn't offer any details on that matter."

I was disappointed. I don't know why he brought up this painful subject, and my anger towards him is growing. Why did he continue to stay in touch with her after we broke up?

In the end, I couldn't hold back. "Was it serious between you two?"

I knew I was asking a very loaded question. I think Mikhail sensed it in my tone as well.

"Of course not, I knew I was planning to leave Latvia anyway..."

The answer only made me angrier. He was very vague about the nature of their relationship.

"...Just remember, not everything is as it seems."

I froze. That's what Yuli said the last time we met. Even now, I have no idea what she meant, but I prefer not to delve into it. I'm so tired, but the conversation still bothers me. I wish he hadn't brought up this topic at all.

# Chapter 47

## Turkey, near a village called Boztepe, Thursday, May 26, 1938

Mikhail wasn't in the room in the morning. The mattress he slept on was placed in the corner. For a moment, I thought it might be related to our conversation before we fell asleep. I had calmed down, but the pain related to Yuli was still there, deep inside me.

I placed my mattress on top of his, gathered my belongings, and left the room. Ahmet was already sitting in his office and greeted me. It was barely 6 AM I returned his greeting and stepped outside to check on White Cloud. Mikhail was already there, working on it.

Ahmet called me over and offered a cup of steaming hot coffee, without milk. I'm not used to drinking it that way, but the smell of fresh coffee was intoxicating, and I couldn't resist. He also offered some cookies. They weren't particularly tasty, but I ate them anyway. It was better to have something in my stomach before the flight, especially since the food we brought with us was nearly gone.

I tried to explain to him that I needed meteorological data, but he didn't understand. We would have to fly without any weather forecasts. I took some coffee and cookies for Mikhail, thanked Ahmet, and we said our goodbyes.

Mikhail was energetic and very happy with the coffee and cookies I brought, but after tasting one, he refused to eat any more.

"I think they've gone bad," he said. "They taste awful."

He warned me that the engine had been working hard in the past few days and that he was concerned the pipes around it were starting to wear out. "I have replacement pipes, but the engine needs more rest," he said. We decided we would fly less today. White Cloud deserved a break too.

We debated how to dress for the flight. I preferred dressing warmly and sweating rather than risking us getting cold and suffering from hypothermia.

We took off quickly and headed southeast. The leg we were embarking on was very mountainous, so I climbed to about 4,000 feet. It didn't take long to realize that I needed to ascend much higher. The mountains we were crossing were tall. I climbed to 9,500 feet (about 3,900 meters). It was a good thing we decided to dress warmly.

The leg was about 400 kilometers (bearing one-three-four) from Canakkale to an airstrip near a village called Isiklar.[42]

After about three hours of flying, we spotted the peak of the last ridge before Isiklar. It rises to over 4,000 meters and gleams with snow. We couldn't reach such heights, so I maneuvered around the peak to its western side, towards Lake Salda, approaching the village of Isiklar from the west.

After days of flying over landscapes painted in shades of green, we found ourselves exposed to an endless plain of desert-yellow.

We couldn't locate the airstrip when we circled above the village. There was nothing there except a dirt road that crossed one of the nearby fields. We assumed that was the airstrip. I couldn't determine the wind direction either. I briefed Mikhail that we would land from east to west, assuming the wind was coming from the Aegean Sea and the lake.

Fortunately, the wind was actually a light southerly breeze, and the landing was smooth, although we kicked up a lot of dust.

By the time we had shut down the engine, villagers, both adults and children, had already gathered around us. They surrounded White Cloud and touched it in curiosity. It's possible some of them were seeing an airplane for the first time in their lives. When we stepped out, we were immediately surrounded by a crowd of children who touched us as if we were moon men.

One of the adults spoke to us in Turkish. I gestured that I didn't understand. Mikhail addressed him in German and then in broken English. It seemed that English was more common here. Mikhail told him that we had just arrived from Canakkale and were looking for fuel and something to eat. He nodded, shouted a few instructions, and offered us to sit with him under the wing.

A woman dressed in a long black dress, her face fully covered, appeared from somewhere with a type of flat, round bread, placed some kind of cheese on it, and offered it to us. We were hungry enough to eat without asking too many questions. The cheese was very sour, but the thin bread wrapping it was tasty. Another boy arrived holding a kind of leather sack filled with water. I tasted the water, and it was decent. It was fresh. I drank eagerly from the sack until I couldn't drink anymore. Mikhail also got one and drank from it with great thirst.

We stuck to the international tour story, and the English speaker translated our words to those around us. They showed great interest in the plane and what we had to say.

After about an hour, a small cart arrived, carrying several metal fuel cans. A young boy expertly maneuvered the donkey that pulled the cart.

Mikhail opened one of the cans and smelled the fuel. "It's not exactly the fuel we need, but it'll do. There's no alternative anyway."

We got up and refueled. We offered to pay, but the locals refused. We thanked them warmly and prepared to take off.

Our next destination was an airstrip near a small village called Boztepe, not far from a city called Antalya on the Mediterranean coast. Compared to the first flight of the day, this leg was supposed to be relatively easy—a short flight of about 130 kilometers (bearing one-two-four), just over an hour.

However, shortly after takeoff, we encountered fragmented clouds that grew denser until they formed a continuous cloud layer that blocked the entire route. I remembered the meteorology lesson given by Janis Dibovski, which mentioned the existence of this phenomenon, but I had obviously never encountered it in flat Latvia. We had to make a decision: turn back to Isiklar or try to climb above the layer of cloud. Mikhail left the decision up to me.

I think accumulated fatigue had dulled my senses, and I chose the latter option. I found myself climbing through a screen of thick, bright cloud, completely blind and navigating only by compass. From time to time, there were small breaks in the cloud through which we could see the ground. If there had been mountains on the route, I have no doubt we would've crashed into one of them. It was a clear misjudgment on my part.

Eventually, after estimating that I had a rough idea of our general location, I decided to carefully descend through the cloud to find the Mediterranean coastline.

The altimeter needle showed ever decreasing values and, as we descended, my anxiety levels rose. I knew that once the gauge ran out of altitude to show, we would be met by the solid, merciless ground.

I hesitated. Should we climb back above the cloud or continue descending, risking crashing into the ground? And if we were to descend, how far should we go? A jumble of thoughts raced through my mind in fractions of a second.

In the end, at an altitude of only 1,500 feet — a mere 500 meters above sea level — and before I could fully decide how to proceed, we emerged from the base of the cloud and found ourselves directly above the city of Antalya.

A great sense of relief washed over me. I could almost hear Edvins' voice in my head, saying that there are countless flight situations you can't prepare for or anticipate, and that all you can rely on are the pilot's skills, knowledge, and gut instincts. This time, I had failed in my judgment, and we were very lucky. I hope that next time I'll show more professionalism.

Navigating from there was easy. Mikhail quickly oriented himself on the map, found Boztepe, and we landed.

We have enough fuel for the first leg of tomorrow's flight, which will run parallel to the coast. It looks like we'll sleep in the tent under the wing tonight and take off early in the morning. Just to be safe, I took the pistol out from the pocket under my seat. Mikhail took it and said it would be better if he slept with it. I think he's right.

# Chapter 48

**Not far from the Turkish-Syrian border, between the villages of Suvatli and Sacakli,[43] Friday, May 27, 1938**

Today's journey was particularly challenging, involving three refueling stops, flying close to the highest mountains I've ever seen, and over the Mediterranean Sea.

We flew along the coast heading east, with the vast, endless, blue expanse of the Mediterranean on our right, and the towering, intimidating Taurus Mountains on our left, which we couldn't cross over.

Landing on a short agricultural airstrip in the small village of Buyukeceli[44] was difficult. The runway was on a sort of peninsula, or strip of land jutting out from the mountains into the sea. The approach would be difficult no matter which direction I chose. I had to get close to the mountain slopes surrounding the airstrip. Air currents buffeted White Cloud right up to the actual landing. I gripped the stick tightly and constantly used the pedals to stabilize the plane until I felt the wheels touch the ground.

Taking off from there after a quick refuel (there was no suitable fuel, so we settled for regular fuel and hoped for the best) wasn't easy either, but once we took off and headed toward the sea, the turbulent air currents from the mountains faded away.

The next leg of the flight was to an aerodrome in a place called Adana. The route there was along the coastline again, and at one point, we flew over a small bay filled with boats of various kinds. Adana is quite a town, with a control tower and a long asphalt runway at its aerodrome. In fact, it was the longest runway I had landed on so far. Armed with a signed flight plan from Ahmet, I felt secure.

An airport official approached us after we shut off the engine. He eyed White Cloud and the Fire Cross emblem, and asked in Turkish to see the flight plan. After my experience with Ahmet, I already recognized the words and handed him the signed form.

The official began to go over it. I glanced at Mikhail, whose tension was visible in his eyes. I didn't want the official to notice, so I asked Mikhail to start preparations for refueling. Eventually, the official returned our flight plan and cleared us to refuel.

Landing in Adana held additional significance for me. Cukurs had landed here as well on his way to Tokyo. Our journey and that of this incredible aviator intersected for a moment. From here, he continued east, while we will continue on our southeast route.

We had about an hour of flight left, during which we crossed the Gulf of Iskenderun, passed the ridge of hills on the eastern side of the gulf, and then descended toward our endpoint for the day, a small airstrip between two villages in the middle of a large, flat valley filled with patches of agricultural fields in various colors.

It was a narrow dirt strip adjacent to a wide dirt road connecting the two villages of Suvatli and Sacakli, marked with a lone pole with a torn windsock. Without it, I might've landed on the wide dirt road instead.

Aside from that, there was nothing on the airstrip, though during our landing approach, I spotted a gas station right outside the village of Suvatli.

As we landed, we kicked up a large cloud of dust that followed us even as we came to a stop, covering us and White Cloud with dust and sand.

Shortly after we touched down, we undressed. The heat was unbearable, and the humidity was particularly high. We were sweaty, covered in dust, and that's on top of having not showered or shaved for five consecutive days.

The total distance we covered today was nearly 540 kilometers. In the past five days, we had crossed all of Eastern Europe, and today, finally, we reached our first stop in the Middle East. One more day of flying and we would reach our final destination.

As had happened when we arrived in Isiklar, curious villagers from Suvatli soon approached us — men, women, and children. They looked different from the Turks we had met so far, and dressed differently. Their clothing reminded me of the figures in church paintings depicting Jesus and his followers.

An elderly man with a beard, dressed in a kind of long, thin robe, approached us and extended his hand in greeting. I shook it and introduced myself and Mikhail in German. To my surprise, he understood and even spoke to me in broken German. It turns out he had accompanied German officers who had stayed in this area in previous years. He introduced himself as Kemal.

He asked why we had come here, and we used the cover story again. I told him that we had just arrived from Adana and asked where we could get fuel and food.

"I am the head of the village," Kemal said. "My father was the head of the village, and so was my grandfather.

It's been our family's role for generations. You will be our guests, and you don't have to worry about food. We'll also bring you fuel from our gas station. My eldest son, Zeki, will take care of it, and my son, Aslan, will stay here to guard your plane until you depart."

We cleaned the windshields, seats, and dashboard of the dust that had accumulated on them. By the time we finished, Kemal's son, Zeki, arrived with a few fuel cans. Mikhail indicated that it was low-quality fuel, but we had no choice. We poured the fuel into the tank through a cloth rag, hoping it would filter out the dirt.

Kemal supervised the entire process, and when we were done, he invited us to his home. We are at his house currently. Well, it's not exactly a house by our standards. There are no furnishings, just carpets laid on the ground with cushions and small tables on top. The bathroom is outside. There's also a sort of bathtub and a tap nearby, with a large metal bucket underneath.

Apparently, we smelled so bad that Kemal, out of politeness, offered us the chance to wash up. Mikhail immediately accepted, and despite my embarrassment, I followed. One of Kemal's children filled a metal bucket with water for each of us. The water was cold, but we washed ourselves regardless and rinsed off the dirt from the past few days. We put on the same dirty clothes afterward, but felt lighter, almost floating pleasantly. I never thought a wash could bring me such joy.

There's no kitchen in Kemal's house. I don't know where they cook exactly, but we were treated like royalty and served a meal we'll never forget.

The feast began at 7 PM and lasted about three hours, lit by oil lamps. Kemal's daughters served us an endless variety of dishes — different types of pastries, including bread with a red paste that I think was made from peppers, various salads made from vegetables and seasoned with spices I didn't recognize, meatballs in tomato sauce, meat called kebab with yogurt or with eggplant roasted over hot coals, and a stew of mashed beans. There were more dishes; I just can't remember them all.

During the meal, Kemal told us, in his broken German, that there was political unrest and a lot of tension in this area. If I understood him correctly, some of the people here want the region to remain part of Syria under the French mandate, others want it to become a province of Turkey, and there were also those who don't want either and instead want to establish an independent state called Hatay. I realized the topic was very sensitive and wanted to leave the area without getting entangled with the local authorities. From this point on, we no longer had a formal flight plan, making our situation dangerous in that regard.

For dessert, we were served various types of cookies, most of them spiced. I had never encountered such foods.

When Mikhail politely asked Kemal who deserved the thanks for these wonderful dishes, he said his wife had prepared everything, but we hadn't seen her at all.

By the end of the meal, I felt exhaustion overtaking me. I apologized to Kemal when he offered us a smoke, telling him that we wanted to go to bed as we had a long day ahead of us. His children quickly laid out mattresses and moved to another area. I'll sleep in my clothes with the diary beside me.

## Not far from the Turkish-Syrian border, between the villages of Suvatli and Sacakli, Friday, May 28, 1938

I woke up in the middle of the night to the sound of metal walls shaking violently. At first, I didn't understand where I was. A strong wind was raging outside. Suddenly, I remembered White Cloud left outside without any tie-downs.

"Mikhail, get up quickly," I called out, shaking his shoulder.

"What? What happened?"

"We have to get to White Cloud and tie it down; there's a very strong wind outside."

We ran towards the plane in the dark. From a distance, we could already see it had shifted from its position and had been pushed slightly to the side. It was only a matter of time before it would flip over. Kemal's son, Aslan, was lying on the ground next to it, fast asleep. The noise of the wind and the plane's creaking didn't bother him at all.

Mikhail grabbed the propeller tightly and stabilized White Cloud. He managed to turn it by himself so that the nose faced the direction the wind was coming from. Meanwhile, I pulled out the tie-down ropes and tried to secure them to the ground with stakes. The ground was hard, and I didn't have a hammer (I hadn't considered this during our flight preparations). Mikhail let go of the propeller and, using a stone, managed to drive the stakes in and stabilize White Cloud against the wind. Mikhail's great strength was evident. I wouldn't have been able to do what he did.

We decided to stay by the plane. We lay down on the bare ground and fell asleep until dawn.

When I opened my eyes, I saw that the wind had completely died down, but the village was covered in a thick layer of fog. The implication was clear. We wouldn't be able to take off.

The fog only started to lift in the late afternoon, too late to start a long flight and make it to our destination before nightfall. We decided to postpone until tomorrow morning. A great disappointment.

I wanted to show my gratitude to Kemal for his hospitality and offered to take him on a short flight. He refused firmly, but his son Aslan wanted to go. I took off with him for a short flight above the flat valley that surrounded us. This caused a great deal of excitement around us. To be precise, the excitement was mostly around Mikhail, who managed to capture everyone's attention, played with the children who gathered around him, and laughed with them all the time.

We continued to stay here for the rest of the day and once again enjoyed dinner with Kemal, though this time the meal was more modest. We informed him that tonight we would sleep by the plane and take off at first light. Kemal and Aslan accompanied us, and we parted with a warm embrace.

"Do you want to see something interesting?" Mikhail asked me when we were finally alone.

I was surprised. Since our last conversation about Yuli, we hadn't had any heart-to-heart talks that weren't related to the flight or our journey.

"Yeah, sure."

Mikhail pulled a newspaper clipping from his bag, which was folded several times. He spread it out on the ground. The letters were strange and unfamiliar to me. They looked as though they were written from right to left.

"What language is this newspaper in?"

"It's a newspaper from Palestine that I got when I was

in Austria," he explained, barely concealing his pride. "It's in Hebrew. It's a very ancient language that has been reborn."

He pointed to a headline. "You write Hebrew from right to left, unlike Latvian or German."

"You know how to read this language?"

"A little, from the Jewish school I attended. It's the language everyone speaks in Palestine today, so once we get there, I'll learn it easily."

"But there are also Arabs there, right? I mean, we've already talked about how there have been a lot of problems with them recently. Do they speak Hebrew too?"

"I suppose not, but it's our land, the home of the Jews. I'm sure we'll manage to sort things out with them in the end."

Mikhail's anticipation of a new life, full of substance and purpose, was contagious. He managed to make me want to reach this land already and get to know it.

# Chapter 49

**Northern Palestine, near the border between the British Mandate and the French Mandate for Syria and Lebanon, Sunday, May 29, 1938**

We took off as planned. Mikhail and I wanted to get out of there before the local police heard about us after spending two days in that place.

We knew we were roughly four hours of flight away from Palestine. Last night, Mikhail refueled again with Zeki's help, and we had enough fuel for three and a half hours. We knew we would have to land at least once more to refuel.

According to the map, today's flight would take us over high mountainous terrain and then over the mountains of Lebanon. So, we planned to fly through the valleys between the mountains. We marked a series of waypoints according to prominent terrain features, like the Orontes River, its fork, and large settlements that we assumed we would see from the air.

We climbed to an altitude of 4,000 feet, and I maintained a speed of about 130 kilometers per hour to avoid wasting fuel. The air was clear in the early morning, and visibility was excellent. The route spread out beneath us, and there was no need for a map. We flew southeast, with Mikhail guiding me along the course of the Orontes River. I knew the Mediterranean Sea was to the west of us, but the mountains hid it from view.

I was very excited about us nearing the end of our journey. I can only assume Mikhail was no less excited, but we barely spoke during the flight.

From time to time, I heard him mutter the names of various settlements that he tried to identify along the way.

After an hour and a quarter of flying, Mikhail said, "I see a large settlement and lake. I think it's the lake near the city of Homs."

He was right, as usual, because shortly thereafter, we saw the fork in the Orontes River. Since we were flying from north to south, we saw everything in reverse, that is, opposite to the river's flow. This was a waypoint we had marked on the map because it indicated where we were supposed to direct White Cloud southward, enter the territory of the French Mandate, and fly along the Beqaa Valley in Lebanon until we reached the territory of the British Mandate.

"Should we continue flying or land and refuel?" he asked over the intercom.

"We still have enough. I suggest we continue to the next waypoint we marked on the map. That point should already be inside Palestine. Agreed?"

"Agreed. You're the pilot, you decide."

The Beqaa Valley widened, and I took advantage of this to move away from the mountains of Lebanon to our right. We already had a bad experience with winds blowing from the mountain peaks, and I didn't want that to happen again when we were so close to the end of our journey.

From above, we could see the scattered settlements on the slopes of the mountains on both sides. The Beqaa Valley itself was covered with agricultural fields and crisscrossed with numerous water channels.

About three hours after takeoff, I remembered to check my fuel gauge. I had been so focused on flying that I hadn't checked it since we passed Lake Homs.

"Mikhail, we barely have any fuel left. We urgently need to find a place to land. Start looking."

I saw him lift his head and start looking down.

But the Beqaa Valley was narrower in this area, the entire region was mountainous and rugged, and to our left, we clearly saw the summit of a high mountain, still snow-capped.

I climbed slightly, carefully, to avoid consuming too much fuel, so Mikhail could get a better view ahead.

Suddenly, a large body of water appeared before us on the horizon, greenish in color. The sun's rays reflected from afar on the water's surface. I didn't recall seeing a lake marked on the map in this area.

I knew that deep within the territory of Palestine, we were supposed to see the Mare Galilea, but not this early. A nagging fear began to creep in that we might have made a navigation error and were flying somewhere else entirely. That couldn't be; we had been flying south along the mountains and valleys the whole time; we couldn't possibly have veered off course, I tried to reassure myself.

"Mikhail, do you see that lake on the horizon? Do you have any idea what it is? Do you think that's Palestine?"

"It's not on the map, but I recognize the valley it's in. I think we're getting very close to the border. Another ten minutes of flight, I think, and we're over my promised land," I heard him respond in my headset, his voice calm and reassuring. A certain tone of excitement crept into his words.

I could feel my heartbeat in my throat.

"We're almost out of fuel; we have to land now. Find a

suitable place fast. Do you see those green fields before the lake? There's a village with houses with domed roofs not far from there, on the mountain slope. We'll try to find a place to land in the valley and walk to that village from there, but we need to start being more cautious now, so English planes don't spot us. We have to fly as low as possible from now on."

The temperature rose as we descended. The heat of the engine also increased, and the needle started to climb. That wasn't good. I hoped the engine wouldn't overheat too much, and that we would manage to land safely.

The lower we descended, the more White Cloud began to wobble, and I found it increasingly difficult to control. The thermals, air currents created as the ground warms up that rise rapidly upward, grew stronger as we approached the hot surface.

I learned in my meteorology classes that flying into an upward-moving air mass causes turbulence and that thermal columns can sometimes cause an aircraft to gain or lose significant altitude within seconds.

"In such situations, you have to be very focused and respond quickly, but carefully, to any wing drop," Janis Dibovski explained in that class. At the time, it sounded completely theoretical to me because Latvia's climate doesn't get anywhere near as hot as it does here.

Mikhail also felt the change, "Everything okay? Are you in control?"

He didn't sound worried, but with Mikhail, you could never really tell what he was feeling.

"Everything's fine. The turbulence is due to the hot air."

I hoped I was right. Controlling White Cloud became more difficult. I increased the speed, hoping it would stabilize it more, but this led to an increase in fuel consumption, and the fuel gauge approached zero.

We were very close to the lake, which looked more like a large swamp than the lakes in Latvia. The vegetation around it was dense, and I didn't see a soul anywhere.

"Have you found a place to land yet?"

"I'm looking, I'm looking, just a moment."

"I don't have a moment; we have to land."

He pointed toward a wheat field that, from the air, looked like it had just been harvested. I descended and circled around it. "Prepare for a hard landing. Are you securely fastened?"

"Yes."

Shortly thereafter, I set White Cloud down in the middle of the field, with only the fumes of fuel left in the tank. We landed at the very last possible moment. But we survived. The plane and we were both safe and sound. That's what counts.

"That's it, Mikhail, unbelievable, but we're probably in Palestine! We did it." I patted the dashboard of White Cloud and said, "Thank you. Thank you for bringing us here safely."

Mikhail didn't answer. Apparently, he had already disconnected from the intercom, but he heard me because he waved his hands excitedly and gave a thumbs-up, indicating that everything was okay.

We got out of White Cloud and embraced with incredible satisfaction and accomplishment.

After over three hours of flying, I was exhausted. The warm clothes, which were suitable for high altitude, were completely unsuitable for the ground. We took off our coats and other layers.

It was clear that we couldn't continue flying south immediately in this heat. The rising hot air currents would be strong and make flying very difficult, and besides, the engine could overheat beyond its limits. I had simply overlooked this issue during our preparations. I hadn't brought this heat into consideration at all.

A warm breeze caressed my skin and cooled me a bit. The dark soil stood out sharply against the golden color of the wheat remnants in the field around us. A strong, fresh smell of cut hay filled my nose. You could also smell the faint, unpleasant odor of stagnant water, probably from the lake or swamp, whatever it was. I estimated that we landed about two kilometers north of it.

The tension and stress of the past few days swelled and threatened to overwhelm me. We still hadn't reached our final destination, near the big city of Tel Aviv. Another flight awaited us. But the need to stop for a moment and rest was too strong for me.

Mikhail also looked tired, but his face was glowing, and his smile didn't budge. He bent down and picked up some soil from the ground, rolled it between his fingers, and repeated the word "Palestine" over and over. He looked happy.

We lay down in the shade, under the wing, and fell asleep.

I awoke to the sound of a loud noise near my ear. I opened my eyes and saw a man in his thirties leaning over me and looking at me. For a moment, I was scared; it seemed like he was attacking me, but that instinctive feeling quickly passed. I saw that he was extending his hand to help me up.

He said something and pointed to White Cloud and then to us, but I didn't understand a word of what he said. I looked towards Mikhail, but he was sound asleep.

Although I didn't understand what he was asking, I

assumed he was asking if the plane was ours, and I nodded in agreement.

There was something in his accent that made me think he knew Russian.

"Do you perhaps speak Russian?" I asked, and to my surprise, he answered that he did.

"Where did you come from?" he asked.

"We're part of an international reconnaissance mission to explore the Middle East. We just arrived from the north. What's this place called?"

The stranger started laughing. "I saw you land here at around nine AM It's two in the afternoon. You call that 'just arrived?' You've probably been sleeping here for a good few hours."

He paused for a moment, "Besides, I don't really buy that story of yours, and maybe it's better if you stop speaking Russian and start talking like a human being!"

I was stunned. He was speaking to me in Latvian.

Out of the corner of my eye, I saw that Mikhail had woken up, and his face also showed great surprise at hearing Latvian.

The stranger continued, "Nice to meet you. My name is Monya, Monya Gershtik, and I can recognize Russian with a Latvian accent from a kilometer away. I'm from Rezekne."[45]

Mikhail and I continued to stare at him, completely astonished, unable to say a word. Could this be a trap? Maybe the Latvian authorities received a message from the Turks about our route and reported it to the authorities, and this was a policeman who came to look for us? The thought crossed my mind for a moment, but I immediately dismissed the possibility. No one knew where we were flying to, so why would they search for us here, of all places?

The stranger who introduced himself as Monya saw that

we were still in complete shock and continued, "Why are you so surprised? There are many comrades here from Latvia. I arrived here six years ago, in '32. We're a large group at Kibbutz Afikim, much further south from here. My comrades asked me to survey this area because we want to establish a kibbutz here, and I'm looking for a suitable plot. So, what are you doing here?"

"We flew here from Latvia," I managed to say with difficulty.

"You're joking, right? You flew here in that? Just the two of you?"

"Yes. We left on Monday, almost a week ago, and arrived here this morning. But no one knows about it. At least no one knew about it when we left. We want to continue south now to the city of Tel Aviv."

Now it was Monya's turn to be surprised. I seized the moment, "Is this lake or swamp the Mare Galilea, I mean, the Sea of Galilee? Are we in Palestine?"

Monya began to laugh and replied that we were far from the Sea of Galilee, but indeed in a place called 'Galilee.' He added that we were not far from the border between the British and French Mandates, but within British territory, "So you're definitely in Palestine."

We felt safe enough and told him what we had gone through during the past few days. He found it hard to believe. I showed him the maps and the marked flight route, and he was very impressed.

"*Yeder gaun hat zayn shigeun*," Monya said.

Although I know German, I didn't understand his words.

Monya noticed this and asked if we spoke Yiddish. Mikhail replied that he understood a little but couldn't speak it.

He laughed. "*Nu*, you don't understand; every genius has his madness," he said in Latvian. "This is quite a story, what you did. No one in the group will believe me when I get back and tell them, and you even dared to come here with a swastika on your plane." I saw he was debating how to proceed. "And what now?"

"We're waiting for it to cool a bit and then take off towards Tel Aviv, but first, we need to refuel. Where can we get fuel? Do you think that village has some?" I pointed towards the village we saw from the air and added, "If there are multiple options, we'll choose the fuel with the highest octane. We need eighty-seven octane fuel."

Monya's face grew serious, and he said, "Don't go there, it's an Arab village. It's not a safe time to go there now, and it's not advisable. There's a lot of trouble these days with the Arabs here, a lot of incidents on the roads. You'd better wait here, and I'll go with my truck and bring you some; there's no gas station here. I'll bring whatever I can find. It'll take some time, but in any case, the heat will last for at least three more hours, so you have time."

Only then did I notice a battered, dirty truck parked not far from us.

And so, Monya drove off, and I took the time to finish describing what we'd done today in my diary.

He returned about two hours later with a full metal tank and sat down to chat with Mikhail. From the side, it seemed as if they had known each other for years. They searched for mutual acquaintances, chuckled about various things I didn't understand, and didn't stop talking. It was clear that something was bringing them together which I had no part in.

After a while, I mentioned that we should start preparing for the continuation of the flight, since it was getting late.

I estimated that we had about an hour of flight left,

but we would need to reserve enough time to find our destination, the new aerodrome near the city of Lydda. Mikhail and I planned to identify it from the air because we didn't have a marked location for it on the map.

Monya helped us refuel and, as we began preparing for the next leg of our journey, he bid us farewell, wished us luck, and drove off.

But when we tried to start White Cloud, we couldn't. Mikhail turned the propeller over and over, but the engine refused to start. The same damn problem again.

This time, we knew what the issue was and what we had to do.

"It'll take some time until I finish working on the fuel system. Maybe we should stay here tonight, get up early tomorrow morning, and fly south without any pressure?" Mikhail suggested.

After waiting on the sidelines as Mikhail and Monya chatted, I was impatient. I felt we were on the verge of completing the journey and that we could succeed in getting there in the time remaining before sunset.

"You're the pilot, you decide," Mikhail said as he began to disassemble and clean. "It'll take me about an hour until we're ready to fly again."

The sun had already disappeared beyond the mountains, and I knew we had to hurry. I used the time Mikhail was working on the plane to finish writing what had happened after Monya returned in my diary. The next time I write, we'll be at the end of our journey. I can't believe we made it.

# Chapter 50

Mark and Lilly looked at each other.
"Did you hear that, Lilly? It's Uncle Monya, Monya Gershtik, Dad's friend."

Lilly nodded, "Yes, this story is incredible. I'm shocked that Dad never mentioned any of this to us. Honestly, until now, I thought Uncle Monya was a relative of ours. What's also strange," Lilly continued, almost to herself, "is that as far as I can remember, Dad didn't know Yiddish, not even a little."

Mark shrugged.

"That's it, that was the last page of the translation," said Attorney Rubin as he closed the booklet, glancing at everyone present.

He took a deep breath and added, "I don't see any continuation. There's no sign of torn pages either. It seems this was the last page Miku managed to write in the diary before they took off towards Tel Aviv."

"I wonder why there's no more, why there's nothing written about what happened afterward," David said. It was the first time he had spoken since the meeting began in the morning. His words lingered in the air. No one had an answer.

Rubin closed the booklet and placed it on the table.

"Since we've finished reading the translation, I'll continue reading the cover letter and instructions."

He flipped through the pages until he reached the right spot, cleared his throat, and began to read.

We flew at an altitude of about a thousand feet (roughly three hundred and ten meters); high enough to feel safe and low enough that British planes wouldn't spot us. We passed over the Sea of Galilee, with Tiberias to our right, and continued along the Jordan River, which had much more water back then, though compared to the rivers we had crossed on the way here, it was but a tiny stream.

We knew there was a British squadron in Samaria, near a town called Jenin, so we tried to bypass it from the east. We passed the junction between the Jezreel Valley and our flight path, and saw a small settlement there. It seemed to be a new one.

Later, Mikhail identified the town of Beisan, and after a few minutes, we recognized the entrance to the Jiftlik Valley. This was the point we had predetermined to turn west.

"I know where the Jiftlik is," Daniel said, "It's in the northern Jordan Valley. But where is Beisan?"

"I think that's the original name of Beit She'an," Rubin replied, "but let's move on and save the questions for later, okay?"

We started climbing to a higher altitude to cross the Samarian Mountains. Once we ascended high enough, I recognized the Mediterranean Sea and the coastline. To my right, I saw a large settlement, probably Nablus.

The sun was already beginning to set, and the light was fading. We didn't have much time left, and I hoped we would make it to the Lydda aerodrome before dark.

And then the troubles started.

The engine suddenly began to sputter. The temperature and oil pressure gauges were just fine. I added power to pump more fuel. I hoped we didn't have a blockage from the fuel Monya brought us.

"What's happening?" I heard Mikhail, but before I could respond, the engine went back to normal.

We continued west. We passed Samaria and turned south. We were flying over the plains of Palestine. I saw lights of small and large settlements, both to my right and to my left.

I felt we were very close. All that was left was to identify Lydda aerodrome and land there.

But the engine started sputtering again. I added more power in the hope of improving fuel flow, but this time it didn't help and, after a brief moment, the engine stopped working. The vibration of the engine that had accompanied us for the entire flight ceased. The silence that fell on the cockpit was palpable.

I tried to restart the engine, but to no avail. The engine was dead, and we were in big trouble.

"Mikhail, find me a place to land, fast," I called out on the radio. There was no response. Of course. My attempts to restart the engine must have drained the battery, and once the engine stopped, we had no more electricity, so the intercom stopped working. I had to find a landing spot myself.

To the west, I saw a stream flowing towards the sea, with abundant vegetation on its banks. To the east, there was a village on the slopes of the Samarian Mountains, with a mosque minaret in its center. The village lights were clearly visible by now. I spotted an orchard with a wide path running through it, between the stream and the village. We were very low. I tapped Mikhail's head with the emergency landing sign. He signaled back that he understood and immediately began the emergency procedure, tightening his seatbelt, tucking his hands inside the cockpit, and bowing his head as much as possible.

I lowered the flaps, but it was very difficult to stabilize White Cloud in the air by that point, and it swayed from side to side. I had to push the stick forward again. I knew this would increase the landing speed, but there was no choice. If I hadn't done that, the plane would have stalled, and we would have fallen from the sky like a rock.

The ground was approaching quickly, and the treetops filled my field of vision. A moment later, I could already see the tops of the trees beside me. I hoped I'd managed to direct White Cloud to land on the path between the trees, but I could no longer see anything ahead of me.

I pulled the stick with all my strength, but the nose didn't lift.

All I could do was hope it would hold up during the landing, despite the high speed, and not fail us at the last moment.

We were heading for the ground.

White Cloud hit the dirt hard, bounced up while continuing to move forward, and hit it again with tremendous force. The left wheel touched down first and collapsed from the impact. The plane tilted to the side and continued to skid along the ground. Everything spun around me, and I heard a deafening noise of breaking and crashing.

Suddenly, I felt a tremendous blow to the head. I lost consciousness.

I don't know how long I was unconscious, but when I opened my eyes, I was enveloped in complete darkness. I felt that I was hanging on my side, strapped in by the seatbelts, with White Cloud lying on its right side.

It took me a while to figure out where I was and what had happened. My flight goggles were shattered. I pulled them off and threw them aside. I touched my face and body. Other than a few scratches on my right hand and forehead, I didn't find any other injuries.

I couldn't see anything in front of me, just shards of my windshield. I looked up, that is, toward the left side of White Cloud, and saw a sky full of stars. It took me a moment to realize that the double left wing wasn't blocking my view. It simply wasn't there. White Cloud was completely wrecked.

With much effort, I freed myself from the seatbelts. I pulled myself from the cockpit and looked toward the front seat. Mikhail wasn't there.

His seat was crushed; the engine was almost entirely pressed against the partition that separated our seats. The engine was still smoking, a strong smell of fuel filling the air, but there was no sign of fire around me. Complete darkness.

I started circling White Cloud, stepping over debris, thinking that maybe Mikhail was on the other side. I finished circling what was left of the Flamingo and stood again by the engine. Now I saw the propeller blades bent as if some higher power had violently warped and twisted them on their axis. There was still no sign of Mikhail.

"Mikhail, where are you?" I first called out loudly and then started shouting, "Mikhail, where are you?" But there was no answer from the darkness that surrounded me. Fear and dread surged through my body.

I began to make my way back along the path of the landing, which was a trail of destruction. The starlight was the only thing that slightly dispelled the darkness, and once my eyes adjusted to it, I managed to see quite well.

I felt my way between broken trees and parts of White Cloud until I reached a dirt road. I managed to see that I had landed White Cloud on the path, but the moment it flipped over, it kept on rolling into the orchard.

And then I saw Mikhail.

# Chapter 51

He didn't survive.

"I can't believe it," Lilly covered her mouth with her hand, tears filling her eyes.

"That's rough," Tom said.

"I don't understand anything, anything at all," Mark said. For the first time in three days, his voice was calm, sad even.

Attorney Rubin took a sip of water from his glass and continued.

> His body was stuck between two large branches of one of the orchard's trees. From where I was standing, it looked as if he was hugging them.
> 
> I moved closer to him. The right side of his head was crushed. I think his blood was still dripping, slowly trickling down the tree trunk. I thanked God for the darkness – I didn't want to see any more.
> 
> I needed to decide what to do, fast. It was only a matter of time before people would arrive and start asking questions about what had happened here. I had to get out, but not before I buried Mikhail. Finding an unfamiliar plane wreck is one thing; finding a body next to it is another matter entirely.

With great effort, I pulled his body down from the tree. His blood soaked my face and stained my coat.

I tried to lift him, but I couldn't. I had to drag him to the far side of the orchard. I found an iron pipe lying next to one of the trees and used it to dig a deep hole. The earth was soft and sandy, so the digging wasn't difficult.

I stripped him of all his clothes and made sure no identifying markers were left. Then I buried him, covered him with soil, and scattered branches around the site.

I didn't know any Jewish prayers, so I tried to repeat what I'd heard the pastor say at my father's, grandfather's, and grandmother's funerals. I probably didn't say the right words, but I couldn't let him go without saying something.

Afterward, I returned to White Cloud and took everything we had hidden under my seat, including the bag of diamonds Mikhail had brought. With great effort, I opened the storage compartment and retrieved the backpack that held my diary, my plane logbook, the photos we took, and the cloth bag where Mikhail kept his personal belongings. I had my passport on me. I placed the diary in the front pocket of my coat.

After making sure I hadn't forgotten anything, I started walking through the orchard to the west, with the backpack on my shoulders. I was still in my flight clothes, including the flight cap and gloves. I don't remember how long I walked before I reached a road that stretched from north to south.

I had to stop and rest. I took off my coat, removed the flight cap and gloves, and sat by the side of the road. That was the moment when the full weight of everything that had happened finally hit me — the crash and Mikhail's death. I broke down in tears.

It took me a while to calm down. I wasn't sure what to do. Somehow, I hadn't given much thought to what

I'd do once we completed our journey to Palestine. My assumption had been that Mikhail would take care of us until I could return home. Now, I was alone, and I had to make a decision, fast.

I decided to try to reach Tel Aviv, as we had originally planned. I knew I had to keep walking west, as Tel Aviv was by the coast.

I pulled a few British Palestinian pounds from my backpack, along with the cloth bag that held Mikhail's personal items. Inside, I found his passport. I put it in my pocket alongside mine. I returned everything else to the backpack and began walking south along the road, hoping a car would pass and pick me up.

After about half an hour of walking, I reached a junction with a road that led west, toward a settlement whose lights glimmered in the distance. I started walking toward the outskirts of the settlement. Close to the first houses, I spotted a car with the word "taxi" written on its side in English. The driver stood a short distance away, smoking a cigarette. I approached him in German and asked if he could take me to a small, inexpensive hotel in Tel Aviv. Luckily, he understood and drove me to a hotel not far from the beach. On the way, he told me that the place we had come from was called Moshav Ein Ganim.

I estimate that I arrived at the hotel around 10 PM I requested a room with a shower and private bathroom in German. I rented it for three days in advance and paid with the bills I had ready.

It was Mikhail's idea to prepare usable local currency, and now I was putting it into practice, all alone.

When the receptionist asked for my name, I hesitated. I don't know why I made it, but the decision I made in that moment changed my life.

# Chapter 52

"**M**y name is Mikhail Golber."
I presented Mikhail's passport.
I entered the room given to me on the second floor of the hotel, and after placing the backpack on the bed, I headed to the bathroom. Only then did I notice the bloodstains on my face, neck, and shirt in the small mirror above the sink.

I felt filthy. I stepped into the shower and scrubbed myself from head to toe, standing for a long time under the soothing hot water. Afterward, I collapsed onto the bed and immediately fell asleep.

---

Attorney Rubin fell silent, raising his head to look at Mark and Lilly. Mark stared at some imaginary point in the distance. Lilly blew her nose into a tissue she took from the box in the center of the table. Mirkin's head was bowed, and the rest of the room remained still.

This story is getting even more complicated, Rubin thought to himself. The significance of the information he had just read aloud was dramatic.

Lilly reached out and took Mark's hand. "Do you understand what this means? Do you see the gravity of what we just heard?"

Mark looked at her in silence.

"Mark, our father is Miku, not Mikhail – do you understand that? It's not Mikhail."

Mark turned to the attorney and asked, in a subdued voice, "Is what Lilly saying true? What does this mean for us?"

"I don't know. I just found out about it, same as you, but it doesn't seem to matter, as long as your father left behind a will."

Lilly stood up. "I need a moment to process this," she said, walking out of the conference room. Her children quickly followed her.

After about fifteen minutes, they all returned, and Attorney Rubin asked, "There's more. Shall we continue?"

---

I slept for a long time. I woke up sometime in the afternoon, tired and with a sharp pain in my back. I could see the sea from my hotel room window. It looked as turbulent as I felt. I hadn't eaten in more than twenty-four hours, and my stomach was letting me know.

I emptied the backpack onto the bed. This was all I had in the world right now. I found clean pants and a shirt, and put them on.

Then I went downstairs to the street and entered a nearby workers' restaurant. It was the kind of place where you could see the food heating in large trays, and I just pointed to what I wanted – no need for much conversation. After I ate, I returned to the room and lay down again, but I couldn't go back to sleep.

My mind was tormented by the thought that none of this would've happened if I had listened to Mikhail. Mikhail had trusted me to make sound, professional decisions right up to the end, and he hadn't argued with me. What a shame. I recalled Ozols' saying: 'It takes courage to choose not to fly too.' Yesterday, I hadn't found that courage—I had failed, and the result was tragic. On the other hand, the engine would have failed even if we had flown in the morning. My thoughts were all over the place. I hated myself, and I hated *White Cloud*.

I reached for the clothes I'd worn during the crash and pulled out everything that was in them. When I shook out the coat, my diary fell out. There was a bloodstain on the front cover, Mikhail's blood; I threw it at the wall, and its leather cover crumpled.

"This diary is cursed," I said to myself. I didn't dare throw it away or destroy it, but I couldn't write in it anymore.

In my frustration, I tossed everything from the bed onto the floor. I couldn't shake the feeling that Mikhail had died because I had failed professionally, and because White Cloud had abandoned us at the last moment. Tears began to roll down my cheeks. I swore to myself I would never fly a plane again, and I ripped my plane logbook to pieces.

I tried to figure out what I should do. Riga felt so far away, a place where a different life had taken place. I didn't really have anyone to go back to. Here, I had Mikhail. In honor of our friendship and the dreams he could no longer fulfill, I decided to stay in the land that Jews like him were building. I would live the life he could have had, in my own way and with his help.

I cried until I fell asleep. Again, I slept for a long time. When I woke up the next morning, I felt better.

I knew I couldn't continue hiding from myself in the hotel room. I had money, and I had Mikhail's diamonds. I needed to start planning for my future.

I went out to the main street, General Allenby Street, and began wandering the city aimlessly.

Tel Aviv was in the midst of a building boom. Nearly every street I walked down had residential buildings in various stages of construction and roadworks being laid out. The city looked completely different from any other I had visited: very bright, with many of the buildings painted white.

So different from where I had come from – Riga, the most beautiful city in the world, with its old, colorful buildings, towering church spires, scattered green gardens, and the Daugava River running alongside it. Even after all my travels around the world throughout my long life, I had never found a city more beautiful.

The gap between Riga and Tel Aviv was so vast that my first few days here, without knowing any Hebrew, were incredibly difficult. My saving grace was that I knew German, and there were enough German speakers around to get by.

In the next two months, I managed to rent a room in a small apartment with two other bachelors. I wandered around the city and bought new clothes and a hat.

I knew I needed to sort out my legal status since I had entered Palestine illegally. During my wanderings, I heard about an official in the Jewish Agency's immigration department who, for a fee, could help with such matters.

I met him after his work hours, paid him what was needed, and he added me to the list of immigrants who had arrived by ship to Palestine the day before I'd arrived at the hotel. Now I had a certificate of immigration with a new name – Michael Golber. That was it. I gave up my old name, my past, and even the remnants of my hopes for Yuli. It hurt, but there was no other choice.

I did one more thing regarding my past. I went to a photo studio on Allenby Street, wearing my jacket and hat, and had my picture taken. On the back of one of the copies, under the stamp with the studio's address, I wrote the date and the words: "We arrived. Mikhail is dead." I placed the photo in an envelope and sent it to Yuli. She would always be dear to my heart. I felt she needed to know.

During my strolls through Tel Aviv, I entered several stores that I identified as real estate agencies. I befriended some of the agents, especially those who spoke German, and got a sense of the land prices for orchards. They were indeed low, just as Mikhail had told me.

I traveled to Ein Ganim and found the orchard where we had landed. The owner thought I had come to inspect it for purchase, so he let me walk around freely. I found the wreckage of White Cloud. My heart broke seeing it shattered like that in the daylight. I took advantage of the opportunity and, after a short negotiation, bought that orchard — my first in Palestine. You all know it. It's the 'Bergs Orchard.'

I hired a foreman and workers, and one of the first things I did was instruct them to dig a large hole at the edge of the orchard, bury the remains of White Cloud, and roll over the site with a steamroller. The plane had ultimately let me down, and I didn't want any reminders of it.

I located the spot where I had buried Mikhail and placed my grandfather's gun with him. It was illegal to hold on to it anyway and could only bring trouble. Then, I instructed the foreman to cut down the trees in that area, pave it with tiles, and build a nice pavilion over it so that corner could serve as a resting place for the workers during their breaks. Over time, I made sure to connect it with electricity and water, and planted flowers and climbing vines around it.

At the same time, I devoted my attention to learning Hebrew. It seemed strange at first, but it was clear I couldn't get by without knowing it well. Soon enough, I could understand almost everything, even if I wasn't fluent. I even went to a surgeon at Hadassah Hospital on Balfour Street in Tel Aviv, who performed a circumcision on me.

I bought a large wooden box, placed Mikhail's passport

in it, along with the photos we had taken, my diary, and my Latvian passport. I kept them all these years in a locked cabinet. My past and future are stored in it.

# Chapter 53

I never looked back.
You already know this next part of my life. I bought more and more orchards, set up a packing business, and that's how 'Michael Citrus & Sons' was born. When he was a child, Mark asked me why it was '& Sons.' The answer was so that clients would think the company had a long history. That's the company that's known today as 'Citrus Investments.'

Work was abundant, and it managed to quiet the thoughts and longing for the life I had lost.

I always acted according to what seemed right. I expanded the business to include agricultural equipment. I successfully competed against the socialists' cooperatives and against those of the large orchard owners. In one case, I managed to beat them on their home turf, and they never knew why. I found out that the head purchaser for the kibbutz of Latvian immigrants in the north was a man named Monya Gershtik. Yes, Uncle Monya. I convinced him to purchase equipment for the kibbutz from me rather than from their cooperative. We remained friends until he passed away. Monya only knew me as Miku Golber. I never told him anything about the fuel he brought, which likely caused the disaster that had befallen us. After all, he only wanted to help. Monya never asked me about Mikhail either—

he probably understood that something had happened between us. We both preferred, each for his own reasons, not to talk about him.

I married Frida, your mother and grandmother, in 1949. By then, I had an office in Tel Aviv and my own apartment on Ben Yehuda Strasse, from which we could see the sea. After the wedding, I bought a house in the new Tel Baruch neighborhood. Our neighbors were immigrants from Bulgaria and Turkey. Frida, who was born in Sofia, Bulgaria, felt at home there. I never told them that I had visited there too.

In the years when money was tight, Mikhail's bag of diamonds, which I kept in the locked wooden box in my closet, saved me.

Every diamond I sold gave me the financial breathing room to hold out until I could stand on my own two feet. Each time I went to the dealer at the corner of Allenby and Ben Yehuda Streets and sold him another diamond, I felt like a piece of the friendship between Mikhail and me was slipping through my fingers. Sometimes it took me an entire day to recover from it.

The last sale I made was in the 1950s. After that, only one diamond remained in the bag. That's the diamond you see on the blue velvet tray at the center of the display in our large conference room. The 'Citrus Investments' logo is a copy of it. Mikhail's diamond being duplicated, thousands of times, every day.

In December 1939, a messenger arrived with an envelope and said, "I think this is for you."

Inside was a signed letter sent to the photo studio on Allenby Street. On the envelope, written in familiar handwriting, were the words: "For Miku, who took a picture with you a year ago." It was Yuli's handwriting.

I have no idea how the photographer knew it was for me or how he tracked me down.

My hands trembled as I opened it. Inside was a photograph. I pulled it out and immediately recognized Yuli. In the picture, she was sitting on a padded chair, wearing a wide dress. Her face was a little fuller than I remembered. She looked straight into the camera with that same confident, self-assured gaze.

In her arms, she held a baby. He bore a striking resemblance to Mikhail.

I turned the photo over and saw a single sentence written on the back: "Mishka, born at the end of February 1939, and I. A surprising farewell gift from Mikhail on the last evening before your flight to Palestine. Everything has changed. Take care of yourself."

I was in shock. There was no doubt that this was Mikhail's son. I had never imagined that their relationship had reached such a stage. He never hinted at it in any way.

For some reason, I felt that some justice had been done by him. Although he had died, he had left behind a son.

This photo, too, is kept in my wooden box.

## Chapter 54

The thought that their father had hidden these events throughout his life paralyzed Mark.

Lilly's sobbing grew louder beside him. "I can't take it anymore," she whimpered.

Rubin stopped reading and looked at Mark with a questioning gaze, but Mark couldn't respond. He sat still, wringing his hands. Tears streamed down his face, which he wiped with a tissue. Even at the funeral, he hadn't felt this sad and confused.

The attorney seemed helpless, unsure of how to proceed. Mark assumed Rubin was only now realizing that his longtime friend and client, Michael, had hidden a terrible truth from him, a real tragedy buried deep within, never shared with anyone.

Tom and Hannah looked horrified, while Mark's sons stared into space, trying to process the information and its implications.

A long silence once again filled the conference room.

Suddenly, Miriam's voice broke through: "I suggest we take a break here, bring you some refreshments, and then continue. We have to move forward."

No one responded at first but, after a few moments, Hannah said, "I need some fresh air; I feel like I'm suffocating in here." She stood up and left the room, followed by Tom, Daniel, and David.

Mark and Lilly stood and embraced.

"Come," he offered his hand, "let's take a short walk." Only Mr. Mirkin and the translator remained in the room.

They stood in the lobby near one of the windows. Lilly continued crying as she hugged her brother, who tried to calm her and get her to drink some water that someone had poured for her.

*This whole thing is starting to get out of hand. I need to focus and regain control of the situation,* Mark thought to himself.

"Lilly, we need to pull ourselves together. We're showing shock and weakness. That's not good. It was already clear yesterday that Dad had some surprise for us. We need to deal with this differently."

Lilly looked at him and said in a broken voice, "It's so hard, Mark. I know you're right, but it's just so hard. You realize where Mikhail is buried, don't you?"

"In Dad's corner," he replied softly, "in the Bergs orchard."

Mark began to realize that events he hadn't understood before were starting to make sense and take on new meaning. His father's severe attitude toward him since childhood, and to some extent toward Lilly, which left such deep scars on them to this day, was probably his way of coping with what he had gone through. That was likely also the reason Dad fought so hard against the attempt to expropriate the Bergs Orchard in the 1970s, agreeing to it only after ensuring that his corner would be left out of the discussion.

"Mark, maybe that's why Dad disappeared for a week in '75 without anyone knowing where he was. I think that happened after they started paving the road through the Bergs Orchard. Now I remember reading in the papers that they found remains of a German plane with a swastika there."

He felt she sounded more composed.

"Right, great job remembering that. There was some article in the paper, even on the news. They thought it was a lost German plane."

"And they were all wrong. It was Dad's White Cloud, and he just couldn't handle it. So, he took off until he could calm down."

Lilly was silent for a moment. "But who are we, Mark? If we're not Golber, then who are we?"

"I have no idea. As far as I'm concerned, I'm a Golber. Maybe the rest of this will clarify that but, for now, let's go back and finish this saga. Do you feel better?"

"Yes. Thank you, Mark. I needed your hug."

Lilly started to walk but suddenly stopped and turned to him. "Could it be that Mr. Mirkin is related to that child Yuli had?"

By the time they returned, everyone was already seated. Each took their place, and Mark noticed out of the corner of his eye that Mr. Mirkin had placed a large brown envelope on the table.

The attorney spoke, "Shall I continue?"

I was tempted to adventure out of stupidity and arrogance. I acted irresponsibly, and my best friend paid for it with his life. I managed to survive all these years with this truth only because I chose to take my fate into my own hands and not let my emotions overcome me.

You will never understand that, thank God, but this is the lesson I tried to pass on to you, my children and grandchildren, throughout my life. I made an effort to lead you to good lives from a position of strength and influence. I did it with good intentions and concern for you, even if you didn't always agree with me, and we sometimes clashed because of it. So, I ask for your forgiveness and that you understand my motives.

In October 1992, a year after Latvia declared independence from Soviet occupation, I flew to Riga without your knowledge. I wasn't ready to explain it then.

It was the first time I returned to Latvia since leaving in 1938. More than fifty years of longing.

We landed in Latvia's international airport, a small airport back then, with a small, gray, polygonal building serving as the terminal. The drive to the hotel revealed that little had changed in the city center since I had left, except for the visible neglect present everywhere.

I chose to stay at the Riga Hotel. I didn't know the hotel from before; I picked it for its location and asked for a room overlooking the opera house.

I couldn't resist and immediately left the hotel for a short walk around the city.

My feet led me toward the building at 10 Antonias Street. It was cold, and I was wrapped in a warm coat and scarf that covered my face. I crossed the Pilsētas Canal and reached the Freedom Monument. More than fifty-five years earlier, I had stood right there, witnessing its inauguration with Yuli and Mikhail by my side.

I struggled to process the emotions I felt standing there. Tears began to stream down my face. Afraid that someone might see me, I kept walking until I reached Esplanade Public Park, where I sat on a bench to rest. I noticed that it hadn't changed at all since I last saw it.

I continued walking until I stood in front of what used to be my home. The building looked very run-down. Some windows were boarded up, and it looked like it hadn't been cleaned on the outside in years. The entrance gate was wide open. I went in, climbed to the third floor, and stood in front of the familiar door. I knocked a few times, but no one answered.

As I started to walk back down, I heard a nearby apartment door open. An elderly woman approached me. "What do you want? What are you looking for here?" she asked in Russian. Her tone was pleasant; not aggressive, just curious. "No one's lived there since the Russians left and the Russian officer moved out," she added.

"I used to live here many years ago," I replied in Russian.

She looked at me again, this time with an examining gaze. Suddenly, she began to tremble and covered her mouth with her hands.

"Miku? Are you Miku Lange? You're alive? I'm Sveta. Don't you remember me?"

I hesitated. I did remember the neighbor's daughter. She was about ten years older than me, so we didn't have much interaction, apart from the times my father asked her to watch me when I was a little boy. But I had been Michael Golber for more than fifty years now. Miku Lange had died a long time ago.

I approached her, took her hands in mine, and whispered in her ear, "Yes, Sveta, I remember you well. I was once Miku, but now I'm someone else." I continued to hug her, feeling the tears tightening my throat. The thought that there was someone who still remembered who I used to be only added to the overwhelming emotion.

She invited me into her apartment, which had previously been her parents', and we sat together drinking tea. She clearly remembered the events that had taken place in the building after I disappeared. According to her, there was a big commotion and a lot of rumors, but no one really knew where I had gone.

"There was even a rumor that you had stolen a plane from Spilve and flown to America," she said, adding, "In any case, you made the right decision. You were very lucky because, two years later, the Russians came and deported all the building's residents to Siberia, including your Martha and my parents. I was at university, so I wasn't sent with them. None of them ever returned. They did that to the entire middle class in Riga. I've lived here alone ever since. All those years, Russian officers lived in your apartment, but according to the new laws, you can reclaim the apartment."

Though she may have expected it, I preferred not to tell her what had happened and where I had been all those years. After years under the harsh Soviet regime, she knew better than to ask.

The next day, I went to the building at 20 Stabu Street. There was no trace of the Bergs family. I decided to skip a visit to Spilve Aerodrome—I wasn't sure I could handle it.

Later that day, I hired a private investigator and a lawyer. I asked them to trace the property that was still registered under my family's name. I left them a copy of my Latvian passport, which I had kept all those years in the wooden box, along with my diary.

Additionally, I asked them to find out what had happened to the Bergs family, to Yuli and her son Mishka, as well as to the Golber family.

A few months later, I received a detailed report regarding all my family's assets, most of which I had never known about. Surprisingly, the factory in the market on Gaizina Street wasn't included, nor was there any mention of my father's Ford Junior. I didn't know why, and I didn't ask. I instructed them to sell everything to the highest bidder, except for the apartment at 10 Antonias Street, where I had lived with my father, and that was the end of it.

I also received the reports on the Bergs and Golber families. The report on the Golbers was very brief. It stated that the entire family had been transferred to the Riga Ghetto in October 1941 and later murdered in a massacre in the Rumbula forest on the outskirts of Riga. I knew nothing of this event and only learned about it later. No one from that family survived.

As for the Bergs family, as I suspected, the report confirmed that they had all been deported to Siberia by the Russians in 1940. The report noted that neither Yuli's name nor her son's appeared on the deportation list. They added that, since I had mentioned that she studied aeronautics, there was a chance the Russians had recruited her. The report's authors suggested I try to search for her in Russia.

I found a private investigator in Moscow and hired him for the task. After more than two years, he informed me that he had found the grave of a woman named Yuliana

Mirkin in a cemetery in St. Petersburg. The information he found in government records stated that she was born in 1917 in Riga and held a degree in aeronautical engineering.

I informed him that there was a high chance this was the Yuli I was looking for, and asked him to continue searching for her family. He found that her husband was a man named Mirkin who had died many years before her, and that their son was named Mishka Mirkin.

When I drafted my will, I contacted that same private investigator and asked him to find out whether Mishka Mirkin was still alive and to get his address if he was. This time, the answer came much quicker. Mishka Mirkin was no longer alive, but he had left behind a son named Alexander Mirkin, who lives in St. Petersburg.

I instructed Attorney Rubin to arrange for Alexander to attend the reading of my will and to ask him to bring any family photos he has. Who knows? You might find among them the picture of the three of us at the entrance to Spilve, which I had left with Yuli in my last letter.

There's a good chance that Mr. Alexander Mirkin, who should be sitting with you now, is the grandson of my dear friend Yuli and my beloved friend Mikhail.

I began my life as Mihails, Miku Lange, the son of a Christian family in the city of Riga, Latvia, and I will die with the identity I adopted for myself in 1938: Michael Golber, a Jew and a loyal citizen of the State of Israel, which I wholeheartedly embraced as my country and my home.

I believe everything should now be clear.

# Chapter 55

"That's the end of the cover letter," said Rubin. All the attendees turned their gaze toward Mr. Mirkin, as though expecting him to say something.

He seemed flustered by the sudden attention directed at him. With a trembling hand, he reached for the brown envelope in front of him, pulled out a photograph, and placed it at the center of the table, in front of Mark and Lilly.

The photograph showed three young people, two men and a woman, smiling happily at the camera. Each of the men had an arm around the woman in the middle, and one of them was holding a leather jacket with a thick wool collar and flight cap with a pair of flight goggles. Behind them was a two-story building. The word "Spilve" could be seen painted in white on the side of the building.

Lilly carefully picked up the photo, as though it were a precious jewel. She looked at it and then showed it to Mark.

"Look," she said, "that's Dad, no doubt about it. Look how handsome he was. That's Yuli, such a beautiful girl, and this must be Mikhail." She pointed at the young man standing on Yuli's other side. She raised her head and fixed her gaze on Mr. Mirkin's face. "Mark, look how much Mr. Mirkin resembles his grandfather—the face, the nose, even the expression; he's the spitting image of his grandfather, there's no mistaking it."

She turned to him, "Alexander, I'm so, so happy you're here with us. This is the first time in my long life that I'm truly proud of something my father has done—bringing you here today."

Her voice trembled slightly with emotion, and her eyes filled with tears of relief.

The translator finished relaying her words, and Mr. Mirkin rose from his seat, approached her and, after she stood up to meet him, embraced her for a long moment.

Afterward, he returned to his seat, visibly moved as well. He pulled a series of photographs from the envelope and spread them out on the table.

The photographs showed Yuli dressed in aviator gear. In some, she was leaning against a military plane; in others, she was inside the cockpit. In one, she stood at attention in a lineup with other female pilots, while an officer stood in front of her, pinning something to her chest.

Mark and Lilly looked at the photographs in silence, then passed them on to their children.

"This is my grandmother, Grandma Yuli," Mr. Mirkin began, waiting for the translation.

"The man I thought was my grandfather died very young, and I never knew him. My mother left my father when I was four, and she didn't really stay in touch with us. In fact, it was my grandmother, Yuli, who raised me.

"I knew that Grandma Yuli was born in Riga, that her father was Russian and her mother was Latvian," he continued, "but that's about all I knew. I don't think even my father knew much more than that. And I'd never seen this photograph of her with Miku and Mikhail until I went looking for pictures after receiving Advocate Rubin's invitation. Now that I think of it, it was the only picture of her that wasn't in her photo album— it was in a drawer in her wardrobe.

"From what she told me, I know that when the USSR annexed Latvia in 1940, they gathered all the aeronautics students who were in their final year or studying for their master's degrees, like her, and gave them the opportunity to join the Soviet Air Force. She requested to become a pilot and was assigned to pilot training at the end of 1941. She left my father with an aunt who lived in Moscow.

"After completing her training, she was assigned as a pilot in the 588th Night Bomber Regiment, which became known as the 'Night Witches.' That's the nickname the Germans gave them. She began flying a plane called the Polikarpov. Grandma really loved that plane; she always spoke of it fondly.

"In 1942, she flew intelligence and bombing missions over German-occupied territories, mostly at night. She told me about it many times. The night bombing technique involved flying low, close to the ground, until they were near the target. At that moment, they would climb slightly, cut the engine, and glide silently to the point where they would drop the bombs on German forces. This way, they managed to surprise the Germans, who never heard them coming. The Germans saw them as witches flying on broomsticks, which is how they earned the nickname 'Night Witches.'

"Grandma told me she shot down two German planes with the machine gun on her Polikarpov. She would laugh and say that to do that, you had to get very, very close to the German planes, and that male pilots would've never dared to do such a thing.

"I know she logged nearly 300 combat flight hours by the day they shot her down. It happened during a daytime bombing mission. A German fighter spotted her and tried to shoot her down, but couldn't. She managed to outmaneuver him, taking advantage of the fact that her plane flew very slowly, while the German fighter couldn't fly that slowly without stalling. Ultimately, she was hit by ground fire and had to make an emergency landing in an open field. She was rescued by local partisans and stayed with them until she recovered enough to be evacuated back to Russia.

"The photo where you see her standing at attention with an officer in front of her was taken at the ceremony where she was awarded the Order of the Red Star. She returned to the regiment, continued her bombing missions, and managed to shoot down two more German planes. At the end of the war, she was also awarded the title of Hero of the Soviet Union."

Mr. Mirkin fell silent, seemingly having finished his story.

"So, in the end, she became an extraordinary pilot and a true hero," said Lilly. "I'm really happy for her, even though it all happened so long ago, and even though they're all gone now anyway."

# Chapter 56

"We still have a bit more to go," said Attorney Rubin.

I ask that you now proceed with the reading of the will. Remember that I loved you, Mark, Lilly, and all my grandchildren, with all my heart, even if it didn't always seem that way.

This is it, Mark thought to himself, the moment of truth. Now we'll know just how much this revelation about the esteemed Mr. Alexander Mirkin has cost me.

Lilly reached out her hand and held his. He looked at her and received her familiar, loving, and optimistic gaze in return. He needed it. They continued holding hands as they prepared to hear the will.

Rubin pulled another envelope from the wooden box, opened it, and took out a printed document a few pages long. On the first page, in bold letters, was the word 'Will.'

He cleared his throat and began reading:

"Whereas no one knows the day of his departure, and as I wish to make a will and express my final wishes regarding what shall be done with my property upon my death, after a long life, I hereby bequeath, being of sound mind and under no undue influence from any party, what is to be done with my estate after my passing, as follows..."

# EPILOGUE

When Attorney Rubin finished reading the will, he stood up and turned to Mark. "That's it. It took considerably longer than we all expected, but now we're done. You're officially the head of the family and the majority owner of 'Citrus Investments.' You bear a great responsibility, and I wish you much success. I'm leaving your father's wooden box in your care."

Mark thanked him and gave him a warm handshake. A weight had been lifted from his heart, and he felt much calmer. His father hadn't let him down after all. On the contrary, he had given him the largest share of 'Citrus Investments' stock, "to ensure my son Mark's control of the company without anyone's interference."

But it was the heartfelt words from his father, words he had never heard during his father's lifetime, that moved him more than anything else. Now, he could finally reconcile and heal the ever-gaping wound in his soul regarding their relationship. That's important too, Mark thought to himself.

His father hadn't slighted anyone. Lilly received a share of the company's stock and many other assets, which would provide her with wealth for the rest of her life. Each of their children had also received a fair share, distributed equally. "I leave this to you to make your lives easier, though not to exempt any of you from the need to work and support yourselves," his father had written.

His father had bequeathed the apartment on Antonias Street in Riga to Mr. Mirkin, as well as all the proceeds from the sale of his family's properties in Riga, "so that the grandson of Yuli and Mikhail would never have to worry about his livelihood again."

But his father had saved the biggest surprise for the end.

When Rubin reached this part, Mark noticed that even he was emotional and struggling to read. "Finally, after all your needs have been met, I instruct my dear children, Mark and Lilly, to carry out two additional tasks.

"The first is to establish a memorial stone for the Golber family at the site commemorating the Jews of Latvia who were murdered in the Holocaust, located in Rumbula Forest on the outskirts of Riga. You will find the details on how to do this with representatives of the Jewish community there.

"The second is to establish an investment fund in Israel of ten million shekels, dedicated to financing flight studies for any girl in Israel who wishes to do so. I instruct that the fund be named after my dear friend Yuli, and called the 'Yuliana Bergs Fund.' The fund will be managed by a professional team, headed by my daughter, Lilly."

For the first time in his life, Mark felt proud of his father.

Mr. Mirkin stood up, warmly shook Mark's hand, embraced Lilly for a long time, exchanged a few words of farewell, and then left the room with the interpreter.

"Well, Mark, open the wooden box already, let's see what else is inside," Lilly said to him.

Mark walked over to the box which had been left on the table in the conference room, and opened the lid. Beneath the documents of the will and the cover letter, additional old photographs peeked out. Lilly reached in and pulled one out. It was the photo from 1939 of Yuli sitting in a chair with her son, Mishka, on her lap.

The next photograph she retrieved was identical to the one Alexander Mirkin had shown them, the picture at Spilve.

One more photo remained. It showed their father and Mikhail, both dressed in black jackets, black trousers, white shirts, and bowties. To their father's right stood Yuli, radiant, with his right arm around her shoulders and his left hand holding a large umbrella over them all. She wore a long, dark evening gown, her hair pulled up and her left arm wrapped around his waist.

The three of them looked at the camera, their faces radiating happiness and joy, filled with the confidence that life would bring them carefree bliss.

The last two items in the box were an old passport and an envelope with yellowing stains, wrinkled and partially disintegrating. Lilly picked up the passport and opened it. On the first page was the name 'Mihails Lange,' and on the second was a photograph of their father in his youth.

Then she carefully lifted the old envelope and examined its contents. Inside the envelope was another passport, its pages yellowed, wrapped in a cover made of thick brown paper. She opened it carefully, and they saw it was in the name of Mikhail Golber. They recognized the picture of young Mikhail inside.

As Lilly held the brown paper covering Mikhail's passport, the passport slipped out. Along with it, a thin sheet of almost transparent paper, which had been hidden in the gap between the passport and its cover, slowly fluttered to the ground.

Lilly bent down and picked it up. The paper seemed to have been folded and hidden for many years, with its creases stuck together. It appeared likely that even their father hadn't been aware of its existence.

Very carefully, she unfolded the creases until the entire page was revealed. Before them lay a letter, written in an unfamiliar language, in cursive, feminine handwriting.

"Mark, I can't believe what I'm seeing. I think this is Yuli's handwriting. Go call the interpreter quickly before he leaves. Tell him there's something urgent he needs to translate."

Mark rushed out of the meeting room and, a few minutes later, returned, panting from the effort, with the interpreter beside him. "He was just about to get into a cab; I caught him at the very last moment."

Lilly presented the open sheet of paper spread out on the conference table, and asked the interpreter to examine it and see if he could translate what was written.

Miku, my love,
I had no choice. If I hadn't broken up with you, you never would have agreed to fly Mikhail to Palestine.

Mikhail told me about your plan from the very beginning. By then, I had already fallen in love with him as well, torn between my love for you and my love for him. Miku! I fell in love with Mikhail without ever stopping my love for you. On the contrary, my love for him only strengthened my love for you—my first love, my great and special love. You made me so happy.

I know I should have told you, but I didn't know how to explain it. I don't even fully understand it myself. I was afraid you wouldn't understand, so I said nothing and kept delaying until, really, it was already too late.

Mikhail told me he had no future in Europe, nor in Latvia. The hatred for Jews was only growing, his family's business would crumble, and everything would only get worse, especially with what was happening in Germany. He claimed that the safest place for him, and the nearest, was in Palestine, but immigrating there was impossible through official channels; the only way was to go illegally. When he asked me if I thought you could smuggle him there by air, I thought he was joking and told him that I was sure you could do it, because you're an excellent pilot. But he was serious and, when he approached you and suggested it, you refused, saying you didn't want to part with me under any circumstances.

Mikhail told me that if I truly loved him, I needed to help him get to Palestine with your help and then continue to love only you. But to get you to agree to his request, I had to break up with you. I did it out of love, with a very heavy heart.

Mikhail made me swear not to tell you anything until you were on your way, and he swore to me, by all that was dear to him, that he would protect you with his life until you've reached Palestine, and only then would he give you this letter before your return to Riga.

I hope that now, as you read my letter, you understand what happened and why I'm asking you to forgive me. Please come back to me quickly. I'm waiting for you.

Your love,
Yuli

# Acknowledgments

Writing a novel set in the distant past is a complex task. When the story unfolds in a distant land whose language I do not speak, the challenge becomes even greater. I couldn't have completed this work without the help of several individuals who accompanied and assisted me along the way.

First among them is my dear friend Mr. Roman Blumental, a resident of Riga. Without the immense help he provided, I doubt I would've been able to complete this book. Words are insufficient to describe the extent of Roman's assistance. He accompanied me on each of my visits to Spilve Aerodrome, a gem now sadly standing in desolation on the outskirts of Riga. Roman arranged my visit to the Latvian War Museum (Medieval and Modern History Department), provided me with maps of Riga from the 1930s, helped with the correct formulation of Latvian names, and even located experts to assist in selecting some of the alcoholic beverages mentioned in the book. Thank you, Roman!

Mr. Dainis Poziņš, head of the Medieval History Department at the Latvian War Museum, helped me find information about aviation activities during the period covered in the book. I am grateful for his patience and for his help answering all the many questions I posed to him.

I also owe my thanks to Ms. Ligita Betaga from the Aviation Department at the Latvian Ministry of Transport (Aviācijas Departaments, Satiksmes Ministrija), who guided me to relevant historical materials located in the Latvian National Library; to Mr. Igor "Sniper" Ristolainen, the founder of the Riga International Vodka Museum, who professionally assisted in selecting the alcoholic beverages mentioned in the book; and to representatives of the Latvian National Opera and Ballet, who provided me with a list of premiere performances held between 1935 and 1938.

Additional thanks also go to my friend Yuval Nadel, who provided me with rare information and photographs of aviation in Palestine between 1934 and 1938, as well as to Iris Epstein, Orit Kedem, Dror Ottenzoser, Tomi Yoel Pinkovich, Tzachi Frishberg, and Guy Kehila, who provided various comments on the book's initial draft.

I owe a special thanks to my brother, Captain Asa Gutkin, who had been asked for the fourth time to read an early draft of one of my manuscripts. His professional insights regarding aviation and his comments on the text have contributed significantly. In fact, several characters in the book owe him a great deal for their role in the final manuscript.

Thank you to the editorial team of 'Bet-Haorhim' and to Liron Fine, who leads it. Thanks to Shir Rosenblum-Man, the copy editor who identified and corrected my copy errors, and endless thanks to my literary editor, Rina Brosh, for her absolute professionalism, patience and, above all, her deep understanding of my psyche and sources of inspiration, and for skillfully applying them to the text.

Thank you to the team behind the English version of the book at eBookPro. To Michael Waisfeld, the translator, for his impeccable work, dedication, musings, and personal insights from his own historical knowledge and past service as an aircraft mechanic; to Joya Peri, for her outstanding editing; to Corrine Hadar, Oren Klass, Aya Noah and Amir Philos; and, of course, to Nave, Tali and Benny Carmi.

All these people generously dedicated their time to helping

me gather the information I needed for this book and to offer comments and corrections on the original manuscript. If I have omitted anyone's name, please accept my apologies.

While writing the book, I consulted several sources to expand my knowledge of Latvian aviation between the First and Second World Wars. Few people are aware of this, but Latvia was extremely active in the field of aviation during those years, including the design and construction of aircraft and engines. I learned much about the extent of this activity from the book *Of Struggle and Flight: The History of Latvian Aviation* by Kārlis Irbītis, one of the founders of Latvian aviation. Another important source was the website *http://latvianaviation.com*, which also provides extensive information on Latvia's aviation history. I also used various websites that provided supplementary information in different areas.

On the subject of citrus farming in pre-state Israel during the 1930s and 1940s, I learned much from the book *The Jewish Citrus Orchards in Palestine* by Dr. Menashe Davidson, published in 2003 by Ariel Books. Dr. Davidson is an agronomist, businessman, and third-generation farmer whose family was among the pioneers of Rishon LeZion, one of the first Zionist settlements in Palestine.

The inspiration for the character of Michael Golber and the description of his ongoing struggle with the agricultural establishment, came from Mr. Yair Kaplan, an outstanding farmer and brilliant businessman who built an agricultural empire with his own two hands. Along with Dr. Davidson and others, Yair Kaplan led a persistent, decades-long fight against the agricultural establishment for legal recognition of private farmers' rights to market and export their own produce.

I had the privilege of accompanying both Yair Kaplan and Dr. Davidson during some of the struggles that eventually led to the granting of licenses to private farmers for export of agricultural produce from Israel. Both of these men have long served as role models and exceptional mentors in my understanding of Israel's private agricultural sector, and for this, I owe them my sincere gratitude.

Finally, as always, I wish to thank my wife, Hannah, for her patience whenever I disappear into the basement for long hours of research and writing, and for her support and encouragement throughout the writing of this book.

November 2024
Reuven (Robby) Govrin

# Diary's – Translator's Notes

1. The original name written in the diary – Antonijas.
2. The original name written – Kārlis Ulmanis.
3. Apparently referring to an airport or an airstrip.
4. Apparently referring to the Daugava River that flows through the city of Riga and out into the Baltic Sea.
5. The original name written – Nicolajs Pūliņš.
6. The original name written – Liepāja. The city is also known as Libau.
7. Likely referencing the steeple of the church of St. Peter in the Old Town of Riga.
8. The original names written – Aizsargu Aviācija.
9. The original names written – Latvijas Aeroklubs.
10. The original names written – Zilais Putns.
11. The original names written – Latvijas Universitāte.
12. VEF – apparently referring to the factory named Valsts Elektrotechniska Fabrika.
13. The original name written – Jūrmala. Apparently refers to the resort town of Jūrmala, located about 25 km west of Riga, on the coast of the Baltic Sea.
14. The original name written – Gaiziņa iela.
15. The original name written – Centrāltirgus. Apparently referring to the central market of Riga.
16. The original name written – Spīķeru.
17. The original name written – Liepajas Menciņš.
18. The original name written – Kartupeļu Pankūkas.
19. The original name written – Biešu Zupa.
20. The name originally written – Rīgas Doms. Probably

referring to the cathedral in the old town of Riga.
21   The name originally written – Kuze Café.
22   BFW U 12b Bachmann Flamingo.
23   The original name written – Kristīna Bakmane Factory.
24   The original name written – Ugunskrusts.
25   The original name written – Vērmanes Dārzs.
26   The original name written – Kurpnieku Sala.
27   There are signs of the existence of pages covering entries between September 22 and November 4, 1935, but they were missing from the diary provided for translation.
28   The original name written – Brīvības Piemineklis.
29   The original name written – Treulich Geführt, also known as the Bridal Chorus.
30   The pages covering the entries between November 23 and December 15, 1935, are worn out and illegible.
31   The original names written – Kundziņsala, Sarkandaugava and Ķīšezers.
32   The original name written – Kara Aviacijas Fonds.
33   The name originally written – Bērziņš.
34   The original name written – Matīsa.
35   The original name written – Tris Zvaigznes.
36   The original name written – Pērkonkrusts. Likely referring to the "Thunder Cross," a pro-German organization that had operated in Latvia and whose members were antisemitic.
37   The name originally written – Jaunākās Ziņas.
38   The original name written – Baltais Mākonis.
39   The original name written – Marijampolė.
40   The original name written – Pančevo.
41   The original name written – Çanakkale.
42   The original name written – Işıklar.
43   The original name written – Saçakli.
44   The original name written – Büyükeceli.
45   The original name written – Rēzekne. Apparently referring to a city located in the Latgale region of Latvia.

Printed in Dunstable, United Kingdom